by Beth Nixon Weaver

Marshall Cavendish
New York • London • Singapore

Acknowledgments
A special thanks to my editor, Francesca Crispino, and her "magic wand" pen.

Library of Congress Cataloging-in-Publication Data
Weaver, Beth Nixon. Rooster / Beth Nixon Weaver.—1st Marshall Cavendish paperback ed.
p. cm.

Summary: On a small Florida orange grove in the 1960s, fifteen-year-old Kady Palmer is
burdened with housework and caring for her senile grandmother and mentally handicapped
neighbor, so when a rich, handsome boy from school becomes interested in her
she devises a plan to spend time with him.

ISBN 0-7684-5218-4
[1. Conduct of life—Fiction. 2. People with mental disabilities—Fiction. 3. Family problems—Fiction.
4. Farm life—Florida—20th Century—Fiction. 5. Florida—History—20th Century—Fiction.
6. Oranges—Fiction. 7. Marijuana—Fiction] I. Title.

PZ7.W3583 Ro 2005]
[Fic]—dc22
2004058491

Printed in the United States of America
First Marshall Cavendish paperback edition, 2005
1 3 5 7 9 10 8 6 4 2

Reprinted by permission of WinslowHouse International, Inc.

This book is dedicated to:
Jim, Ryan, Jeff, Katie, and Sara

I woke in the gray dawn to Rooster's screams. At first I thought I was having a nightmare, but the screams persisted, slicing through my gauzy cocoon of sleep like sharp knives. I flung off the covers, threw a T-shirt over my nightgown and shook my sister, Minnie.

"Wake up! Something terrible's happening!" I hollered, then gave up as she buried her head under a pillow.

No one else seemed to have heard Rooster, even though our little wood frame house had its windows wide open to catch the faint breezes of the hot Florida night. When I got to the henhouse, where the racket was coming from, I saw Rooster's slight body poised with a heavy stick over a huge snake. An egg was clutched in its powerful jaws. The snake began swallowing the egg whole, while its yellow eyes glared defiantly at the boy.

"G-G-Give it back!" Rooster shrieked as he waved the stick wildly. His face was flushed and tears streamed down his cheeks.

The egg cracked and a trickle of blood ran out the side of the snake's mouth. Rooster stared in horror as the lump of egg slid down its throat. He began jumping in the same spot, the stick flying dangerously over his head as he screamed, "You c-c-can't steal m-m-my *egg!* G-G-Give it BACK!"

I tried to wrench the stick away from him, but it came crashing down on my shoulder. I reeled back in pain as he continued to yell, his corkscrew hair bouncing with a life of its own.

"Rooster!" I started to scold him for being so careless, then bit my tongue, knowing it was pointless. Rooster just didn't understand things the way an ordinary thirteen-year-old did. I sighed. "Give me the stick and stand back!"

He did, and, squeezing my eyes shut, I raised the stick above my head and brought it down as hard as I could. I missed, and we both screamed as the snake writhed at our feet.

My brother, Wendell, rushed toward us, shouting, "What the heck's going on, Kady? Mama kicked me out of bed and told me to . . ." He saw the snake—at least six feet long—and froze.

"Here," I said, putting the stick in his hand. "Kill it!"

"Me?"

"Yes, you!"

His freckles stood out on his ashen face as he backed away. "I got bit the last time I messed with a rat snake." His voice cracked as he spoke. At fourteen, he was a year younger than me, but tall and gangly for his age, with a voice that was beginning to change. One minute he sounded like a kid and the next, these deep, bullfrog noises erupted. The new voice didn't fool me a bit. He was the same pain-in-the-butt kid he'd always been.

"You WIMP!" I yelled.

The snake finished its egg breakfast and slithered into the yard, its long body weaving through the patchy grass like oiled thread.

"I'll do it, then!" I exclaimed and, snatching the stick back, I ran after the snake. I raised the stick again and was about to bring it crashing down when Rooster's brother, Tony, showed up. He was wearing a rumpled T-shirt thrown on inside-out over some cutoffs. At seventeen, he'd been watching out for Rooster ever since their mother died.

"What are you *doing?*" he asked, running his hand over his black hair. It was as curly as Rooster's, only cropped short.

I brought the stick down and missed the snake. It whirled into position, ready to strike me. "What does it look like?" I replied sarcastically. "Wonderful *Madrina,* O Mighty Protector of the Chickens that I am!"

"*¡Dios mío*, Kady!* It's only a rat snake." He slowly leaned over the nervous snake and picked it up. "He won't hurt anyone."

I was stunned by how nonchalantly he'd picked it up. "Tell that to your brother. He's mad that it ate one of his eggs."

"You were just hungry, no?" Tony addressed the snake.

The snake whipped its head around and bit him on the wrist.

"Ouch!" I cried.

Tony's jet-black eyes regarded me with amusement. "That's my line, no?"

"Yeah, and you're not even flinching. Why not?"

"You go around barefoot, don't you?"

I glanced down at my bare feet. "Yeah. So?"

He shrugged. "Is no different from stepping on a sandspur."

"Oh *really?*"

"*Sí.* Snakebites don't hurt much. Is only the venomous snakes you have to steer clear of. And that's because of the poison, not the bite."

"Wendell doesn't think so. He just about had a cow back in the coop."

Tony rolled his eyes. "What doesn't that brother of yours have a cow over? Yet he's the one who's always playing practical jokes. He came over for dinner last night and sat on a whoopee cushion while *Papi* was saying grace. Rooster couldn't stop laughing. Spit food all over the table, a big gob splashing into *Papi's* tea. You don't want to know what happened next."

"I guess we both have crazy brothers."

"*Sí. Loco.*" The snake inched around Tony's neck, then slithered down his other arm. "Come here, I'll show you how to hold this guy."

I backed away, shuddering. "No thanks. I can kill 'em if I have to, but I don't like 'em. Especially when I see bulges in their stomachs."

"*Ay*, Kady, put him in a cage and feed him for a week like you would a pet and you'd start seeing him differently. Snakes gotta eat like the rest of us." He started to brush away something white, like a piece of rice, where the snake had bitten his wrist.

"What's that?"

He picked it up as the snake started coiling itself around his other wrist. "One of his teeth. Snakes sometimes lose their teeth when they bite you." He held it out to me. "Want it?"

"No!" I shuddered.

"I used to have a jar of these back home."

"A *jar?*"

"*Sí,*" he grinned. "We had plenty of these guys hanging around the cane. Bet I got bitten at least a hundred times." Tony's family had owned a sugar plantation back in Cuba. That was before Fidel Castro had taken over in 1959, in what Tony called the "*Revolución.*" A few years after, the Rosados fled the island on a homemade raft the size of a king-size bed.

"I think I'll stick to sandspurs if it's all the same to you; maybe even collect a jar of them."

He flinched slightly as the snake bit him again. "See if you can calm down Rooster while I take this sucker to the woods." Then, grabbing the feisty snake by the back of the head, he cried, "*¡Vamos!*"

After Tony left, I couldn't find Rooster anywhere. Not in the orange grove. Not by the lake. Not even among the towering stalks of bamboo between our properties where he liked to play. I was just about to give up when I heard sobs coming from inside the widowmaker that loomed over the chicken coop in our side yard.

A widowmaker, according to Papa, was any tree threatening to topple over and kill some poor soul passing by, thus making his or her spouse a widow. This particular tree had been struck by lightning years before and its lower trunk was only a shell of bark. It shocked people that such a hollowed-out tree could continue to grow. But its top half kept putting out new leaves every year. Rooster hid inside the trunk whenever he felt scared.

That's where I found him, his head buried in his bony knees, his birdlike body trembling. When he realized I was there, he clung to me, wetting me with his slobber. *"¡Madrina! ¡Madrina!"* He was so small for his age that it was hard for me to imagine that I was only two years older.

"Everything's okay now, the snake won't hurt the chickens anymore," I said as I wiped the back of my hand on my T-shirt.

"Noooooo," he sobbed. "It will c-c-come back and—and—and—come back and—and—and—*KILL* my chickens!"

"No, Roos, Tony took it away." Something stung my head and I felt a spider with my fingers. It curled itself into a ball and I was horrified by its size. I flicked it through the opening of the tree.

He smiled at me briefly before his face clouded back over. "But the sn-sn-sn-ake—"

"Just one measly egg. The rest of the chickens and their eggs are safe."

"But th-th-that egg was *sp-special.* No scr-scr-scrambled egg, n-n-no s-s-siree! It was g-g-gonna grow into a-a-a *ch-ch-chicken!*"

"Well, bad things happen sometimes, Roos."

He grabbed my hand and squeezed it so hard I thought a bone might break. "*Madrina* makes bad things go away."

"I've told you a million times that I can't always do that."

"Yes *Madrina* C-CAN!"

Madrina meant godmother in Spanish, a role I had no desire to assume. He'd been calling me that practically from the day we met at this very tree, over seven years ago when I was eight and Rooster was six. I sometimes wondered if he even knew my real name was Kady. "No, I can't!" I snapped. "You've gotta realize, Roos, that sometimes life just plain stinks!"

"N-N-N-Nooo!" He gave a determined shake with his head. "*Madrina* makes b-b-bad things go away!"

"Listen, kiddo," I said with an exasperated sigh as I realized this was going nowhere, "*you've* got powers, too. We don't call you Rooster for nothing! You're my fellow O Mighty Protector of the Chickens."

He blinked at me in astonishment. "*R-R-Rooster* O M-Mighty Pr-Pr-Pro—"

"Yes! You're a big strong guy now!"

"*Rooster* . . . str-str-strong?" His lower lip began to tremble.

"Yes! You could've handled that silly old snake if you hadn't been such a scaredy-cat."

He gave me an uncertain look, then slowly nodded his head as if he desperately wanted to believe me. As if being the O Mighty Protector of the Chickens was the most important thing in the world.

From the moment his family had moved in next door, Rooster had been fascinated but also terrified, for some odd reason, of the squawking chickens my family kept. He'd watch them for hours at a time with his mouth half open and his head cocked, but always standing at a distance. If I tried to talk to him, he'd run away.

But slowly over the weeks, as I fed those birds, he edged closer to me, usually hiding behind a rusty refrigerator or a pile of old tires (his father was starting a junkyard business). Then one day I heard shrieks of laughter coming from inside the widowmaker tree. The next day, the same thing happened, and so it went for several days.

From time to time, I saw an arm or leg poke out, streaked black from the charred insides of the tree, but Rooster never showed his face. And he always waited until I was gone before he slipped back out.

I'd already met his older brother, Tony, while swimming at the lake bordering our properties. He'd started talking to me right away in his strange-sounding English (he'd learned the language of Shakespeare in his Cuban school). He told me not to worry about getting to know Rooster, that he'd come on out of that tree if, and when, it suited him.

Rooster's mother told me the same thing in her broken English (the little English she knew was from waiting on American tourists as a teenager in Havana). She added that life back in Cuba had frightened Rooster badly and that you couldn't reason with him the way you could an ordinary kid. I came to realize that was putting it mildly.

I liked his mother, Señora Rosado. Her name was Evangelina, but Señor Rosado called her Angelina. Sometimes I slipped and called her that, too. She was always smiling, and if I so much as sneezed, she would cry out, *"¡Jesus, Maria y Jose!"* to bless me. She would often invite me to their house and serve me steaming cups of *café con leche,* which is a very strong Cuban coffee poured into a steaming cup of milk. I would always dump in about half the sugar bowl. She'd serve me a pitcher of water on the side and gesture that I was to drink it to "chase down the coffee."

The first time she did this, I couldn't imagine drinking an entire pitcher of water, but I didn't want to be rude, so I smiled and started sipping away. Tony took one look at my expression and started laughing, saying that later on when I started drinking "real" coffee (the bitter, black coffee his mother sipped), I'd understand what the water was for.

Sometimes, if it was later in the day, Angelina would serve me a *batido,* which was like an American milkshake but made with tropical fruits or wheat. The fruit *batidos* were great, especially when she used ripe pineapples from our patch, but the wheat *batidos* reminded me of a bowl of Sugar Smacks that had been put into a blender—weird!

While I sipped my drinks, she told me about Cuba in a flurry of words I barely understood while her hands flew about like birds' wings. Slowly, though, I learned about cloud forests, which were mountaintop woodlands filled with orchids and giant ferns, and about the various types of huge, colorful worms that Rooster used to play with. I learned about the majestic ceiba tree, which was so large that in olden times the Taino Indians had used a single tree to build a canoe for a hundred people.

Rooster's energetic mother seemed the opposite of his father, who was quiet when his temper wasn't flaring. He wore fancy, pleated shirts called *guayaberas* every single day. They were starched and blindingly white in the early days, then wrinkled and disgustingly food-stained after Señora Rosado died. Nobody ever called him by his first name, he was "Señor Rosado" to everyone. He was the only person I knew who chewed whole garlic cloves. If I stood too close to him, the garlic was so strong that it burned my eyes.

The Rosados' house was smaller than ours and filled with artificial plastic flowers. They were stuck in every imaginable place, including an upended roll of paper towels! In the tiny foyer was the family's most cherished possession, a statue of the Virgin Mary. They called her *"La Virgen de la Caridad,"* which meant "The Lady of Charity." I thought she was lovely. "She's always with us," Tony once told me. I wondered if seeing her statue every day had something to do with Rooster confusing me with a patron saint.

Even when I visited the Rosados' house those first times, Rooster would hide from me. He'd dart behind couches and chairs, or seemingly disappear through the walls like Casper the Ghost. His skin and clothes were streaked black from spending hours inside the widowmaker tree, which was his favorite hiding place. I'd seen his mother hang up his wash, covered with black streaks that she couldn't get out, and yell, "Son of a goon!" in her thick accent.

Finally, I decided to take matters into my own hands. I hid behind the widowmaker tree before feeding time, and as Rooster darted inside the tree, I filled his hands with chicken feed. He started to bolt, then froze when he saw the chickens swarm around his feet and gobble up the feed as it sifted through his fingers.

That's when something clicked inside him, and from then on I became, "Wonderful *Madrina,* O Mighty Protector of the Chickens." I'm not sure who came up with that title. Probably Tony.

I quickly regretted getting him out of that tree, because after that, when he wasn't hanging around the chickens, he followed me *everywhere.* If I was picking blackberries, he'd start picking blackberries; if I was climbing a tree, he'd start climbing the same tree. He was always bringing me stupid gifts, like Spanish moss "stoles" full of tiny red bugs that made you itch like crazy. He'd watch TV with me, too, and sing along with the commercials, making up his own words: "Plop, plop, frizz, frizz, oh what a real beast it is!"

Since we owned a color TV and the Rosados didn't, Mama invited him to watch *The Wizard of Oz* with us when it came on once a year. He'd show up in his pajamas and within minutes he'd be laughing hysterically at just about every scene, especially the talking tree. For weeks afterwards he'd babble about lions and tigers and bears and "oh mys." Nobody could explain to him that there was no such animal as an "oh my."

Then, when Rooster was eight years old, his mother died suddenly. She'd made a hurried trip to the grocery store to pick up cream cheese to fill her freshly baked *pasteles*, a type of pastry. Tony had suggested she just use guava paste, which she had on hand, but she insisted on adding the cream cheese, too. She told Rooster he couldn't come along to the store unless he found his shoes. As usual, he couldn't find them, so she left him behind. The last image he had of her was bumping down the pot-holed driveway in her rusty Rambler that she'd just learned how to drive. Minutes later, her car was struck by a tractor-trailer while making a left-hand turn into the A & P parking lot, and she was killed instantly.

Rooster refused to believe his mother wasn't going to return any moment with cream cheese to fill the *pasteles* she'd left sitting on the kitchen countertop. She'd simply gotten "lost" coming home. After she died, he spent hours at the top of his driveway waiting for her, always with his shoes on. Day after day, week after week, month after month. He wore his shoes everywhere, even in the shower, and only took them off to change pairs. His father kept him well-stocked with secondhands, but Rooster had a hard time deciding which pair to wear for which occasion—loafers sometimes went swimming, Keds sometimes went to church. Not only that, but he was always changing his mind. So he began carting his whole supply around in an old, beat-up suitcase.

Five years after his mother's death, with the suitcase long fallen apart, Rooster still never went barefoot like the rest of us did. He'd finally stopped wearing his shoes in the shower, and took off his flip-flops when he went swimming, but when something sparked the memory of his mother, like the smell of freshly baked pastries, he'd wait for her at the top of his driveway for hours. As dopey as he seemed, Rooster was loyal to anyone he loved, and his worship of me became unshakable. Before long, I came to the grim realization that for better or worse, for richer or poorer, in sickness and health, I would probably go on being his *Madrina*—until death did us part!

Maybe I should've felt honored—after all, nobody else idolized me. But the truth was, I felt trapped. Because when it came right down to it, all I'd really done was coax him out of the widowmaker tree, and that was only because I wanted to see what the goofy kid looked like.

"Come on, Rooster, let's get some breakfast," I told him after he'd finally calmed down over the snake. One sure way to make him happy was to give him food. "Afterwards, if you're nice, I might let you look at my dollhouse."

My dollhouse! That was my pride and joy. I'd found the kit at a garage sale at the beginning of the summer buried under a pile of dumb toys, including a "Creepy Crawler" maker that Wendell had snatched up. The kit only cost me three dollars compared to the four-fifty Wendell spent for the stupid bug maker.

While Wendell started popping out bugs, I started working on the dollhouse every spare minute I had. Wendell thought I was crazy for making a dollhouse at fifteen years old, and teased me every chance he got. No one else could believe it either, as I'd never been one to play with dolls. Working in the few spare minutes I had between chores, I slowly transformed a pile of sticks into a sunny yellow Victorian mansion. It had a real cedar roof I'd glued on shingle by shingle and tiny green window boxes I'd made myself from scraps of wood from the Rosados' junkyard, and filled with dried flowers.

The dollhouse sat on top of the card table in the living room on a green terry cloth towel of "grass." I'd painted a miniature NO TRESPASSING sign on the lawn, but everybody kept dumping stuff there anyway, not realizing what a masterpiece I'd built. Once Wendell put his Creepy Crawler bugs in the rooms, along with a sign that said HOUSE CONDEMNED!

Sometimes, late at night, when everyone was asleep, I'd stand in front of my dollhouse for hours, just looking at it. I didn't imagine I was much different from a rich man who'd pull out his hidden stash of gold and run his hands through it when nobody was around.

I'd wish I were Alice in Wonderland with a little bottle I could drink from to make me small. The dollhouse would be just my size and I'd be the mistress of that small, perfect world. I'd wear a ruffled gown, and have creamy porcelain skin, instead of freckles and a sunburn.

Maybe that was why I'd taken twenty-seven dollars and fifty-three cents out of my savings account—nearly the entire amount I'd saved over two years—and ordered a china doll. She was exquisite. Her sweet face was set off by a tiny nose and a rosebud mouth. Her gown had a flounced skirt and a tie-back bow of pink sateen.

Mama called her a silly indulgence and asked me how much money I'd spent. I lied and said only three dollars.

"Three dollars!" she'd scoffed. "Why, you could buy an entire dollhouse family at K-Mart for only two-ninety-five. Not that you need to be wasting your money on dolls. You're nearly in high school!"

I nearly died when I realized the dolls she was referring to—a tacky plastic family with seams running down their arms and legs, with painted-on clothes and hair. Who was she kidding! I told her my dollhouse was going to have real class, unlike anything around this dump!

Nobody was around when Rooster and I went into the kitchen, so I pulled out the boxes of cereal. They were smashed boxes that Mama got from the bargain bins at the local A & P, priding herself on how much money she saved.

"We've got smashed Lucky Charms and smashed Rice Krispies," I told Rooster as I held up the boxes.

"Want *tostones*!"

Tostones were salty fried plantains, a Cuban dish. "Sorry, Rooster, but we don't happen to have any plantains lying around." The only time Mama bought them was after they'd turned completely black and were marked down. And even then, she usually didn't buy them. She'd been suspicious of Cuban food ever since Señora Rosado had given her a bottle of *mojo,* a Cuban barbeque sauce that she'd made from our oranges. Mama said it had ruined her chicken, that it had turned it into something that looked and tasted like a great big pickle.

"T-T-Tony always b-b-buys th-them."

"Well, Mama didn't buy them this week. She didn't buy my favorite food, either, which happens to be Lorna Doones."

"L-Lorna D-D—" He looked at me questioningly.

"Never mind. You guys eat a lot of weird stuff that we don't, like those nasty black beans that look like rabbit droppings. You gotta choose between this and this." I plunked down the boxes before him.

"¡*Tostones!*" He jumped up and down. "¡*T-T-Tostones!* ¡*T-T-Tostones!*"

"Sorry guy, but this restaurant only serves Lucky Charms!" I retorted as I opened up the box. "What's *with* you today? You usually gobble up every pink heart in the box!"

Wendell sailed into the kitchen and picked up a banana.

"We don't have plantains today, but how 'bout if I fry this sucker?" he asked Rooster.

Rooster nodded eagerly.

Wendell flashed me an arrogant smile. "You can at least give him something he likes, Kady."

"Well, aren't you the smart one? And my, but didn't *you* come to our rescue earlier this morning?" I rolled my eyes. "Tony picked up that snake and it bit him and he didn't even flinch. Said it felt like stepping on a sandspur."

"Is he crazy or what? Who wants to step on a sandspur?"

"Admit it, Wendell. You're a wimp!"

He ignored me as he pulled out a heavy iron skillet, oiled it with Crisco, then placed it on a burner. "Ever see a match burn twice?" He held out a kitchen match.

I looked at him warily. Wendell always had a trick up his sleeve.

"That's once," he said, striking the match and lighting the gas burner. Then, blowing it out, he pressed the hot match against my wrist. "That's twice!"

"Ouch!"

Wendell doubled over in laughter. Rooster, hearing him, mindlessly laughed along.

"What's going on?" Mama asked as she entered the kitchen. She was wearing a shapeless housedress with faded orange flowers that smelled like Vick's Vap-O-Rub and a stretched-out headband with little nubbies all over it. Her springy hair looked like mown alfalfa sprouts the way it stuck straight up in a blunt cut. It was the same sort of ridiculous hair that sprouted from Rooster's head, only dull brown instead of coal black. Her plain, broad face didn't have a scrap of makeup on it.

"Wendell's being a jerk as usual!" I retorted as I moved the pile of dishes out of the sink and ran cool water over my wrist.

"What now, son?" she asked.

Wendell shrugged. "I'm just frying some bananas for Rooster."

"And burning me with a match!" I added.

Mama ignored both of us when she realized Rooster was in the room. "So, you've come to join us for breakfast." She beamed. "How wonderful!"

My shoulders slumped as I watched her turn her attention to Rooster instead of tend to my burn. Ever since Rooster's mother had been killed, the little spark of maternal instinct she had went to him. Try as I could, I couldn't imagine why she had so much patience with him while being so harsh with the rest of us.

Rooster went on and on in his gibberish about how I'd saved the chickens by chasing away the big snake. Even Mama had come to realize that in spite of all her mothering, it was me he idolized. And it bothered her to no end. Instead of thanking me for helping him like any normal mother would, she told me to hurry up and eat because I needed to start weeding before the sun came up full strength.

"I promised Rooster I'd let him see my dollhouse first," I firmly replied, then busied myself pouring Lucky Charms into a bowl so I wouldn't have to see her eyebrow—a fuzzy brown caterpillar—shoot up the way it did when she disapproved of something.

After Rooster had eaten his fried bananas, I whisked him into the living room and told him to wait by the couch while I cleared the most recent pile of clutter next to my magnificent mansion—naked Barbie and Ken dolls left by my sister.

"Doesn't anybody around here have any respect for my stuff?" I shouted. "Well, anyways," I said to Rooster when nobody answered me, "this is it."

He walked up to the house with his eyes popping like a kid about to see Santa.

"It's got doors, see, that really open and shut"—I opened and shut the front door that I'd spent an entire week of stolen moments installing—"and real wallpaper. Not bad, huh? For free samples from K-Mart? Feel the surface," I said as I guided his fingers along the embossed pattern. "Just like velvet. And best of all, here's my first doll."

I pulled my china doll from the tissue-lined box I kept in the attic of the dollhouse, and held her out to him. "Look, don't touch!"

"PEE PULL, PEE PULL," Rooster babbled.

"See her dress? Isn't it amazing how they make such tiny ruffles? It's made of real sateen. If you look at it in the light, it shimmers."

"W-W-Wowwwww," he breathed.

"These are called leg-of-mutton sleeves because they look like a leg of mutton. Do you know what mutton is?"

He shook his head.

"It's sheep meat."

"Oh," he said in that clueless way of his.

"Anyway," I carefully replaced her in her box, and slipped it back into the far reaches of the attic, "I'll have her sitting at the dining room table when I get it. It'll be a round mahogany table with flowered print chairs. And underneath the table I'll have one of those *Savonerrie* rugs like I saw in *Small World* magazine." I peered into the lower rooms, caught up in my vision. "Against this wall will be a china cabinet with beveled glass doors, and over here, a *Venus de Milo* statue—"

I heard a terrible crash and saw to my horror that Rooster had managed to pull my doll back out and dropped her on the floor.

"Rooster!" I screamed. The beautiful doll's head was split down the middle of her face; her tiny nose and rosebud mouth had shattered on impact. Half of her head slid under the couch. I shook him in anger. "You idiot!"

His eyes grew huge and he began to cry. "*¡Idiota! ¡Idiota!*" he echoed.

"You'll have to pay for this, including shipping and handling!"

"Good golly!" Mama roared as she stepped between us. "You're mighty worked up over a piece of china! I'll give you the three bucks myself!"

I wanted to tell her that the doll was worth a lot more than three measly dollars, but instead I retrieved the broken pieces as best I could and put them carefully back in the box—a box that suddenly resembled a coffin. My stomach knotted. Sometimes I wanted to kill Rooster. I'd been a fool to think I could show him my dollhouse.

Twenty minutes later, I stood outside blinking at the weeds that had sprouted between the rows of prickly pineapples. The sandy soil glinted like shards of glass.

How I hated living on the orange grove! Our wood frame house didn't even have air-conditioning. Just a tin roof hot enough to fry eggs on. Well, almost. I'd actually tried it once, but the eggs had slithered off, leaving a brown stain that was still there. The sides of the house were painted a horrid aqua blue. It seemed to me that the uglier the house, the happier the color. The Rosados' hovel was painted a shocking flamingo pink.

There were seven of us in that "happy" house—my parents; myself; my younger siblings, Wendell, Minnie and Sammy; along with my lunatic grandmother. For a while Jewel had stayed with us, too. She'd been the maid for the family who had lived on the grove before us, and had stayed with them whenever her husband took a fancy to beating her up. Now, Jewel only came twice a week to help with the washing and ironing since my folks didn't have the means to support a full-time maid. Especially when they've got me for free.

There was lots to do besides manage the grove, such as tend the garden, the chickens, and "Rosy," our three-hundred-and-fifty-pound hog. Papa had never gotten around to killing her since she'd saved my little brother's life several years before. Sammy had gotten cramps from swimming after eating four servings of beanie-weenies, and Rosy had rushed into the water after him. The rest of us—who were grabbing floats to toss to him—had stared in amazement as she'd pushed him to shore with her snout. Her picture had appeared in the paper along with Sammy's, but hardly anybody believed the story, since it came from a bunch of hicks.

After that, Rosy got so full of herself that all she did was eat, sleep, and grunt. And grow. Which meant a lot of pig to feed and keep clean, especially when Sammy should've known better than to have gone swimming after eating.

I often found myself staring wistfully at the new houses across the lake—all similar, yet as sunny and clean as my dollhouse, with lawns the color of Easter basket grass. And people inside who didn't have calluses on their feet or dirt under their fingernails. From a distance the houses even looked like dollhouses, with miniature doll people. Sometimes the doll people walked their miniature dogs. I never saw anybody walk a pig.

"Them houses look like toadstools sprouting up on a cow field, the way they're built so close together," Mama had snorted as we'd watched them go up a few years back. They were built on land that had been orange groves until the "Big Freeze of Sixty-Two" had killed most of the trees. "Can't imagine living in a place without a tree to rest your dogs under on a hot afternoon!"

"They've got air conditioners and swimming pools instead," I had pointed out. "And besides, they're pretty."

"Humph!" she'd snorted again. "I'd feel right naked."

Papa couldn't understand why anyone would want to live without trees, either. He never saw the egg stain on our tin roof that I was so painfully aware of, or the uneven concrete blocks propped under our house like broken teeth, or the screen door sagging on its hinges. All he saw were the acres of citrus trees he'd planted.

"When they reach maturity, we'll get close to two thousand oranges from a single tree. Can you imagine that?" he'd marvel. "I planted them far apart so they'd have room to grow. Lots of growers don't do that, they plant 'em all bunched together for the short-term profit."

We clearly weren't in it for the short-term profit, that was for sure. After seven years we hadn't made a single dime. It was only this year that there was enough fruit on the branches that we could finally look forward to our first cash crop.

In winter, when the days were short, I could see the glow of Papa's pipe flickering through the leaves and smell the rich cherry scent that lingered, as if his very spirit dwelled in our grove. He loved every stage of the growing season, from the fragrant blossoms that burst forth each spring to the tiny green balls that swelled with the summer rains, turned orange in the cool fall nights, and sweetened in the winter chill. Since he'd bought the land following the Big Freeze, he'd replanted the grove in Valencia juice oranges, which matured in March. He'd also added other citrus varieties to our yard that ripened throughout the year, plus added banana, papaya, mango, and avocado trees.

Sometimes when I helped him plant a new addition, our hands caked in mud, our feet rooted to the earth, he'd remind me of how far we'd come since that bleak winter following the freeze. And I'd think to myself, *Here I am up to my neck in mud, and he's telling me how far we've come!*

But when I considered the way we were living then, I guess he was right. I remember the day we arrived so clearly: I was eight years old, piled in the back of our old Chevy pickup. Wendell and Minnie sat among the few belongings that we hauled from state to state as we followed the cotton-citrus-peach-strawberry-and-tomato crops. Mama was eight months pregnant with Sammy.

It was surprisingly chilly for March, so Wendell, Minnie and I had built a tent over the lumpy mattress we were sitting on. We'd opened up a card table and draped a couple of blankets over it to make a little house.

We'd been nestled under there for about an hour—each of us holding down a table leg so our house wouldn't fall over when we hit potholes—when Papa pulled to the side of the road. He shooed us out and helped Mama lay down on the mattress. I remember there were crows all about, shrieking and carrying on as they gorged on rotten oranges, which lay thick on the ground among the dead trees.

The oranges had a sharp smell and were covered with blue-green mold. Papa told us that the crows were drunk from eating them, which stunned us. Who had ever heard of a drunken crow? I couldn't imagine why Papa had picked such an awful place to stop. But a short time later, as Mama's screams mingled in with the crows', she delivered Sammy right there in our tent. Papa cut the umbilical cord with his hedge clippers.

The owners of the land where we stopped, a couple by the name of Clark, took one look at us—MIGRANTS!—and told us not to bother stealing the oranges because they'd all been ruined in the freeze. Then they realized what was really going on and brought us up to the house.

We never left it.

The Clarks sold both the house and the grove to us for next to nothing. They told us they didn't like farming in Florida, anyway, where there was an ongoing battle against snakes, bugs, and oppressive heat, and seemed relieved to move back to Kentucky. Papa and Mama pawned their wedding bands and nearly everything else they owned to make a down payment, and managed to secure a loan through friends of the Clarks. Papa had been wanting his own land for a long time and thereafter referred to this little turn of events as the "Act of Providence."

We went right to work on our Act of Providence, clearing out the old trees and planting new ones. Papa took a job at the local orange plant to make ends meet while we awaited our first cash crop. During the processing season, he worked as much as seventy hours a week and came home as drained as the oranges he squeezed. Mama stayed home and ran the house as well as our lives.

I would've likely gone crazy these last boiling hot months if I hadn't had my dollhouse to retreat to. I wished I were working on it now, staining the dining room floor I'd carefully laid with Popsicle sticks. But instead I had to weed our Act of Providence!

From between the rows of pineapples I could see Rooster by the chicken coop. He was kicking at the earth, brooding over his lost egg. It amazed me how a kid with the I.Q. of a turnip could get all worked up over an egg.

I wondered what his life would've been like if his mother hadn't gone into labor during a hurricane back in Cuba. The roads were washed out and the power lines were down, so his father had ridden on horseback to get the doctor. But Rooster decided to come early, and a maid went into a panic and crossed his mother's legs to keep him from being born before the doctor arrived. Rooster, whose real name was Carlos, was born "oxygen-deprived."

Except for his wild hair and his shrunken size, he was a surprisingly ordinary-looking boy. It was the way he moved that made him strange, the way his arms and legs jumbled together. And the way he would stare at you with his mouth half open, as if he forgot he even had a mouth. He talked funny, too. Stuttered over most of his words, with spit flying everywhere, and shrieked at the slightest cause.

I often wondered how he would've turned out if his birth had gone normally. Would he have been full of himself like Tony? Or would he have turned out like his father, wasting away like the rusty junk he sold?

I felt a sudden ooze of mud between my toes and yelled at my sister, "Turn that hose off, you're making a mud hole!"

"I'm thirsty," ten-year-old Minnie whined, "it's hot out here." She had a broad face that looked like a younger version of Mama's. Today, her face was so red from the heat that you could barely see all of her freckles underneath—*a lot* more than I had! Sometimes, to tick her off, I called her "Mini-Mama."

"Tell me about it," I said as I twisted my long hair into a knot atop my head. (It was limp and reddish blonde, like Papa's before it started prematurely turning gray.) I started to get some water, too, then wrinkled my nose. I'd never gotten used to the sulfur water from the well—warm and smelling like rotten eggs.

It was August, the hottest month, when summer had gone on forever, with no promise of ending. Day after day the clouds hovered over the sweltering land, soaking up the heat like giant sponges until they exploded in angry bursts of rain and lightning.

I was wearing my bathing suit to keep cool, not that it helped.

Tony revved up his pickup, a pile of junk propped up on cinder blocks he'd been piecing together from scrap. A cloud of exhaust fumes belched forth. He told me the reason it didn't run was because he hadn't put the wheels on yet, but it looked as if there was a lot more wrong with it than that.

I'd been amazingly tolerant of that farting machine he'd been working on all summer. I'd even helped him tinker on it, until he confided to me that he needed a car to take out Lily Finch. I couldn't imagine Tony picking Lily for his first girlfriend. She had a sharp nose, sharp eyes, and sharp spikes of hair yanked into a ponytail with one of those rubber bands that came around the newspaper. He'd met her in his shop class—she was the only girl.

Once, I overheard Lily tell Tony that if his fan belt ever happened to break, he could use a woman's nylon stocking as a replacement until he got to a repair shop. I couldn't believe it when he told her he'd have to take *her* wherever he went! Didn't he notice that she was hardly the type to wear nylons?

Right now, Tony was driving me nuts the way he was revving up that engine and polluting the air while the truck sat stuck there. I felt my own engine revving up, my own life going nowhere. I screamed, "GET A MUFFLER!"

He looked over at me, amused by my outburst. "Why don't you help me with this water pump that won't fit on right? I could use a hand."

"What do you think I am, an octopus?" I snarled.

"*¿Qué te pasa?* You wake up on the wrong side of the bed?"

I almost yelled something back when I heard the craggy voice of Bob Dylan singing "Mister Tambourine Man" blast out of his car radio: *I'm ready to go anywhere / I'm ready for to fade / Into my own parade / Cast your dancing spell my way / I promise to go under it.*

It was a refreshing change over the cha-cha-cha music Tony usually played almost nonstop.

The words mesmerized me:

> *Yes to dance beneath the diamond sky*
> *with one hand waving free*
> *Silhouetted by the sea*
> *Circled by the circus sands*
> *With all memory and fate*
> *Driven deep beneath the waves . . .*

Hot sand fell like sifted flour from the weed in my hand as I wondered what it would be like to dance beneath a diamond sky. I wanted a life! "I'm outta here," I announced to Minnie.

"What!"

"I'm outta here!" I started running, then called over my shoulder, "Get Rooster to help you!"

"I'm telling! You're gonna be whooped! Kady! *KADY, COME BACK!*"

That song was still jangling in my mind as I floated on the lake. The magic swirling water tickled my ears as it lapped against them, washing away my cares. I kept my eyes closed to the sun, but whenever it slipped behind a cloud I opened them to watch the sky.

I loved to watch the clouds change into fanciful shapes and wondered how they could hold thousands of gallons of water yet float so high. How I wished I could stay here forever and never go back home! I could become a sea goddess, spending my days drifting under a diamond sky.

I even felt like a sea goddess, dressed in the best swimsuit I'd ever had, a shimmering green bikini Mama had gotten only because it was a deal "too good to pass up." The way the light struck the material made it look as if there were hundreds of tiny rainbows on it.

Even if Minnie and Rooster tracked me down and dragged me home, for these few stolen minutes I could at least pretend I was a sea goddess. My subjects were the little fish nibbling at my toes. I closed my eyes. . . .

I was about to be crowned the Goddess of Lake Pomelo by a school of sunfish carrying a seaweed garland when the distant whine of a ski boat interrupted my fantasy. I blinked at the harsh sunlight, startled. There were lots of motorboats on the lake now as people crowded into the growing subdivisions. Not that I really minded. In fact, I had chosen to swim near the subdivisions to pretend I really lived there.

As the noise grew louder, I looked up and realized the boat was headed right toward me. I waved my hands, shouting, "Watch where you're going!"

The driver of the boat swerved, sending the skier he was pulling headlong into the water. "What are you doing in the middle of the lake? I almost hit you!" he shouted as he slowed down.

"I live here!" I shouted back as the wake of his boat washed over me. "Don't you know to stay more than thirty yards from shore?"

The skier surfaced and gave me a dazed look, his hair sticking up from his head in comical tufts from the sudden impact. "You *live here?* What are you . . . a mermaid?"

I started to say something nasty, but his face crinkled into a smile and I found myself smiling back at him.

"We are more than thirty yards out. Take a look for yourself," the driver pursued.

I looked toward shore, realizing I'd drifted out. "Oh, well . . . sorry . . ."

"Are you sitting on some kind of a float?" the skier asked.

"No."

"Then you've got to be a mermaid." He swam closer and peered at my face. "With violet eyes."

"Violet eyes?" I pulled away from his intense stare. "They're blue."

He looked at me from different angles. "They're violet, I swear."

Nobody had ever paid attention to my eye color before, especially some nut with silly hair. "So?"

He shrugged. "They're pretty, that's what. But then, fish have all sorts of neat eye colors."

"Very funny."

He dove underneath me and resurfaced a moment later. "What do you know, Mark! She's our same species!"

"Cut it out!" I splashed him with my feet to show him just how human I was.

"Okay, okay!" he laughed as he held up his hands against the onslaught of water.

I stopped kicking. When I looked at him again he was smiling at me, a dimple appearing in his right cheek. "I'm Jon."

I smiled back. "Hi, Jon."

He looked about seventeen, with sun-bleached hair—now plastered to his head—and a deep tan, except for the tip of his nose, which was bright red and peeling, same as mine. I was relieved to realize I wasn't the only person who looked like Rudolph the Red-Nosed Reindeer.

"And I'm Mark," the driver called out. He was a muscular guy—the weight-lifting type—with dark hair pulled back in a sweatband and silver-tinted sunglasses that masked his eyes.

"Hi, Mark."

"You ought to try out to be one of those Weeki Wachi mermaids," Jon went on, that dimple showing again. "You'd be perfect."

Although I'd never been to the popular attraction, I'd seen the mermaids gracing the covers of the brochures and they were all beautiful girls. "Sounds kind of rough swimming around with your legs crammed in a tail," I said self-consciously, "and smiling all the while."

"Oh, but think of all those bananas you'd get to eat." Weeki Wachi mermaids were famous for eating bananas underwater.

"It'd drive me bananas I'm sure," I retorted with a laugh.

"She's as quick as Maddy," Mark called out to Jon.

"Who?" I asked.

They exchanged glances. "Oh, just some girl we know," Jon said.

Oil from the puttering motor floated across the water, painting swirls of color around him. I poked my finger in a swirl, embarrassed by his confident grin. He wasn't as cute as the driver—his nose was too long, his lips too thin—but his hazel eyes mesmerized me the way they seemed to change color.

"So how do you stay afloat all the way out here?" he asked.

"Well, I just keep my lungs full and"—shrugging—"float. Or dog paddle, like I'm doing now."

"And you don't worry about alligators coming along and— "

"No," I laughed, "just ski boats."

"You won't have to worry about us, we'll be more careful."

"I'm sorry I almost hit you," Mark said, his sunglasses glinting in the sun. "What's your name, by the way?"

I started to tell them, but blurted out "Katerina" instead. It sounded more regal than plain old Kady, a name that none of my teachers even knew how to spell. They always misspelled it as "Katie," which was what my mother had meant to name me when she'd written it on the birth certificate. But since she'd only made it to the third grade, she misspelled it. I'd tried to explain all this to my second-grade teacher, Miss Rose, but she made such a big deal of how ignorant my mother was in front of the whole class that it made me ashamed.

"So, do you go to Pomelo?" Jon asked.

"'Bout to start."

"So you're just a sophomore."

"Yep."

"That's why I haven't seen you," Jon grinned.

"Jon makes it a point to know every pretty girl in school," Mark said.

"Oh?"

"I do too," Mark admitted. "He just has the advantage of being in the water with you right now."

I couldn't believe this! I started to say something back, such as, "I make it a point to know all the good-looking guys," but since I'd never flirted with guys before, the words wouldn't come out. I giggled like an idiot instead, which wasn't like me at all.

"Would you like to take a spin with us?" Jon asked. "We could sit up in the bow while my private chauffeur drives."

"Gee, thanks," Mark protested.

The invitation caught me off-guard. There was no telling what would become of me if Mama saw me flying past the house on a ski boat. I was already in enough trouble. "Maybe another time."

"Come on. Just a short ride." He shot his skis over the water to Mark, then climbed aboard and offered me his hand.

I found myself unable to resist those blue-green-golden eyes that seemed to be teasing, coaxing, almost toying with me. Suddenly, I was rising out of the water on a wobbly metal ladder.

Mama wouldn't notice me on a boat, I told myself. *I'd just be another dot of waving hair.*

Jon led me to the bow and sat next to me while Mark reeled in the ski rope, muttering, "Chauffeur—ha!" Then Jon offered me some brownies out of a Tupperware container.

His eyes twinkled. "These aren't just any brownies."

"Oh really." I took one. "Did you make 'em yourself?"

"Yep," he nodded, "with all my secret ingredients."

I told him I thought it was neat when guys cooked.

I was trying to pick the crumbs out of my teeth a few minutes later when Mark shouted, "Hold on!" and thrust the throttle to forward.

Crumbs from my brownie flew past my face, and my hair

whipped to life as we lurched forward. I'd been on plenty of boats, but nothing this fast. My body hummed with vibrations as the motor tore through the water.

It was too loud to talk, so Jon and I sat side by side, our wet calves knocking together, his soft with long hairs and mine prickly with stubs. It'd been three days since I'd shaved and I felt like a cactus. He didn't say anything about it. He just kept passing me brownies as he shouted whoops of joy into the wind.

Afterwards, I remembered the little details of that ride: the whipping wind, the dancing sun, the low-flying birds we kept catching up to and riding directly underneath, the shoreline that seemed to shake when we hit the wakes of passing boats, the little chip on Jon's front tooth as he drew me against his ski vest and kissed me good-bye.

Kissed me good-bye!

His lips landed mostly on my cheek but the corner of his mouth landed on the corner of mine.

I stumbled off that boat in a stupor, the whole world spinning giddily around me, as if I'd just stepped off a carousel ride. I could feel my heart racing as it never had before, pumping new life through me. I'd never realized there were so many colors, sensations, or sounds. I could still feel the tingle of Jon's lips on mine—my very first kiss—as he waved good-bye and slowly shrunk into a little dot of red-and-white. I slowly brought my hand to my lips as a silly smile spread across my face.

I'd asked them to drop me off at the ravine about a half mile from my house, knowing that Mama would "skin me 'live" if she saw me getting off that boat.

The ravine had always been one of my favorite hideaways, a delightful tangle of magnolia, sweet gum, and live oaks, so different from the grove trees that stood in straight lines, like soldiers at attention. A vine of confederate jasmine jumped at me in a vibrancy of whiteness. I playfully draped it around my shoulders and inhaled its cloying sweetness. Then I covered my hair with sticky pink tarflowers growing in clumps by the water and giggled at my reflection.

"LOVE IS A MANY SPLENDORED THINGGGG-GGGGGG!" I crooned. I sang softly at first, but was soon pouring my heart out to the oak-pine-palm-plum-persimmon-bamboo-sweet-gum-and-magnolia trees that surrounded me: *THEN YOUR FINGERS TOUCHED MY SILENT HEART AND TAUGHT ME HOW TO SINGGG! YES, TRUE LOVE—*"

Something stirred in the bushes.

I froze, my face scarlet with embarrassment. "Who's there?"

A twig crackled and I whirled around. "Who's there, I said?"

Rooster rushed up to me. "¡Madrina! ¡Madrina!"

"Geez, Rooster! You nearly scared me to death!" I cried, then laughed with relief. If Minnie or Wendell had caught me singing about true love, they'd never let me live it down.

His face—smeared with blackberries that grew wild in

the woods—beamed with pleasure. "Found ya! F-Found y-ya! Found y-ya!"

I could almost hear glass shattering as the real world crashed over me. "So much for privacy," I grumbled. "So what are you up to now? Finger painting your face with blackberry juice?"

What amazed me about Rooster was that he was so infatuated with me that he never caught on to my little acts of cruelty. I could say almost anything to him, even reduce him to tears as I had over the china doll, and he would still follow me around as though we were best friends.

The wind had started to blow as it often does before a storm and Rooster motioned for me to be quiet. "C-C-Come," he said, grabbing my hand.

Thinking he was taking me to a blackberry thicket, I was surprised when he pulled me to the stand of bamboo between our houses. His face lit up as he stared—entranced—at the bamboo as it swayed back and forth with a creaky groan.

"What is it, Rooster?"

He clung to my hand, his eyes following the bamboo from its very roots all the way to the tips of the towering stalks, to its feathery leaves trembling in the wind.

"It's like Jack's beanstalk, isn't it, the way it climbs into the heavens," I said. "Is this what you wanted to show me?"

I often stared at the bamboo the same way, especially on breezy nights when the moon was full and the stalks became graceful dancers. Anything was possible on nights like those. . . .

Rooster threw up his hands and yelled to the wind, "LAND OF THE FREE!"

I couldn't help but grin. Rooster often yelled about the land of the free when the huge stalks began to creak and groan. They reminded him of the creaking mast of the bamboo raft on which his family had made the treacherous crossing to America. His mother had been so excited when they drifted ashore that she yelled, "LAND OF THE FREE, HOME OF THE BRAVE!" She'd learned the words when "The Star Spangled Banner" had been broadcast in Havana during American baseball games.

I'd seen Rooster screaming "LAND OF THE FREE" in the pouring rain about a hundred times. It used to annoy me, but today the word "free" made me think again of Jon and a warm blush lit me from my cheeks to the tips of my toes.

"LAND OF THE FREE!" I shouted as the rain began to fall, the lightning to crackle.

"LAND OF THE FREE! ERRR—ER—ERRR—ER—ERRRRRRRRRR!" He flapped his arms and ran through the stalks, shouting, "I'm Rooster! O Mighty Protector of the Chickens!" without the slightest stutter.

I flapped my arms crazily and sang to the roaring wind, "*Once on a high and windy hill—*"

"I AM NOT AFRAID OF ANY SN-SN-SNAKE! I AM N-N-NOT AFRAID OF *ANYTHING!*" he screeched. "NOT L-L-LIONS, N-N-NOT TIGERS, N-N-NOT BEARS, N-N-NOT O-O-OH-*MYS!*"

"—in the morning mist—"

"ERRR—ER—ERRR—ER—*ERRRRRRRRR!*"

"—two lovers kissed—"

"ERRR—ER—ERRR—ER—*ERRRRRRRRR!*"

"—and the world stood still—"

"ERRR—ER—ERRR—ER—*ERRRRRRRRR!*"

"—Then your fingers touched my silent heart—"

"ERRR—ER—ERRR—ER—*ERRRRRRRRR!*"

"—and taught it how to singgggggg! Yes, true love's—"

"ERRR—ER—ERRR—ER—*ERRRRRRRRR!*"

"—a many splendored thing!"

"ERRR—ER—ERRR—ER—*ERRRRRRRRRRRRRRR!*"

"ERRR—ER—ERRR—ER—*EERRRRRRRRRRRRRRR!*" I crowed back exultantly.

I was giddy when I came into the house a half hour later, soaked to the skin. We'd crowed right through a severe thunderstorm. I couldn't remember such a wild, wonderful afternoon. And it had all started with that song pouring out of Tony's radio about some silly tambourine man.

Mama swooped down on me, so close I could see beads of sweat jostling on those caterpillar eyebrows. "What was all that racket about? You'd think the sky was falling the way you and Rooster were running around, like Henny Penny and Cocky Locky."

"You know how Rooster is."

"Rooster's one thing, but I've never heard you crow. Especially during a thunderstorm. You're likely to get fried. A woman died walking to her mailbox just last week. Blam!"

"You ought to try it sometime, it's good for the soul," I giggled.

Her eyes drilled through me like a mean old woodpecker's.

"You're twenty minutes late and news is about to start. And I ain't too happy with your behavior earlier, upsetting Rooster over a piece of china—"

"How dare you call my beautiful doll a *piece of china!*"

"—and leaving Minnie with all that work. You're walking on thin ice."

"What ice?" I retorted as the joy faded completely from my face. "It's hot as hell around here!"

Those beady eyes just kept drilling and drilling. "I'll give you two minutes to get changed."

It was my rotten luck to get stuck with the worst job in the household—getting Grampsie ready for the news.

Grampsie had been living with us since Grandpa—who she always called by his full name, Leopold Baines Palmer—died of a heart attack three years before. He'd been getting a root canal at the dentist's office when he keeled over in the chair. She wouldn't go near a dentist after that and was relieved that her teeth had already rotted out and been replaced with dentures. All she had to do was pop 'em in a cup of water before she went to bed and pop 'em back in her mouth in the morning, like wash 'n' wear clothing.

When she first arrived, she was always setting us straight about this or that, and working her knitting needles to the beat of her temper. Some of my best sweaters—generally bright reds and hot pinks—had come from those flashing needles.

Well into her seventies, she'd been able to scale the few towering survivors of the Big Freeze and pluck the "shiners" right off the top. The shiners were the fruit that had been overlooked after a tree had been picked. They were called that because of the way they shone like little lights. My sentimental father called them "lights of hope."

Grampsie had a pair of tree-climbing boots with spikes on the bottoms a half-inch long and had once killed a frog by accidentally stepping on it while wearing them. We could always tell when she was wearing the boots by the scraping sound they made on the hardwood floors. Mama said that she was going to make Grampsie stop wearing them one of these days because they were ruining her floors (not that they weren't already ruined!). But whenever Mama said "one of these days" on the subject of Grampsie, you knew it was just a lot of talk.

That was all before she was afflicted with what Mama called the "spreading decline." In this particular disease a small worm feeds from the roots of a tree until the tree slowly dies from the top down. I wasn't sure what kind of worm was eating at Grampsie until one night during the Lawrence Welk Show— the "old fogie's show" as Minnie and I called it—a silver-haired man kissed a silver-haired woman during a Geritol commercial and she burst into tears. We stared at her, shocked, for we'd never seen her cry.

"I've never known the love of a man," she whispered hoarsely.

We nudged each other, whispering, "What did she say?" for we couldn't believe our ears. After all, she'd been married to Grandpa for half a century!

"My life is nearly over and I've never, never known—" She began sobbing so hard that she went into a coughing fit. Mama pounded her on her back and gave her water until she came around. Soon Grampsie stopped crying, but she never really recovered.

Just a week or two later she got the silly idea that Walter Cronkite was paying her a personal visit every night when he anchored the news. She began leaning forward in her recliner and gazing at the TV with huge, dreamy eyes.

"Can you imagine such a charming man wooing a country gal like me?" she asked our family one night over chipped beef and strawberry Jell-O. "He looks right into my eyes, just right into them!"

Wendell started to snicker. "He looks into *everybody's* eyes, Grampsie. He's on TV!"

"And that's the way it is . . . ," Grampsie went on dreamily.

"*What's* the way it is?" Wendell asked, baffled.

"That he loves me, of course. He says it every night as he gazes into my eyes."

Wendell looked at her as if she'd gone mad. "Are you hearing things? The guy's on television, delivering the news! Not talking to you personally! And he's certainly not GAZING into your eyes!" He turned to Papa and guffawed. "Can you imagine Walter Cronkite GAZING at anyone?!"

Grampsie's eyes went all liquidy as she went on, as if in a trance. "'*I love you, Sadie Palmer, and that's the way it is.*'" She sighed blissfully. "I've never known real love from a man until . . . until sweet, kind Dear Walty came into my life."

Wendell burst into laughter.

Papa ordered him to simmer down.

"But what about Grandpa?" Minnie asked. "Didn't he love you?"

Grampsie snorted, clearly insulted by the question. It took her a moment to recover enough to speak. "Why, Leopold Baines Palmer was an S.O.B.!"

"Ma!" Papa cried as he dropped a squiggly spoonful of Jell-O onto his lap.

She pointed a long, crooked finger at him. "He was an S.O.B. and you know it!"

During the moonwalk coverage in July, Walter Cronkite chummed with the astronauts on TV and told the world how great Tang was (the beverage that helped sponsor the moonwalk). Grampsie insisted that Mama buy some to offer him when he came calling. Papa was appalled, not just because Tang was nothing like fresh orange juice, but because he realized his mother was getting worse.

What shocked me about Grampsie's behavior was that a lot of unbelievable events were happening in the news right then, events she'd normally be pitching a fit over: guys were growing their hair long, burning their draft cards to keep from being sent to Vietnam, and calling cops "pigs"; acidheads were jumping off tall buildings; hippies were sticking flowers into the ends of gun barrels; and women were burning their bras.

I kept expecting to see those knitting needles flash when I turned on the news, but, instead, Grampsie's hands remained limply in her lap as she made lovey-eyes at Dear Walty.

On last night's news she'd seen a bunch of teenagers skinny-dipping at an outdoor rock concert in Woodstock, New York. She'd just smiled dreamily when the show was over and mouthed, "I love you, Sadie Palmer, and that's the way it is on August 16, 1969. Yes, that's the way it is." It was hard to believe this was the same woman who just the year before had told me quite proudly, "Your Grandpa never saw me buck nekked in the fifty-two years we were married." I began to pray that I never lost my mind.

She was so honored by Dear Walty's "visits" that she had to "get respectable" for him. Every night. Grampsie had never been one to dress up, except on Sundays when she went to church in one of three calico prints she'd had for years, all with droopy hems and silly bows she'd never learned to tie correctly. She began wearing those dresses every night, with pantyhose that bunched around her bony ankles, and clunky heels that were years out of style. I'd see Jewel spending her short visits carefully washing and ironing them, muttering good-naturedly under her breath. At least Grampsie had stopped wearing her tree-climbing boots.

She did her own makeup, but the years of toiling in the fields (she and Grandpa had eked out a living on a dirt farm near Lake Apopka) had stiffened her fingers and she had difficulty rolling her hair, especially with those "newfangled" hot rollers that burned her fingers. She didn't understand why the Clairol company had named them "Kindness." Since Mama didn't have any patience with hair, the job usually fell to me. Just last week I'd offered to give her a permanent, but she wouldn't hear of it. "I've no intention of looking like a broccoli stalk!" she'd sniffed.

"A what?" I'd asked.

"That's what old people with permanents look like. Broccoli stalks! I'll have no part of it."

"Then how about getting a blunt cut and let it hang straight? That's the style now."

"And look like a pot-smoking hippie?" She waved me away. "I don't think Dear Walty would go for that."

The afternoon I met Jon she was especially difficult. "I can't find my 'Flames of Fire'!" Grampsie wailed as I picked up a brush and began attacking her hair.

"Try this peach stuff." I tossed her a tube of lipstick from the pile of makeup strewn before her.

"It's much too pale. I need my 'Flames of Fire.' And quick! News is about to start."

I walked over to the tiny TV set on the counter, turned it on and fiddled with the coat hanger antenna Mama had rigged to improve the reception. Then I explained as if she were three, "This is a television. The people inside it can't see you."

Grampsie clapped her hands over her face. "I won't have Dear Walty see me like this!"

Mama handed her the "Flames of Fire" lipstick—a garish orange-red color—then glowered at me as she flipped the TV switch back off.

Grampsie seized the lipstick, carefully twisted the stick all the way out, and applied a quick dab to her lower lip. "There! Now I'm respectable!" she announced with a sparkle in her eye.

That same night I had a dream I was sitting in my Victorian mansion awaiting my gentleman caller. "There! Now I'm respectable!" I announced as I added a dab of lipstick to my rosebud mouth. There was a knock on the door and the butler whisked in my gentleman caller. He smelled faintly of gasoline and his hair stuck out in comical tufts. In his hand was a bunch of violets, the very same color of my eyes. But as he tilted my face to meet his, I felt a splitting headache coming on. I collapsed on the floor, the whole world going black.

"A little more to the right," Papa said as he puffed on his pipe. The scent of tobacco mixed in with the fresh dirt.

I moved the palm a bit, then held it still while he scooped shovelsful of soil around the roots. It was rich black earth he'd hauled from the woods. He tramped it down firmly, making sure there were no air pockets, then stood back to admire it. "Whaddya think?"

"Great," I replied flatly.

I heard the whine of a boat motor and turned toward the lake, searching for the boy who had burst into my life as suddenly and beautifully as a night-blooming cereus. But it turned out to be a houseboat, and my shoulders slumped in disappointment.

Maybe Jon was waiting for me at the ravine. But could I slip away with Mama following my every move? She was glaring at me from the kitchen window, daring me to run off again. I'd been helping Papa for hours, chopping up the rotten branches of the orange trees, then pulverizing the wood and spreading it around the garden, and now planting palm trees.

Minnie gave me a smug smile from underneath the widow-maker tree where she sat with Rooster. I gave her a dirty look.

"A little soaking and we're done," Papa said.

I turned the hose on, filling the air with the dreadful smell of rotten eggs.

"This really isn't my job," I grumbled.

"Maybe you'll think twice about skipping out."

"Shoot, Papa, all we do is work around here."

There were dozens of palms now lining both sides of the driveway the half mile or so it stretched to the highway. "Someday these'll make the finest entranceway of any place in town," he said as fat clouds rose from his pipe.

It seemed silly to plant such magnificent trees when they only led to a hovel. Even the driveway leading through them was a disgrace—full of so many potholes that it looked like an old rag. But it was pointless to tell that to Papa, who was caught up in his Act of Providence.

Papa dumped his ashes on the ground and refilled his pipe. "It wasn't my plan to make an entrance with 'em, ya know. Just needed a place to put 'em until they were ready for harvest. Ain't nothing better than hearts of palm."

"You eat the heart?"

"You ain't much of a Florida gal not knowing about our finest delicacy," he smiled, the lines creasing on his weather-beaten face. "But you can blame your Mama for that. As I recollect, Grampsie invited us over for dinner right after we moved here. Your grandparents were native Floridians, as you know. Always just getting by, by farming the scrub country. But Grampsie sure did cook up a storm when we came around. She'd fry up a heap of squirrel heads—"

"Gross!"

His blue eyes sparkled. "People just don't know good food anymore. She made pecan pies you'd die for, fish chowders oozing with cream, kumquat marmalades, possum pies. Cracker cooking. It's too bad that's all changed since . . ."

He never could say, "Since she lost her mind."

He pushed back a wisp of gray-blond hair on his balding forehead. "Well, her hearts of palm dish surpassed all others. Swamp cabbage we called it."

"I remember going out to their place. They had that outhouse where I found the water moccasin curled up on the seat."

"Yep," he nodded. "I remember chasing him outta there."

I shuddered. "I don't remember eating anything called swamp cabbage. And with a name like that, who'd want to?"

"Well, your Mama thought it was the grandest stuff in the world."

"It figures."

"Kady," he frowned.

"Well, I'm sorry. But of all the mothers in this world, it isn't fair that I got stuck with her."

"When we got back home," he went on with a stern look to silence me, "I went out in the wilds and dug up a couple of palms. I planted that first pair right up there." He pointed to the tallest pair next to the house. Then he took a long drag on his pipe and slowly let it out. "But when your Mama realized the trees die when you cut out their hearts, why, she wouldn't let me touch 'em."

"Oh?"

"Nope. Not a single one. It surprised me, learning that about your Mama. So"—he gave me an almost imperceptible wink—"I just keep planting 'em and they just keep growing. She says this way she gets to enjoy her hearts of palm year round."

"That so?"

"That's so."

So Mama had a soft spot other than her love for Rooster. For trees of all things!

Rooster rushed up to me as I was washing the mud off my feet a few minutes later. "Lookee!" He held up three dolls cut from the papery bark of a punk tree that grew in his yard. He'd glued on acorn heads and Spanish moss hair. Stuck cloves served for the eyes, nose and mouth. Torn pieces of one of Jewel's colorful but faded old scarves served for clothes. Obviously, Minnie had helped Rooster make them.

"Lovely." I forced a smile. I'd made many things from punk bark, too, mainly because I liked the feel of tearing the huge sheets from the tree. It had a wonderful smell, like Doublemint gum, and felt like leather. It didn't seem to hurt the tree, either, pulling off the bark; there were layers and layers of that wonderful stuff. I'd made sailboats, little houses, but never anything so ugly as these dolls.

Minnie sauntered up to me, her short brown hair bouncing just like Mama's. "We made them for the dollhouse. Rooster wanted to replace the doll he broke."

Rooster nodded excitedly. "I m-m-make new PEE PULL, *Madrina!*"

"You mean to tell me that these are to replace my china doll?"

"New PEE PULL!" he cried again.

I looked at him, aghast.

"Don't hurt his feelings, he spent hours on them," Minnie whispered to me out of the side of her mouth, then said to Rooster, "Come up to the house and we'll put them in the rooms."

"Don't touch my dollhouse!"

"We're not going to hurt it. Good golly, Kady, you get uptight over nothing!"

"Nothing! Did you see what he did to my brand-new doll?" I'd stayed up late gluing her head back together. Now she looked as if she'd contracted leprosy.

"Yes, but Mama said she'd give you three dollars to replace her. That's pretty amazing for her. Especially since you're the only fifteen-year-old I know who still plays with dolls."

I wanted to tell her that three dollars would barely cover one leg, but instead sniffed, "It wouldn't be the same."

"Will you stop making such a big deal over a stupid doll!" she hissed, then spoke loudly and clearly, "ROOSTER HAS MADE SOME VERY NICE PEOPLE FOR YOUR DOLLHOUSE."

"PEE PULL! PEE PULL!" he echoed, thrusting them in my face.

"I'm warning you, Mini-Mama, don't touch my dollhouse!"

A fuzzy little eyebrow raised up. "Don't you dare call me that!"

"Then stop acting like Mama!"

"*Anybody* would tell you the same thing!" Then, tugging Rooster's hand as he continued to shout, "PEE PULL! PEE PULL!" Minnie pulled him toward the lake. "We don't need a house to play with our people. They can go on a picnic instead. Right, Rooster?"

"Right, Rooster!" he echoed. "I c-c-can be their O M-M-Mighty Protector!"

The last week of August as I got ready for the coming school year, the lake drew me toward it like a giant magnet. I found myself constantly searching for the red-and-white boat.

"Turn," Mama commanded, her mouth filled with straight pins as she altered my clothes.

I was staring dreamily at the lake, feeling that kiss on the corner of my mouth. . . .

"You got cotton in your ears or what? I said, 'TURN!'"

"Sorry!" I cried, startled, as I turned to one side.

"The other way. You ain't heard a word I've said in days."

"Sure I have," I lied. I wasn't about to tell her about the boy with the blue-green-golden eyes. My mother was definitely NOT a romantic.

It was stuffy in the tiny living room and my back ached from standing still for so long. A pile of cheap clothes lay at my feet. Preparing my clothes was a yearly ritual I hated, especially since Mama would spend hours trying to salvage an outfit anybody else would throw away.

The minutes stretched into hours. The only relief was a fan that blew a blast of warm air my way every few seconds.

"You've got to stop wiggling," Mama said as she yanked my dress and inserted a pin at knee level, the recommended dress length from the school handbook. She didn't care one bit that most girls ignored the handbook and wore minidresses about six inches above the knee, and never got sent home for indecent exposure of a female leg. "All this wiggling's giving me a headache."

"The hem doesn't have to be perfect. Especially on these rags."

"Hush up and turn slowly so I can have a look," she said. "This particular 'rag' happens to be made of an indestructible fabric, a brand-new material called Orlon Acrylic. Got it for only three-ninety-five at the Bargain Barn."

"Oh great, I'll be stuck with it forever."

If the price was right, Mama was a sucker for anything. I had a closet filled with oddities to prove it, including a pair of loafers that felt like concrete blocks, a plaid skirt with mismatched seams, and an embroidered peasant dress marked down because one of the yellow flowers at the back of the neckline had started to unravel. Mama had filled it in with orange thread—the closest color she had to match—and told me not to worry about it, that my long hair would cover it anyway. I kept meaning to redo it with yellow embroidery floss, but was so lousy at sewing, I was afraid I'd only make it look worse.

"*¡FELIZ NAVIDAD, ROOS!*" Tony hollered from the Rosados' dock. Every time Rooster caught a fish, Tony yelled *Merry Christmas* in Spanish. It was his way of protesting against Castro for banning the Cuban celebrations of Christmas because they interfered with the sugarcane harvest. Rooster beamed as he held up his fish.

Mama looked out the window. "Oh Lordy! Rooster's caught another big fish." She narrowed her eyes and examined the fish as closely as she could from such a distance. "Thank Goodness it's a bass this time," she remarked.

Just the day before, Rooster had caught a huge carp, which he'd carted all the way up to the clothesline where I was helping Jewel pin up the wash. Its iridescent scales had shone like tiny rainbows as Rooster—straining under the weight— swayed its heavy weight before us. "We have b-b-big fish dinner, no?" he'd cried with excitement. "Jewel c-c-can even stay for d-d-dinner!"

"Oh Lordy, Rooster, that's a beauty!" Jewel had exclaimed.

Neither of us had the heart to tell him that it was nothing more than a ridiculously oversized, totally inedible goldfish. Not only that, but it looked as if it was sickly, for healthy carp were almost impossible to catch. Mama had come out and taken it from him, then gone off to the store and bought fresh bass, which she cooked for him instead.

I ran to the window and waved through a rip in the screen.

"Come see, Kady!" Tony hollered. "It's an honest-to-goodness large-mouth bass! Roos did most of the work reeling it in."

"I'll be right there." I started to take off the dress. It was uglier than the rags we used to clean the house with.

Mama pulled me back by my skirt. "Not until we're through."

I yanked free, pulling pins loose as I went back to the window. "Mama's holding me hostage!" I yelled back.

Mama had just started reinserting the pins when a piece of punk bark sticking out of my dollhouse caught my eye. I rushed over to it, half dragging her with me, picked up a handful of punk bark PEE PULL and waved them in front of her. "What are these tacky things doing in here? I told Minnie she wasn't allowed to touch my dollhouse!" I exclaimed, then ripped them up.

"Stop it! Rooster put them in there."

"You *saw* him and didn't stop him?"

"He didn't mean any harm. After all, it's just a dollhouse."

"Just a dollhouse! Mama, he broke my china doll the last time he went near it." I marched back over to the window and yelled to Rooster, "STAY OUT OF MY DOLLHOUSE!"

At the sight of me, his face broke into a huge grin. *"PRETTY—PRETTY—FISH!"* he hollered back.

I turned away in disgust. "I've told him and *told* him to stay out of my dollhouse and he never listens! What an idiot!"

Mama's face went wooden. "Great Spirit!"

"Oh, Mama," I moaned, "he *is* an idiot!"

"GREAT SPIRIT!" she barked, and I had to repeat an old Indian prayer that my parents made us quote whenever we insulted anyone: "Grant that I may not criticize my neighbor until I have walked a mile in his moccasins."

I'd barely finished rattling it off before she lashed out, "I can't believe you'd want to hurt that boy! There he is dancing all around his dock, so happy about his fish, and all you can think about is your silly dollhouse. Hard to believe you're fifteen!"

"It's not silly to me. Especially when I live in this hovel," I added under my breath. "Rooster needs to learn to respect my stuff."

"Tsk! Tsk! Why that boy adores you, I'll never know. You barely lift your finger for him!"

"Who was in the chicken coop with the rat snake? Not you!"

"It just about broke my heart when he brought those dolls over the other day," she rushed on. "He'd spent hours on them, carefully gluing on the hair and making faces out of my own supply of cloves. Whole cloves ain't cheap, either, and he managed to spill what he didn't use. Might've even eaten a few. But do you hear me complaining?" She pursed her lips. "I was amazed he was so capable. And he did it all for you, because for some confounded reason you're the only one he—"

"Mama, he broke the one decent thing I owned!"

"I told you I'd give you the money to replace that doll." She stalked over to her purse and yanked it open. "Here you go!" She threw three one dollar bills at my face like confetti.

"I lied to you about how much I spent on that doll. Flat out lied! It was twenty-seven dollars, not three!" I blurted out.

She looked at me, stricken.

"And fifty-three cents!"

"You don't even have that kind of money."

"I got it out of my savings account."

"You spent twenty-seven dollars and fifty-three cents on one doll?"

I wished I hadn't blurted it out, but it was too late now. I nodded.

She was so flabbergasted she couldn't let it go. "Twenty-seven dollars and fifty-three cents on *one doll!*"

I stared at her hair, marveling the way each strand quivered as if it were a raw nerve ending. "Yes! That's why I'm so upset—"

"Well," she clucked as a fuzzy eyebrow arched up, "you know what they say about fools and their money! I know who the real idiot around here is!"

I remained Mama's hostage for another hour while she lectured me about the value of a dollar. As she spoke, she kept yanking at my hems and jabbing in those needles. I could barely keep my legs still for fear she might stick me, too. Finally, she let me go.

As I carried my horrid new clothes back to my room, who should rush up to my window and plaster his nose against the panes but Rooster.

"*¡Madrina!*" he yelled exuberantly. His nostrils were spread wide against the glass like a pig's.

I cracked opened the rows of jalousie windowpanes and barked, "Stay out of my dollhouse!"

"The egg—it is cr-cr-cracking!" he announced.

I stared at him, befuddled. "Egg? What egg? I thought you wanted me to see your fish and I'm sorry, but I'm not in the—"

"N-No, *egg!* In—In—In the coop."

"Rooster, we have dozens of eggs in the coop. Who cares!"

He banged his fist against the windowpanes, rattling them. "BIG, B-B-BIG egg!"

"Stop it! You're gonna break the window."

"BIG! BIG! EGG!" he cried as he continued to bang the windowpanes. "*¡Vamos!*"

"Stop it, Rooster! I'm not in the mood!"

His fist slammed on the windowpane. "*¡V-Vamos! ¡Vamos! ¡R-Rápido!*"

"If *that's* what it takes to get you to stop banging on my window!" I yelled as I stalked out of my room. All the way down the hall and out the front door I muttered that Rooster was the biggest idiot on the planet. Who else would care about an egg of all things? An *egg!*

Yet when he showed me the egg a few minutes later, I jumped back in amazement. Geraldine—the hen whose egg had been eaten by the snake—was sitting next to a large, speckled *goose* egg! As I got over my anger at Rooster—for it *was* an unusual egg—I realized that Tony must've planted it under her.

Rooster pointed to the small cracks running down the sides. "See?"

I leaned over and saw the tip of a tiny beak chipping at the shell from within and became fascinated. Eggs are so fragile that the least change in the environment can keep them from hatching, and there was no telling where Tony had gotten this one from. "Well, what do you know, Roos? It *is* a big egg!"

Rooster began strutting about like an expectant father while I watched the tiny beak chipping away. It was making very slow progress.

By the time dinner was over and the dishes washed, the egg still hadn't hatched. When I went back to check on it, the beak had stopped tapping.

"*¿Qué te pasa?*" Tony asked as he walked up to me.

"What do you think's wrong? This egg's a dud." I looked outside in the falling darkness and saw Rooster flapping his arms as he shrieked with excitement.

"Are you sure?" Tony asked.

"It quit pecking."

Tony frowned, then squat down and put his ear against the egg. His eyes lit up. "I hear—," he managed to say before Geraldine, upset by his nearness, pecked him hard on the wrist. "*¡Dianche!*" he cried, bolting up. He stared with disbelief at the angry welt showing up on his arm. "I'll take a rat snake over you any day!" he exclaimed to the protective hen.

"She doesn't know you very well." I laughed as Geraldine continued to scold him.

He unclasped a safety pin on his shirt that took the place of a missing button and bent it straight. "I think I heard something in there."

"Really?"

He looked through the wire mesh at the sky. "Is nearly dark. Get a flashlight and cover it with red flannel—hens can't see red light. They'll think it's dark."

I blinked. "You're going to try to tap him out?"

He shrugged. "Maybe if we help him out he'll have a chance.

But of course"—he fell silent for a moment—"if he doesn't learn to get out by himself, it's going to be harder for him to survive later on. . . ."

"Well, if he really is still alive, maybe we can help him just a little bit," I said.

When I came back with the flashlight covered with flannel, I held it over the egg while Tony lightly tapped along the crack lines with the straightened safety pin. Geraldine, unable to see us, clucked softly.

"So where'd you get the egg? The Easter Bunny?" I asked him.

He laughed. "Never mind. Let's just hope the little guy lives."

"You're sure you heard something in there?"

"*Sí.*" He motioned for me to lower my head and listen for myself. I heard a faint, "Bib-bib-bib!" I shrugged, grinning.

"Rooster's had enough disappointments," he said with a bitter edge to his voice. He rolled the egg a little with his thumb and exclaimed just loud enough not to frighten Geraldine, "Hey you in there! Don't quit on me! You're supposed to grow up to be a big, obnoxious goose! So obnoxious that no harm will come to you."

"So that's why you picked a goose egg."

He nodded. "Nobody wants to mess with a goose. Not even a rat snake."

"There's something I don't get, Tony," I said, then paused. "I mean, Rooster was really happy when he caught that carp yesterday. And again today when he caught that bass. But he eats what he catches—or at least thinks he does—without a second thought. But it's different with the chickens. He goes nuts if something happens to any of them. And he never eats chicken. Not even Kentucky Fried. Once, he saw a leg poking out of a bucket Papa brought home and went crazy."

Tony smoothed back his hair and stared out the flimsy coop door for a long moment, watching Rooster under the dim moonlight, before he said, "Something happened back in Cuba that I've never talked about to anybody."

"Why not?"

He gave me a guarded look. "I guess because it's painful to remember those days."

"Well, never mind then."

"No," he said, "I should've told you a long time ago because it might help you understand why you're so important to my brother. Why he calls you *Madrina.*"

I stared at him with curiosity. It had never occurred to me that there was any particular reason behind it.

He set down the safety pin as he took a deep breath. "Our family used to raise chickens before Fidel turned everything upside down. Those chickens, I believe, are the last memories Rooster has of a peaceful, secure world."

"Oh," I said, thinking there wasn't much to this story after all.

"One day, when I was about seven and Rooster barely three, some soldiers showed up on our property and demanded a barbecue dinner. They appeared out of nowhere, slithering into the cane from every direction like snakes. I remember the feeling I had in my stomach—like car sickness—when I realized they were invading our *cañaveral*. They were rebel units, dressed in burnt green uniforms that blended in with the cane. Most had beards or were attempting to grow them, which made them look wild."

"What are rebel units?"

"Fidel's supporters. Gathered from all over the country. This was the end of 1958, just before Batista was overthrown. Many people supported Fidel then. They called themselves *barbudos*, because of their beards. Fidel, see, has a double chin and a beard makes him appear strong."

I stared at him, riveted. "Where were you?"

"Catching cicadas in the ceiba tree out front. I was way up in the branches of this very massive, very old tree that I loved to climb. You would love this tree, Kady. Sort of like your widowmaker, only much bigger. I would stay up there during the heat of the day—our *siesta*—watching the old farmhands play dominoes beneath me, or maybe play guitars. Everyone gravitated to the ceiba tree during *siesta*. I tried to hide among the wild orchids and the bromeliads that grew in the upper branches when I saw them coming, but one of the soldiers spotted me and ordered me down. He looked just like Fidel."

"Was it him?"

"No. He said his men were hungry and tired and demanded we feed them a barbecue chicken dinner at once. That entailed slaughtering every chicken we had—about a hundred."

My eyes widened in horror. "You're kidding!"

Tony slowly shook his head. "Chickens are often sacrificed in Cuba for religious purposes, but this was entirely different. *Papi* and I were ordered to do the dirty work of chopping off the heads and feet while the farmhands built a pit and dressed the chickens. *Mami* had to scurry about with the maids to do the rest, make guava pastries, set up makeshift tables, fill whatever pitchers we could find with *guarapo*—"

"What's that?"

"Fresh cane juice. Is very good, not too sweet like you might think. Rooster was always spilling it on his shirts, which made them stiff as cardboard." His eyes narrowed and he bit down on his lip. It was a long time before he spoke again.

"I can still taste the splattered blood, still see the cross-hatched marks in the dirt from the chickens scrambling to get away. Then the *barbudos* had the nerve to invite us to eat with them. The highest-ranking soldier wouldn't take his first bite until we'd taken ours." He shook his head in disbelief.

"Why was that?"

"Part of the new way of thinking. That we were all together in the *Revolución!*" He clenched his jaw in anger. "When it was over, it took us the rest of the day to find Rooster. He was huddled in the middle of *la caña*, this tiny lump of a boy. He must have witnessed the slaughtering, because his hair was matted with chicken blood, and streaks of blood covered his clothes and body."

"That's awful."

"He was never the same after that. Not until the day you drew him out of the widowmaker tree. That day you put chicken feed in his hands."

"But I was just—just feeding the chickens! And he was so weird the way he hid inside that tree." I clapped my hands to my face in stunned amazement. "I had no idea."

"You brought him back to the little boy he used to be. That's why he calls you *Madrina*. His godmother."

"Oh, my God . . ." Tears welled up in my eyes and I blinked them away.

Tony peered at the egg, noting that the beak was beginning to tap from the inside of a hole he'd enlarged. "Hold that flashlight steady now," he instructed. "See its beak? How hard it's struggling to live?"

I glanced at the egg without really looking at it. My mind was still on Rooster. I felt even more trapped in a friendship with him than ever, because I could never again think of him as simply hollow-headed. Now, I could picture him hiding in that cane field, his tiny body trembling, could hear my voice whispering that everything would be all right. That the lions, tigers, bears and oh mys would never hurt him again. Could picture myself as his true O Mighty Protector.

"Rooster's never really trusted *Papi* and me since that day. Never understood why we had to kill all our chickens. Trying to explain it to him is no use, he was too young when it happened for words to matter. Even after all this time, whenever *Papi* or I ask him to do something, he flinches, as though he expects us to hurt him. I can understand why he doesn't trust *Papi,* whose anger is like a Florida thunderstorm. But why he doesn't trust me when I do everything for him—things that *parents* should do—I don't get.

"*Ay,* he trusts me a little, like he's letting me help hatch this egg," he added with a slight smile. "But *Mami* was the only one he really trusted after the chicken fiasco. . . . Did I tell you he was looking for her again the other day?"

"I thought he'd quit doing that."

"I thought so, too. But he heard a car coming down our driveway and ran outside, yelling '*Mami!*' just as some guy selling encyclopedias came knocking."

"Oh no."

"The guy had a blue car exactly like hers. Funny that a kid who can't remember what he ate for lunch can remember certain things so clearly years later."

"You still miss her a lot, too," I observed as he turned back to the goose egg. He put his ear up against it and, hearing nothing, murmured, "Eep! Eep!"

"Eep! Eep!" came from within.

"Eep! Eep!" he called back.

"Eep! Eep!" I echoed.

I grinned at Tony, but he was lost again in his own thoughts.

"I guess when Rooster shouted *Mami's* name the other day, I half-expected her to bustle through the door with that damn cream cheese to fill her *pasteles* with. If she were still alive, she'd probably have a nice little catering business by now. Food was her soul. . . . It's not fair," he sighed, "she went through so much to get us here."

"A lot of things aren't fair, that's for sure."

"*Ay*, but *Mami!* She cradled Rooster on that leaky raft for thirty hours straight, singing until she was hoarse. He was six then, and we were afraid he'd get scared and fall into that dark, tumbling water, or start screaming at the patrol boats—those death ships that shoot you on sight. There were so many of them, this being right after the Battle of Giron, what you Americans so distastefully call the Bay of Pigs. You have no idea how many *balseros* were gunned down. . . .

"*Papi* was put on Fidel's list to be executed," he added a moment later.

"Now isn't *that* a nice way to thank him for his chicken dinner!"

"*Sí,*" Tony agreed with a bitter laugh. "We left hours after he escaped from prison. *Mami* had been slowly making the raft once we realized it was too risky to leave by plane. She scavenged everything she could find around the village—bamboo, old tires, wood from an old dresser, even empty oil barrels. She covered it with sheets and pretended it was her bed. I helped, but she was a pretty amazing carpenter."

"It couldn't have been very big."

"If you saw it, you'd be amazed that we got here. Especially the way she made it in sections so we could get it out of our house and hide it near the shore. I didn't realize how much of a risk we took until she went *loco* when we drifted ashore near Key West, screaming 'land of the free.' I don't know how she could scream at all, as our tongues were swollen from thirst. But she was so happy to be here, to be given another chance. She thought all *Americanos* wore shiny new clothes and were rich, like the ones she'd seen in her youth."

"Oh yeah. Look at my new clothes, shiny with sweat!" I exclaimed, shining my flashlight momentarily on my clothes.

Tony rolled his eyes at me and continued. "She'd worked one summer as a waitress in a nice restaurant in Havana that her father owned, and found her fortune not just in tips, but from the coins that spilled from the pockets of the *Americanos* into the creases of the booths." He looked out over his yard, at the heaps of rusted junk, the piles of used tires that had grown into mountains over the years, and the painfully pink house.

I could feel his sadness by the way his face tilted back as if to meet a wind that was no longer there. He was thinking about the *cañaveral* his family had left behind, with its sprawling ceiba tree out front, that Castro had turned into a "People's Farm." He'd once told me the waving cane looked like sea grass under water and that he felt as if he could rise up in that enormous expanse of sky and float over it.

He turned his attention back to the egg, carefully splitting the membrane inside the little opening as far as he could. "There you go. The rest is up to you," he whispered to the little gosling. "You're in America now, the land of the free!" He set down the safety pin, got up and pulled at the chicken wire. "After the Battle of Giron, when it was clear there would be no overthrow of Fidel, *Papi* said the only future left in Cuba was a street named *El Porvenir*. That road didn't go anywhere, just turned to dust. He told me that just before soldiers showed up at our house in the middle of the night and took him to prison. We never knew why. But now we're in America, struggling like this gosling.

"You know, *Papi's* business, selling second-hand stuff, was just beginning to make money when *Mami* died. It was a lot better than many of the jobs the government found for the exiles. Our doors would be wide open all day, with people coming and going, like back in Cuba. *Papi* would talk to the customers and give them Cuban cigars or maybe tell them how to season black beans. And they'd always find a reason to come back, just to talk. Now he's buying crap like battery-operated cookie presses—wait till I show you those—which I have to sell while he is *ebrio* from too many rum punches."

About the only time I ever saw Señor Rosado get up these days was to lumber through our yard to find a ripe orange or a grapefruit to squeeze into his rum. "Can't imagine why anyone living here would possibly want to drink," I said sarcastically.

Tony turned to me sharply, and I regretted my words. "You think I'm a fool to find hope here, and maybe I am."

"I didn't say that."

"*Ay*, Kady, it's in your eyes. I play 'Mister Tambourine Man,' and you're out of here faster'n a rat snake."

"Tell me you don't ever dream of getting the hell outta here!"

He fell silent and looked down. "So where did he take you?"

"Who?"

"The Tambourine Man. He is like your Pied Piper, no?"

The color rose in my cheeks.

"You always complain about how loud I play my Cuban music, but music is in your soul, too, no?" He smiled at me as my cheeks got redder. "I saw you go past my house on that ski boat with some guy. I'd know your strawberry-blonde hair anywhere."

"So wh-wh-where is it?" Rooster demanded as he came up to us.

Tony nodded at the cracked egg, and Rooster saw a tiny webbed foot freeing itself from the membrane.

"Oh!" Rooster cried, pointing with amazement. "Oh! Oh! Ohhh!"

The minutes ticked by as we watched the gosling free itself.

"*¡Qué bonito!*" Tony cried when he saw the head emerge.

"*¡Qué b-b-bonito!*" Rooster echoed, his own head so close to the gosling's that we had to pull him back.

"He's t-t-talking to me!" Rooster shouted. He put himself right back in front of it. "B-Beep! Beep!"

"Beep . . . beep," the gosling slowly returned.

Tony and I laughed at the scrap of wet, bloody feathers and spindly legs that finally presented itself. Rooster was awestruck by how different it looked from the baby chickens he'd seen hatch. For a breathless moment I thought he was going to reject it. But instead he cried out, "See *Madrina,* see? My chick!" Then he started running around the coop in a frenzy of sputtering drool and flying arms and legs. My heart skipped a beat at the word *Madrina*.

Tony transferred the gosling to a brooder to keep it warm. After a while, Rooster calmed down enough to squat beside his brother to look at it. His eyes grew wide with wonder as he watched the tiny chest rise and fall with each new breath. I stared at both of their faces in the rosy light and for a split second the brothers looked identical, one a shadow of the other, like a ghost on a TV screen. Their eyes shone like liquid chocolate and their teeth both had the same slight gap in front. In that instant, Rooster seemed like any other boy.

"It looks like a dandelion," I told Rooster after the gosling had dried itself off a while later and a yellow puff of feathers covered its fragile body. Tony and I had both come and gone, but Rooster had stayed beside the gosling all the while, peeping softly to it.

"A d-d-dandy?" he repeated, looking at me curiously.

"You know, a kind of flower. You brought one to me once, remember? But all the bits of fluff had already blown off."

He stared at me without comprehension.

"Don't you remember the dandelion?"

"D-Dandy," he repeated, his mouth curving into a smile. "Dandy."

"I think he just named him," Tony said, grinning.

Rooster didn't go to bed till nearly dawn. He remained hovered over the little gosling instead, murmuring that he was his O Mighty Protector and that no lions, tigers, bears or oh-mys would get him. Not even a measly snake.

My heart was pounding as I dressed for the first day of school. What would I say to Jon if I saw him again? I could *not* stop thinking about him! Over and over again I'd relived his kiss, felt his lips on the corner of mine. Thoughts of Jon had crowded out everything else, until I felt that I'd go crazy if I didn't see him again. Yet, whenever I looked upon the lake, I could never find the little red-and-white boat that had darted in and out of my life so quickly, changing everything.

I blushed self-consciously as I pulled a piece of peeling skin off the tip of my freckled nose and studied myself in the mirror. Did I really look like a Weeki Wachi mermaid with violet eyes? I leaned against the mirror and stared at my irises. My breath kept fogging up the glass and I had to wipe it off several times before I saw the tinges of pink mixed in with the flecks of blue. They *were* violet . . . a little bit, at least. I couldn't help but smile.

I tried on one depressing outfit after another, settling on a dark red shift. But when I looked in the mirror, I saw a giant hot dog! I finally decided on the peasant dress with the unraveled yellow flower, and carefully arranged my hair over the irregular stitching.

Mama and Wendell were in the midst of a heated discussion when I sat down at the breakfast table.

"I'm not taking that stupid bike to school!" He was referring to a bicycle that the Clarks had left behind when they'd sold us the place, along with the clothes wringer and a lot of other junk that Mama referred to as "antiques."

"It works, don't it?"

"Not when I get finished with it, it won't."

"Wendell!"

"Mama, it's an old woman's bike! I'd be the laughingstock of the school."

"It's not an old woman's bike. It has a bar across it."

"And a stupid basket in front, a stupid horn, and stupid daisy decals on the fenders! You ride it. I'd rather get to school on Rosy's back."

"What's going on?" Papa asked as he walked to the counter and set down a bag of oranges. His pipe, still smoldering, wobbled in his mouth. The room suddenly smelled of cherry tobacco.

"I need an advance on my allowance," Wendell announced, and explained why he had to have a new bike.

"I don't have that kind of money, son," Papa said as he began to cut and squeeze the oranges. "But I'm sure I can come up with some jobs around here so you can raise it. You might check the neighbors, too."

"I can't wait that long!"

"Here," Papa said, tossing him an orange. "You slice while I squeeze."

Wendell looked at the pile of oranges on the counter and groaned. "Why can't we buy juice like normal people do? Who wants to slice up fifty million oranges every morning? It's stupid."

Papa gave him an incredulous look. "Ain't nothing better in the whole world, son, than fresh juice off your own trees." He reamed an orange and watched with satisfaction as the juice gushed forth. "And with all the varieties I planted in the yard, we got it near year-round."

"Besides, it's free," Mama said.

"That's the real reason," Wendell grumbled, "the money. You'll slave away for an hour just to save a buck. Well, I'm not going to live my life like ya'll do. I'm gonna be rich!"

All this commotion was making me even more nervous than I already felt. "Gotta go!" I jumped from the table even though I'd barely begun eating my waffles. Not that I could eat them anyway.

I was out of breath by the time I met Tony in front of his house. He'd promised to walk with me the first day.

Instead of saying hello, Tony stared at me with such intensity that I felt like an alien.

"What's wrong?" I asked.

"Wrong?" He shook his head. "*Nada.*"

"Then why are you staring at me like that? Do I have syrup on my dress or something?"

"No." His face broke into a slow grin. "*Dichosos los ojos que te están viendo. ¡Estás como nunca!*"

I hated it when he said something in Spanish that I didn't understand. I glared at him, waiting for him to explain.

"Is very pretty dress," he went on in English.

"Oh," I said with surprise and relief. "Well, it's the first day. Why not wear something nice, you know? Not that anything Mama buys is really nice. You'd think she could at least let me pick out my own stuff. But she's afraid I might want something that's not on the bargain tables."

"Wait a minute, what's this on your back? I think it's a loose thread. Stand still." He started to pull at Mama's stitching.

I jumped away from him. "Don't!"

"What's wrong?"

"*Nothing's* wrong!"

"But there's a loose—"

"Don't worry about it!"

"*Dios mío,*" he muttered. "What's eating you?"

"NOTHING!"

"You shouldn't be nervous about high school," he said after I'd stalked up his driveway in stony silence. "Is no big deal."

I pressed my lips tightly together, then blurted out, "All of my dresses are horrendous."

"*¡Ay, caramba!* This dress is not horrendous."

"Appalling, then. Monstrous. Hideous. Dreadful. Ghastly."

Tony threw back his head and laughed. "None of those! Is

very pretty, like I already told you. Since when did you care about clothes, anyway? When I met you, you and your brother and sister weren't wearing a stitch!"

"Well," I said, coloring, "that was different. Everybody goes skinny-dipping when they're kids."

He shook his head emphatically. "Not where I grew up."

I smiled in spite of myself. "I'll never forget that look on your face when I swung in front of you on that vine."

He smiled, too. "Well, it's not every day you see a naked girl swinging on a vine like Tarzan Jane."

"I remember you yelling at us in that ridiculous Shakespearean English you'd learned back in Cuba, 'All hail! My name is Antonio and I just move in and—and—is not so PRIVATE anymore. I pray you, school yourself, and put your suits on!' I had no idea what you were talking about! *School yourself?*"

"It means 'control yourself.'"

"Yeah well, for the next few months, Wendell, Minnie and I went around saying, 'School yourself!' every time Mama got after us."

"I thought you'd be so embarrassed that I'd seen you swinging naked on that vine. But"—shaking his head—"not you."

"You weren't either after I told you that everybody swam naked," I reminded him. "I jumped off the vine, and when I resurfaced there *you* were—naked!"

"Well," he shrugged with a sly grin, "I figured skinny-dipping was an American tradition I could live with."

"Remember how Mama went nuts when she saw you swimming with us?"

Tony slapped his knee and howled. "I thought she was going to have a stroke! She's a big woman and—not to make fun of her—but her whole body started shaking like guava jelly. Do you remember how she rushed to Woolworth's and bought suits for me and Rooster?"

I nodded. "And Rooster couldn't even swim."

"Ugliest suit I ever had, with green and white stripes. I looked like toothpaste squeezed from a tube!"

"Well, how would you like for her to pick out your clothes all the time?"

"Sounds appalling, monstrous, hideous, dreadful and ghastly. Did I get them all?"

"You forgot horrendous."

"*Sí*. Horrendous. But to be perfectly honest, you don't look one bit like toothpaste in that dress," he added. "Ghastly, maybe."

I nudged his arm.

"School yourself!" he laughed, nudging me back. "I'm only joking. Actually," he went on in a slur of soft-spoken words, "I've never seen you look so pretty."

"Really?"

He nodded. "I don't know when you became a *señorita*. Just yesterday you were all bones and freckles."

"Thanks a lot!"

"I'm trying to compliment you! In Cuba you would've had a *quinceañera* on your fifteenth birthday."

"What's that?"

"A big party to celebrate your new womanhood."

I found myself suddenly blushing.

Tony talked to me about what to expect at high school during the remainder of our mile-and-a-half walk along the highway, then down a path through some woods to the campus. The morning dew from the wet grass that grew along the path made my feet slide uneasily inside my sandals. A green garter snake slithered before me, a blade of moving grass. I watched with envy as it retreated into the dark coolness of a blackberry thicket. Then, the buildings grew visible through the trees— two-story concrete block structures painted an institutional beige. Two grapefruit trees dutifully reigned outside the front entrance, a tribute, no doubt, to the name of our high school, "Pomelo," which meant *grapefruit* in Spanish.

Soon I could smell baking bread from the cafeteria kitchen mixed in with the fumes of the school buses, which began unloading kids in the front of the school, their gears squeaking and hissing as kids poured forth like water gushing from hoses. *Was Jon among them?* My heart started to pound. *How would he react when he saw me on dry land? Would he still think I looked like a Weeki Wachi mermaid? Or had my novelty simply been because of the water surrounding me?*

My insecurities mounted when we got to campus and I saw the number of students—far more than had gone to my middle school. The smells of deodorant, donuts, candy bars, hair spray, body odor, Lysol-washed-hallways, and freshly mown grass hit me all at once. Bodies nudged into mine as everyone seemed to be scrambling in a hundred different directions. I suddenly felt as small and inconspicuous as a carpet fiber. *There was no way Jon was going to notice me among all these faces. And how was I supposed to find him?*

A green convertible roared into the main entrance and braked to a sudden stop in front of the school. A half-dozen kids spilled from the doors and laughed among themselves. The driver sped toward the student parking lot, his sunglasses glinting in the early morning sun. I recognized him as Mark, even though his hair was shorter and he wasn't wearing a sweatband.

"Some school bus," Tony said wistfully. "Did I tell you a field mouse gave birth inside the stuffing of the seat of my truck? I heard this little peeping noise and . . ."

Trailing somewhat behind the rest of the kids who had gotten out of the convertible, with his hands jammed in his pockets and a faraway look in his eyes, was Jon. My knees began to buckle, and it became almost impossible to put one foot in front of the other. Not that I even knew where I was going.

Tony, noticing that I wasn't responding to him, repeated, "Kady? What do you think?"

I grabbed his hand and dug my nails into his palm as I watched Jon walk toward me.

"Ouch!" he exclaimed, pulling his hand away. *"¡Dios mío, Kady!* You need to be declawed!"

Jon's hair, gleaming blond in the early morning light, fell limply into his eyes and I wondered with a little laugh why he didn't push it out of the way. On the boat it had dried in stiff, wind-blown tufts.

"That's him," I breathed. For a heart-stopping moment, I thought he saw me among the carpet fibers.

"Who?"

I fell silent, giddy with dizziness as Jon came nearer. He was wearing a faded cotton button-down shirt with long sleeves casually rolled up to his elbows and the two top buttons left unbuttoned. The shirt was loosely tucked into blue jeans and belted with a wide leather belt and an oversized hand-fashioned brass buckle. I loved the color of those jeans, a rich royal blue, gently faded. They were nothing like the stiff, dark blue jeans that Tony and Rooster wore, the main staple of Sears and K-Mart.

Jon dropped behind the others until a girl playfully slipped her arm through his and pulled him back into the group.

I knew at once who these kids were—everyone in town did. They were the rich kids who lived in the subdivisions across the lake. Back in grade school, you could always tell when the girls raised their hands in class because of the miniature French poodles and pom-poms that clinked together on their charm bracelets—

bracelets that chronicled every major event of their life, from getting a part in a play to taking a trip to an interesting city.

Last year, they had acquired Aigner loafers made of extra-thick cowhide tinted reddish brown, with a big "A" sewn on top, and Aigner purses, also with a big "A", that cost as much as my china doll. The most important girls in the group had purchased the items first, then on down the line until even girls who weren't part of their clique were beginning to show up in those stiff shoes. Their gleaming hair was like the Breck shampoo girls', with a perfectly coiled curl at the end, courtesy of heat-rollers and Dippity-Do. They all wore crisply ironed Villager and Ladybug clothes that they went all the way to downtown Orlando to buy.

This year they'd traded their charm bracelets—crammed with life experiences—for love beads and peace sign earrings. They looked as if they slept under the stars with bands of hippies, judging from the rumpled look of their hair and clothes—embroidered shirts and whimsy dresses that caught the breeze like kites. Their clothes were made from "all natural cotton," with colors that faded and bled if they weren't carefully hand-washed and hung to dry—a material Mama refused to cater to. The embroidered dress I was wearing was the only "all natural cotton" dress I owned. And Mama never would have gotten it if it hadn't been so cheap.

I recognized the girl who had slipped her arm through Jon's as Charlotte Jones. She'd sat in front of me in English last year with her mane of perfectly groomed hair. I remember reaching out and touching her curl one day and marveling how brittle it was. Then I had carefully inserted a paper clip inside it and waited to see if it fell out during class. It stayed there until she got up to give a report on Shakespeare's Globe Theater.

She never said a word to me, not even when she passed out papers (she was the teacher's pet and always got this job), until one day when I was late leaving the room. I'd lost my pencil and was searching under my desk to find it when she whirled around and fixed a huge smile on me. "Kady," she said as if I were her best friend. Her lips gleamed with pale pink gloss. I noticed that we were the only students left in the classroom.

I was stunned she knew my name—most people who barely knew me called me "Katie." Flattered, I immediately responded, "Yes?"

She leaned over and whispered, her breath smelling like Vick's cough drops, which she often sucked like candy, "I just started my period."

"Oh," I said, turning red. *Why was she telling me this? I hadn't even told my mother when I'd started mine.* "It happens to all of us sooner or later," I said with a nervous laugh as I hastily gathered up my books. I was going to be late to my next class if I didn't hurry.

"I'm not wearing anything," she whispered again as students began to enter the classroom for the next period.

"What?" I asked, barely able to hear her.

"I'm not wearing anything!" she repeated frantically. "Hey there!"

she chirped as a boy smiled at her in that goofy way guys smile when they have a crush on someone.

"Oh!" I said as my eyes widened knowingly.

"Will you please walk right behind me to the restroom? I feel really wet and I'm sure there's blood—Hey there!"—she cried hoarsely to another guy—*"everywhere!"*

"Sure," I said, and got right behind her as she stood up.

Sure enough, her pale pink Ladybug dress flocked with white butterflies had a bright red stain smack in the back of it. There was a little blood on the seat, too, which I hastily wiped off with the back of my shirt sleeve.

I must've looked like a love bug stuck to her as I followed her out of the classroom and down the hall, all the way to the restroom, covering up that stain with my body as best I could. She continued to greet students—everyone seemed to know who she was—with her chirpy "Hey there!" as if nothing was wrong, until she pushed through the restroom door and burst out in nervous giggles. "That was a close call!"

She pulled her dress around to have a look. "Oh my God!" she shrieked. "I look like the Japanese flag. Nobody noticed, did they?"

"I don't think so," I said. "Though I'm sure they wondered why I was practically breathing down your neck."

"Talk about embarrassing." She slipped off her dress and began scrubbing the stain with the gritty soap that came out of a pump, complaining the whole while that she was ruining her nails.

As she stood there in her undergarments—a lacy padded bra in soft blue pastel and matching bikini underwear (also stained)—going on and on, I heard the bell.

"Look, I've got to get to class," I said.

She nodded.

"Are you coming?"

"No way. I'll just hang out here until lunch. It's just a period away. *Period!* I can't believe I said that word!" She shook her head and continued to scrub.

"I'll see you, then," I said, then added, "make sure you use cold water. Hot water'll lock in the stain." Jewel had told me that when she'd noticed my underwear stains on the clothesline one day.

She stopped scrubbing for a moment and looked up. "Listen, thanks, you're a real lifesaver."

"Sure," I said, nodding.

It wasn't until I got to my next class and slipped into my seat, the unexcused tardy slip burning in the palm of my hand, that I realized I'd forgotten to wash off the blood from my sleeve, a red-brown tinge that reminded me of the blood that got on my sleeves when I cut up meat.

When I got to my English class the next day and passed Charlotte in the aisle, I asked her how things were going. She barely glanced my way as she chirped, "Hey there!" before resuming her conversation with the boy across the aisle, the one who'd given her the goofy smile the day before.

After that she never greeted me by name again, even though

I continued to greet her by name. I was lucky to get a "Hey there!" After a while I didn't even get that—she stared right through me as if I were invisible.

I told myself I didn't care, yet deep down I was hurt. For in spite of everything, I envied her life right down to her English notebook with its picture of a fluffy Persian cat on the cover. My notebook had a plain denim blue cover with tic-tac-toe games scrawled all over it.

Charlotte was now wearing an orange flowered dress that billowed in the breeze, flapping against Jon, as they joined their friends. Her long hair—three shades blonder than last year—was parted straight down the middle and flowed freely about her shoulders. Oh! But wasn't she a flower blowing in the wind! The faraway look in Jon's eyes disappeared as he started to joke with her in that same easy manner he'd joked with me on the lake. Everyone strained to hear what he was saying, and before long, ripples of laughter rang out.

Suddenly Mama's uneven stitching on the back of my dress seemed to be loosening. I could picture it unraveling without stop until the flower disappeared. I tightly clutched it even though I knew it was a useless gesture, that nothing could stop that flower—or me—from coming undone.

"So, did you talk to him today?" Tony asked me that evening as he set up the Monopoly board on a sagging plywood table in the junkyard. Tony and I often played Monopoly (which we referred to as "Monotony" because some of our games went on for weeks) as he minded his father's shop in the evening. Mama allowed me to sit out with him in that time after I'd finished the dishes and before the mosquitoes decided to make dinner of our arms and legs. In the summertime, we often played for hours, but with fall approaching, the games were getting as short as the days.

"What happened to the game we were playing?" I interrupted, sidestepping his question.

"*Ay, Papi* spilled a drink on it."

I looked at him suspiciously. "Oh, come on! I'd just gotten the Boardwalk monotony and was about to smear you. All you had was that dippy Oriental monotony and a GET OUT OF JAIL FREE card!"

"If you don't believe me, take a whiff of it. It's drying out like he ought to be."

There were ripples on the board and the whole thing reeked of rum, so I let the matter drop.

"Well, did you talk to him?" Tony pressed as he rolled the dice to start the game.

"Who?" I asked, feigning innocence as my stomach knotted.

He got doubles and landed his token of the day, an Alka-Seltzer tablet, on Community Chest. We'd been using unusual tokens ever since he'd accidentally knocked the metal dog that had come with the game onto the ground. Unable to find it in all the junk at our feet, he'd picked up an upholstery staple instead. Right now I was using a Barbie doll head Wendell had pulled off one of Minnie's old dolls. Tony picked up a yellow card and read: "'You have just won second prize in a beauty contest. Collect ten dollars.'"

"I won first!" I shouted with my usual comment.

He got ten dollars out of the bank and repeated, "You know who. Your *novio.*"

I was pretty sure *novio* meant boyfriend, but I didn't want to ask. I looked down and said, "No . . . I don't think I will be, either." I concentrated on rolling the dice and landed on "Body Odor" railroad, which I bought.

"When you saw him with that girl, I watched you grab the flower on the back of your dress—you know, the one that was coming unraveled—so tight that you wrinkled it. I've never seen you like that, so unsure of yourself. I was thinking, this can't be Kady Palmer, the girl who just won first prize in a beauty contest!"

"I wish."

He looked at me, surprised. "You wish?"

I lowered my eyes, uncomfortable with this conversation.

"Why here," he said, pulling a battered saucepan lid from the junk strewn about and placing it on my head, "I crown you Miss Ruby Red."

I wrinkled my nose. "Miss Ruby Red?"

"Well, how 'bout Miss Kumquat?" he suggested.

I shook my head, sending the lid crashing to the ground. Somehow, this wasn't helping. Tony was too observant and this was all too personal.

The next morning, as I started off to school, Rooster flew up to me with his hand cupped protectively over his shirt pocket. "Dandy!"

"In your pocket?" I gasped. "He's too young!"

He gently pulled out the gosling and put him on the palm of his hand. The little guy tried to stand up, then fell back down on his wobbly legs and cheeped. Rooster thought this was incredibly funny and started to laugh, which made his hand shake.

"Watch it, Rooster! You'll hurt him."

"N-N-Nooooo, *n-n-not* hurt," the boy insisted. "Rooster, O M-M-Mighty Pro-Protector!"

"Well, he does look a little better this morning. But you really need to put him back in the coop."

Rooster slipped the gosling back into his pocket and gently patted him. "W-W-Warm."

It would be just my luck if I came home to a dead gosling after all I'd done to help bring him into the world. And yet, I knew that it would be difficult to separate Rooster from his new pet, especially now that I knew about the slaughtered chickens.

"Well, I gotta go. . . . You be careful with that gosling now. Mama says she'll keep an eye on him while you're at school."

Rooster cupped his hand tighter around the gosling, and shook his head. *"Not* go to school t-t-t-today. Gotta w-w-watch Dandy."

"But you have to go to school, Roos. Everybody does." Rooster went to a special school for the learning disabled. A blue van came bumping up his driveway every day to take him.

"R-Rooster g-g-g-go to school *t-t-tomorrow,"* he informed me.

When I got to school, I saw Jon surrounded again by that crowd, larger even than before. This time he was talking and laughing, filled with the frenetic energy of an eggbeater. Near him was a girl who was equally energetic, her hands gesturing this way and that, in sync with his. She was wearing a rather odd but exotic paisley-patterned turban, which matched her dress. I wondered if maybe she was his girlfriend; she seemed very eye-catching, to put it mildly.

At any rate, I was terrified to go anywhere near Jon, terrified that he wouldn't remember me, or worse yet, that he would remember me but pretend not to, and stare right through me the same way Charlotte had. The painful truth was that I wasn't "Katerina, the beautiful violet-eyed mermaid" after all, but simply another carpet fiber. And when I thought back on our conversation on the water, it seemed so terribly ordinary.

I decided to put him out of my mind altogether.

*   *   *

Coming home from school two weeks later, I kicked the screen door open the way I always did since it was warped, and found Mama sitting stiffly in a dining room chair with a smile plastered on her face.

She was playing hostess to our next-door neighbor, Miz Wanda Sanders. After the Big Freeze, Miz Sanders had lost all but a few navel orange trees, and instead of replanting her grove like most folks had, she'd opted to plant pine trees instead. Once matured, the pines wouldn't bring in as much return as the citrus trees. But they didn't require much maintenance, either, which was just the way the old lady liked it.

She looked about two hundred years old, with leathery skin that crinkled up like tinfoil on the rare times she smiled, glittery green eyes and a shock of coarse white hair that stood on its ragged ends. She wore men's overalls over plaid shirts, and work boots with bobby socks rolled down like spare tires on her bony and somewhat hairy ankles. Unlike Grampsie, she hadn't lost any of her marbles, nor the sharpness of her tongue. She was known by just about every old-timer as "Magic Wanda" because she'd made a small fortune selling alligator hides, by killing them with what she called her "magic wand" shotgun.

That was before the government put the gators on the endangered species list. Now she had two freezers jammed full of hides while she figured out a way to sell them on the black market. She was so trigger-happy these days, there no telling just what—or who—she'd shoot at. And at nearly ninety, her vision wasn't what it used to be, a scary thought for those who lived nearby.

Just last fall she'd shot Señor Rosado in the big toe for snitching navel oranges off her trees. We weren't certain if she'd meant to kill him outright or had just meant to scare him off. Several policemen had arrived on her property to investigate the incident, but instead of carting her off to the station for questioning had carted off several frozen alligator hides instead, under the cloak of nightfall.

Magic Wanda didn't come to our place unless something was rankling her, although she used to "set a spell" with Grampsie until Grampsie had gotten the foolish notion about Walter Cronkite.

"Miz Palmer . . . ," she began after she'd helped herself to three biscuits in a row, piled high with real butter (Mama must've gotten it out of the freezer; we never had real butter at the table). Mama flashed me a look of pure dread. *Here it was, coming like a truck down a mountainside without any brakes.* "You've been good neighbors and all, but I was having pork chops last night and the smell of your pig"—she paused and winced—"who happened to be roaming, as usual, outside my window, was so overwhelming that I couldn't eat a single bite."

She gave Mama a piercing look. "Something must be done with that animal. A barbecue at the very least!"

Mama angrily brushed the crumbs from her lap as she

composed herself. "Why, Wanda, Rosy is like a member of our family. She saved Sammy's life just a few years back. He was drowning and she went right in—"

"Why, everybody knows that!" Miz Palmer snorted impatiently. "But it's no reason to keep a three-hundred-and-fifty-pound hog! What a colossal waste of bacon!"

"Why, I believe there was a children's book about a little girl who kept a pig for a pet," Mama piped up. "Wasn't his name Dilbert, or something?"

"Wilbur," I corrected her.

"If she comes on my property again, I'm gonna be the one having that barbecue!" Miz Palmer warned. She stood up abruptly, spilling a lapful of crumbs on the floor. "You give my best to Sadie," she added with a perfunctory smile, and left, her fist still clutching a half-eaten biscuit.

"'Give my best to Sadie,'" I mimicked, rolling my eyes. "I'm sure that'll make Grampsie's day! All that woman needs is a broomstick."

"Kady!" Mama snapped, "you'll clean out Rosy's pen at once. Then you'll find her, bathe her, and make sure she stays in it. There'll be no more roaming for her, I'm afraid."

"Yeah, well, those rotting gator carcasses she used to leave hanging around smelled a heckuva lot worse than Rosy," I retorted. "I have half a mind to go over there and unplug her freezers."

"She'll have you stuffed in one! Stop talking nonsense and

get to work."

There is no job worse than washing a huge hog and cleaning out its pen, especially the moment you get home from school and haven't even had so much as a nibble of a cheese biscuit piled high with real butter, and have had a lousy day to begin with.

When I explained this to Mama, we got into a fight. I called her some terrible names and she called me some terrible names, too. In the end, I was still stuck with cleaning out the pen and cried the whole time.

After that, I had to drag the beast down to the lake and soap her up twice before I rinsed her off. She'd been eating something with lots of garlic in it and really did stink.

As I was hauling her back to her pen—all the while trying to keep her from rolling in the mud, which she liked to do when she was wet—who should come out of the house but Rooster and Sammy.

On his shoulder Rooster held a red plastic shoulder strap purse that had once belonged to his mother. He'd begun toting Dandy in it, who, at nearly three weeks, had more than quadrupled his weight. Rooster was taking his job as O Mighty Protector very seriously and barely let the gosling out of his sight, except when he went to school. He'd built a straw nest inside the purse and there was a mirror in the top flap, which he liked to hold up to Dandy so he could see himself. "That's *you*, D-D-Dandy, the b-b-big chicken!" he'd exclaim. "And this is me," he went on as he peered into the tiny mirror, "Rooster, your O

M-Mighty Pr-Protector!"

It didn't take long for the purse to really stink, even though Rooster dumped out all the old straw every day. The sides got pretty nasty as well, with streaks of milky white goose excrement mixed in with bits of food and downy feathers running down. I told Rooster it wasn't healthy to keep a gosling cooped up in a purse. But Rooster wouldn't listen. He reminded me that Tony had *not* killed that rat snake and that it might come back and get Dandy if he didn't protect him.

As the boys approached me, they began singing the *Mr. Ed* theme song at the top of their lungs. They must've been watching reruns again. Rosy, excited from her bath and the fact that I wouldn't let her roll in the mud, started to squeal along with them. I told them to quit it, but they kept right on. As they practically roared the last line, Rosy broke away and took off, all three hundred and fifty pounds of pink flesh wriggling in the sunlight. She tore right through Jewel's clothesline, yanking down a freshly washed sheet and trampling it, and kept right on going. At least Jewel had already gone home and wasn't around to see the damage! I followed Rosy as far as the ravine where she got winded. She plopped herself down in the muddiest hole she could find and regarded me with a sneer.

"Heck with you!" I hollered to her. "It's my turn to take a bath!" I looked about to make sure the boys weren't around, then went behind the cattails, stripped down to my panties, and jumped into the water. It must've taken twenty minutes to get rid of the horrible garlic smell. When I got back to shore, Rosy was gone, and so were the boys. I didn't care if she ended up on a spit with an apple in her mouth. I wasn't about to chase her down and wash her again.

When I reached for my clothes, I realized, to my horror, that Rooster and Sammy—or probably just Sammy—had hidden them! I frantically searched the cattails and finally spotted them thrown into the lower branches of a punk bark tree, several yards from shore. I started to make a dash for them when I became aware of a boat puttering along the shoreline.

I couldn't believe it when I saw Jon—alone—behind the wheel. The way he was peering at every cattail made my heart leap. Was he looking for me? I barely had time to jump back into the water before he spotted me. He waved and steered his boat toward me.

A few minutes later, he pulled up alongside of me and turned off the motor. I stayed low in the water so he would assume I was wearing a bathing suit. Fortunately, the roots from the nearby trees stained the water the rich color of Coca-Cola.

He broke into a grin. "I'd know those violet eyes anywhere."

"I'd know that boat anywhere." I grinned back. "I haven't seen it lately."

"That's because it's been in the shop. Carburetor problems or something like that. I really don't know much about motors except they either work or they don't." He paused and fiddled with the gear shift. "I was hoping I'd run into you— oops! bad choice of words"—we both laughed—"I mean, see you again."

"Same here."

"Haven't seen you at school and wasn't sure where you lived."

"Around here," I said evasively.

"Well, you might be on the lookout for pigs."

"Pigs?" I croaked.

"Yeah," he laughed. "There's one running wild just up the way. Never saw anything so big in my life."

I laughed nervously, not sure what to say. "Oh, *that* pig."

"You saw it?"

"Yeah. He was a real pig of a guy, so I saw no choice but to change him into his true form."

He stared at me for a moment, startled, then broke into a smile. "Oh, I get it. You're the sorceress who changes men into pigs. I read about you in ninth-grade lit." He snapped his fingers. "*The Odyssey*, wasn't it?"

"Welcome, Great God of the Sea," I said enticingly. "Won't you come onto my island?"

"To be turned into a pig? No thanks."

"Well, I don't turn everybody into pigs." I flashed him a smile, then blushed a little as I continued, "I think I would keep you the way you are."

"Oh you would, would you?" His face became serious.

"Actually, that was Rosy you saw"—taking a deep breath—"our pet."

He blinked. "You have a pet *pig?*"

"Uh . . . yeah." I started to tell him how special she was, but I decided the less I talked about the pig, the better.

"You must live near the Clarks' old grove."

"You know the place?"

He nodded. "My dad was interested in buying it at one time."

"Really?"

"Yeah, right after the Big Freeze. I was a kid and all, but I remember driving around with him looking at groves that didn't make it. The Clarks' was one of the worst hit. The trees looked like kindling wood the day we went out there. With rotting oranges all over the ground. I remember being amazed that orange trees could split apart like that when they froze, all the way down to the roots."

"Yeah, well, fortunately, it doesn't happen very often."

"Dad thought he'd be helping out the poor couple by offering to buy the place. But it turned out they'd already sold out to some migrant worker."

"M-M-migrant worker?"

"Yeah," he said, shaking his head, "most've them can't even spell their name, they just write a big 'X' on the line that says 'buyer.'"

That was exactly what Papa had done!

"It happens sometimes, folks panicking and selling out. Dad would've given them a much better deal."

I took a deep breath as I looked away. "That was my dad who bought the place."

"Ohhh . . ."

"Yeah," I said, splashing at the water so I wouldn't see his embarrassed look give way to rejection of me, the daughter of a migrant worker and not a mermaid or sea goddess. "He fell in love with the place as we were passing through." I didn't add that Mama had gone into labor and had Sammy in the back of the pickup right among the drunken crows. Or that Mrs. Clark had taken pity on us and cooked our meals while Mama recovered—buttery eggs and the thickest slabs of ham I'd ever seen. She'd even given me a Popsicle when I'd split my lip—a Dreamsicle, my very first. I'd always thought it was she, who had never had children of her own and had taken an interest in us, who'd convinced her husband to give Papa a special deal.

"Well," he said, recovering himself, "looks like it's finally bearing again."

"'Bout to." I nodded vigorously, showing a pride I didn't really feel.

"Dad bought another frozen grove instead. Right over there." He pointed across the lake toward the Citrus Club, the most exclusive subdivision around. It was enclosed by a brick wall and a guarded entranceway. Mama had really hooted when she heard of its name, since there was hardly a citrus tree left on it.

"Is that where you live?"

He nodded. "Dad's a developer. Travels all over the state buying and selling. Says that now that central air conditioners are being put in new houses, we're about to see a building boom like you can't imagine."

"I wouldn't mind that. Anything to liven things up around here."

"Looks pretty lively to me, with pigs and sorceresses afoot," he laughed.

"I'd trade it all to be somewhere—anywhere!—else," I remarked. "Except when I was really small and my folks followed the crops, I've hardly been anywhere. The big trip in my life was going to Orlando and walking around Lake Eola at dusk. Watching the fountain turn colors. And once on a school field trip we toured the Merrita bread factory. I've never smelled anything as wonderful as those huge ovens filled with bread. They gave us miniature loaves to take home. Mine was too pretty to eat, so I kept it in my drawer until it turned green." *I immediately regretted mentioning the green mold—I had a tendency to ramble when I was nervous.*

"Well, if you like to travel, you'd get along great with my parents. They're always on the go."

"Really?"

"Yeah. Mom owns that boutique next to Barry's Seafood. Shirley's?"

I nodded, impressed. Shirley's was a dress shop with lavish window displays. I was afraid to even touch the glass for fear I'd smudge it or something.

"She travels to New York City twice a month. Has to have the latest fashions. Peacock feathers and whatnot."

"Peacock feathers! Nobody wears—"

"I'm kidding," he laughed. "Although she does have some feather boas. Little girls like them for dress up."

"I used to have some of those."

His bright smile turned into a stare.

"What?" I asked, suddenly embarrassed.

He continued to stare—simply stare—at me.

"What?" I repeated. *Could he see me topless in the water?* I kicked up the dirt from the bottom to make the water murkier.

"I'm sorry," he finally said, shaking his head. "It's just that here we are talking about orange groves and feather boas and all I want to do is look at you." He raked his fingers through his hair that looked as wind-blown and ridiculous as I'd remembered it.

I didn't know what to say, so I crossed my eyes and made a face.

"Hey, don't do that!"

"Well, you're embarrassing me."

"I'm sorry. It's just that your hair is dripping wet and you don't have any makeup on and you are—well—glistening."

"Glistening?" I giggled. I'd never been described as glistening.

"I've been looking everywhere for you on campus. I even went to the office and there were no Katerinas listed."

"I go by Kady, actually."

"Katie?"

"No, *Kady.* With a 'D'."

"Oh. Well, maybe that explains it."

"I just like the sound of Katerina, you know? And I thought I'd try it out around someone who didn't really know me," I explained self-consciously.

"Well, that's okay."

"I mean, I never really thought it was fair that you can't pick out your own name, do you?"

"I've never really thought about it."

"That you're just stuck with something for your entire life that somebody else picks out. And Kady sounds so ordinary, you know?"

"Not really. Come to think of it, I don't know any other Katies with a 'D.' But I like the sound of Katerina, too."

"You do?"

"Yeah. You don't mind if I keep calling you that, do you?"

"No," I grinned shyly, "I'd like that."

"Well now that I've found you, *Katerina,* I guess I won't have to pester the office anymore."

An image of girls surrounding him every morning flashed before me. "I don't believe you really went down to the office to find me. You're too cute to bother looking for me."

He drew back. "How can you say that? Didn't meeting me on the lake this summer mean anything to you?"

I gulped. "It did. But I didn't think . . ." My voice trailed off.

"Listen, it's not every day that I go around kissing a girl I barely know."

I blushed. "I've seen you on campus," I admitted after a moment. "And I've wanted to approach you."

"You have?"

I nodded.

He looked perplexed. "Well, why didn't you?"

"Because—because—"

"Because?"

"Because"—I giggled stupidly like Rooster—"because I felt like a carpet fiber, I guess," I blurted out.

"Like a what?"

"You know, small . . . insignificant . . . one of many not-very-distinguishable girls."

"A carpet fiber!" He laughed. "That's a new one."

"Well, after all," I went on, glancing downward at the water, at the tiny bubbles caused by my movements, "I live around here." I waved expansively toward Rosy.

"So! What is this—the Dark Ages? Come on, Katerina! I wouldn't care if you lived in a rain barrel."

I gave him a pained look. "I don't believe that, either."

"It's true. I've been looking everywhere for you, like I said. I close my eyes and I see your violet eyes."

I crossed my eyes, feeling embarrassed again.

"Hey, stop it!" he laughed. "I'm serious. And that's not all. I remember how the corner of your mouth felt against the corner of mine."

I stopped laughing. The way he was staring at me again—so intently—made me feel as if an invisible thread was working its way back and forth between us, stitching us together.

Then he was telling me to climb on board, and I knew he wanted to kiss me again. I started to swim toward the ladder he put in the water for me.

THEN I REMEMBERED!

I'd love to kiss you, but I seem to have lost my clothes and wouldn't want you to get the wrong idea! "I'm s-s-sorry," I stammered. "B-But . . ."

"But what?"

I stared at him.

"Okay, so I want to kiss you again. Am I being too forward?"

"No. I . . ." I swam backwards through the water to stay away from him.

"I guess I am too forward. . . . Look, I'm sorry."

"It's just . . ."

"Well," he said after an awkward moment, "I really ought to get going. I'm in charge of cooking tonight. Frozen turkey pot pies. Yummmm. Have you ever counted the carrots in those things?"

"Can't say that I have," I replied as I struggled to sound normal.

"About four microscopic orange squares per pie. Might as well not bother putting them in. Ditto the meat and potatoes. I don't know why they don't just call them gravy pot pies. Course with only three of us now, why should my mom bother to cook?"

"Three of you now?" I asked, wondering if he had an older brother or sister who'd gone off to college.

But he seemed distracted as he drummed his knuckles on the steering wheel, which made the motor wiggle back and forth, then fiddled with the rearview mirror. "Listen," he went on after a moment, "my friends and I have discovered this spring just around the bend from here." He pointed to where the sun was beginning to turn the sky pink through the tops of the trees. "Just inside those trees."

I nodded, familiar with the place. It was a natural spring of clear, cool water that formed a stream that flowed into the lake. It was much prettier than the ravine, with sandy shores as white as sugar surrounding the bubbling water and huge oaks dripping with Spanish moss. Tony, Rooster, Wendell, and I had discovered it several years ago while tracking down a family of opossums that kept getting into our garbage. We'd loved the woodsy, secluded spot with its own built-in swimming pool so much that we forgot all about the opossums and built a couple of forts there instead. For an entire summer we went there whenever we could slip away.

When we weren't swimming, we played "war," pummeling each other with hard, green palm seeds. We used garbage can lids, pieces of plywood, and an assortment of junk mostly from the Rosados' yard to fend off each other's assaults. Then Rooster got hit in the eye and Mama put an end to our fun. It'd been years since I'd gone back there. It was part of a stretch of undeveloped property owned by the same guy who owned the ravine, some businessman from Miami who was never around. I was surprised to learn it had become a hang-out for Jon's friends, since it was so rustic.

"I'd like you to come with me next Saturday, if that's okay."

"Sure," I shrugged, unable to repress the huge smile that was taking over my face. "I'd love to."

I'd love to. I'd heard girls say that so effortlessly on TV shows like *That Girl*, and now I was saying it so effortlessly. *I'd love to.*

"I could pick you up at your dock."

"Okay."

"I know which one it is, with the pig running around that used to be a pig of a guy."

"That's the one." I nodded with embarrassment, even though he'd said he wouldn't care if I lived in a rain barrel.

Something brushed against my leg, startling me.

"Three o'clock okay?"

"Sure."

"Okay, I'll see you then."

"Great."

I tried to keep smiling as he took his time turning his boat around to leave. Yet all the while I felt uneasy. Fish had nibbled at my feet countless times, but whatever it was that had brushed up against me hadn't been a fish. It had been something pretty big. An alligator? There had been recent reports of one sighted in the area, but I hadn't let it get to me. After all, I'd been swimming in the lake all my life and had never been disturbed by one.

Usually they came out at night to feed, then returned to their watery burrows at dawn. I'd see them steal past our dock like floating logs sometimes during the twilight hours. Miz Sanders apparently saw them, too, for occasionally we'd be awakened by the blast of her "magic wand" shotgun. Nonetheless, I panicked as I felt something bump me again.

As soon as Jon left, I leapt out of the water and laughed with relief when I spotted an otter swimming around the cattails.

"*¡Madrina!*" Rooster cried out. His sudden appearance startled me.

"Rooster!"

"Eep-eep-eep!" Dandy echoed.

He got a good glimpse of me standing bare-chested in my panties. I snatched my clothes from the punk tree branch and dashed behind the tree to put them on.

Rooster followed me without the slightest trace of embarrassment and said, "Y-Y-You put-put-put on old *sm-smelly* clothes?" Then he laughed, as if that was a very strange thing to do, and not the fact that I was standing there practically naked.

I knew then that it had been Sammy who had hidden my clothes. "Oh, Rooster," I said with relief, "thank you for being you!"

I was too excited to go home, so when I saw Jewel hanging up the laundry, I went to see her instead. I didn't care that news time was fast approaching and that Mama would be angry I wasn't helping Grampsie get ready for Dear Walty. Mama was always angry about something, so what did it matter?

I danced around Jewel's ample waist, my eyes shining.

She spat out a clothespin. "That big ole smile for me, Miss Kady?"

"For you and the whole world! I've got a date, Jewel."

Her eyes widened. "Say what?"

"You know—" I ran my fingertips lightly across the clothesline, tracing the top of a clothespin—"with a boy."

I glanced at the back of her calves, at the dark scar where her husband had shot her, and wondered if she'd be happy for me when she'd had such a miserable marriage.

"My husband's a good man when he's sober," she'd told us that first winter, "but he gets mean when he takes a drink, which is pretty regular now that all them oranges froze and he can't get any work."

I never met him, because one night shortly after that, he got so drunk that he slammed his pickup into a tree and was killed instantly. Papa called that tree a widowmaker even though it remained standing.

Jewel stayed with us for a year after that, cooking and cleaning in return for a roof over her head. I can still remember the whisper of her bare feet—tough as overcooked steak—padding across our creaky floors, the sound of steam spewing from the iron as she attacked the clothes with the force of a steamroller (especially when something really exciting was happening on *The Edge of Night*, her favorite soap), the sizzle of frying onions, which she added to everything, and the pitchers of lemonade she was forever making, so sweet you could lick the sugar off your teeth.

She had massive arms as strong as an oak and hands like the gnarled roots of an old tree. I loved the way she'd wrap those arms around me when I got hurt and sing to me about the sweet love of Jesus until the hurt stopped. And I loved how her fingernails, no matter how bitten-back, were always awash in color.

The house seemed hollow after she left. She landed a job tending a college professor's family that earned her a lot more money than we were able to give her. Even so, she still came twice a week to help Mama with the washing and to catch up on our comings and goings. Sometimes I even fantasized that she was my mother.

The gold in her teeth flashed as she smiled at me now. "I always knew there was a girl 'neath all that dirt. Figured you'd be showing yourself one of these days."

I yanked a strand of Bahia grass from the patchy ground and chewed on the end of it. "Do you ever go out?"

"Who me?"

"Yes, you."

She fiddled with a clothespin, opening and shutting it several times before securing it to a pair of overalls. "There's a coupla gentlemen I see from time to time. But right now I'm mostly concentrating on Jewel, you know what I mean?"

I shook my head. I couldn't imagine anything more exciting than falling in love.

"I always wanted to be a nurse, mmm hmm," she went on, "and now I'm goin' to school four nights a week. If I was married, I probably wouldn't be able to finish, 'cause a man now, he wants his woman home at night, see?"

"Did a man ever tell you you had neat eye color?"

"Neat eye color?"

"Yeah," I blushed a little. "Neat eye color."

"Can't say one ever did. But a man, now, will say all sorts of things. When I met Tyrone he told me I had a smile like a toothpaste commercial. I just laughed, cause I'm missing two teeth on the bottom and have three gold fillings on the top."

"They don't really mean it then, when they say things like that?" I asked as I ducked under a sheet.

"Why, I don't know . . . you've got right nice eyes."

I pushed at the sheet, letting it billow in front of me, then fall—cool and clean-smelling—back onto my face, which had suddenly gotten hot. "Do you think they're violet?"

"Violet?"

I nodded.

"I don't know 'bout that."

A butterfly fluttered between us and landed on my shoulder. She stared at it, transfixed. "Why, honey," she said with a sudden smile. "Do you know you're fixin' to get a new dress?"

"Huh?"

"A butterfly just landed on you."

I kept still as I pulled my neck back to see it. "So?"

"So! Why, honey, it's a *sign*. When a butterfly lands on a young girl it means she's gonna get a new dress."

I rolled my eyes. Jewel drove me crazy with her constant talk about signs. Like if you bit your tongue, it meant you were about to tell a lie. Or, if you drank lake water your teeth would fall out. (She figured this was the reason Grampsie had lost her teeth!) Or, every time you yawned, you better cover your mouth quick, or your soul might fly out and an evil spirit might fly in. Or that certain trees, such as the big, sprawling ceiba tree that Tony talked about, were possessed by magical powers. Or if a picture fell from a wall, someone was going to die. She firmly believed that if you were faced with bad luck, it helped to spit. Jewel spit more than any person I knew.

"Like I really need another of Mama's stupid dresses," I said wearily. "I just want to know if you think my eyes are violet." If you could get her to talk about something besides superstitions, she had plenty of basic common sense.

"Lemme take a look." I walked up to her and the butterfly fluttered away.

She had me look skyward as she studied my eyes. "I reckon they are violet, Miss Kady. Kind of a blue-violet."

"You ever know anybody with violet eyes?"

"Don't know that I has. Course I never thought 'bout it one way or 'nother. Eyes see just the same no matter what color they are."

"Oh, but Jon makes a big deal about my violet eyes. Says he can close his eyes and see my violet eyes." My face lit into a rapturous smile.

"Grab an end of this sheet," she said, throwing a length of wrinkled cloth my way. "Who is this boy, anyway?"

"Someone I met on the lake a few weeks ago."

I recounted everything that had happened during our two chance encounters, including the kiss, while we pinned up the wash. As I talked, she smiled inwardly—especially when I told her how Jon had described me as glistening—but she didn't burst out laughing and make me feel stupid. I suppose I should've held something back, but I had to tell somebody about the wonderful feelings that were exploding inside of me, and Jewel was the only person, other than maybe Tony, who ever listened.

"I never understood romance before," I went on ardently, "never understood the feelings that just come over you. Jon said the most incredible things to me and not just about my eyes. Oh but, Jewel, he has the nicest eyes, too"—I traced a wrinkle in the sheet—"the color of Lake Pomelo when the sun's beating down—blue, green, and gold all swirled together."

"That right?" She worked her mouth to keep a big grin from spreading all over it as she shook out a pair of overalls. But I could tell her eyes were twinkling just the same.

"Now he's asked me to go to the spring with him on Saturday, this place where he hangs out with his friends, and"—my face suddenly clouded over—"oh, God."

"What is it?"

"Oh, God!" I repeated. "I'm nothing like his friends." I snatched up another strand of Bahia grass and let the bitter-sweet sap seep through my teeth.

"Why, Kady Palmer, what has gotten into you?"

"Don't you get it? Jon isn't the kind of guy ordinary girls like me impress! It's only because he found me on the lake, in an extraordinary place that—"

"Ordinary!" she snorted. "There ain't nothing ordinary 'bout you. Listen up, now." She fixed her eyes upon me as she sucked in her lower lip and chewed it for a moment. "I 'spose you can impress anybody if you want to badly enough. It's like sailing close to the wind. Filling them sails just as full as you can by turning toward the wind just so. And you can go mighty fast that way, mmm hmm, mighty fast . . . but then the wind owns you, see?"

"So?"

"You've got to learn to let your own natural color shine through, Miss Kady. And I ain't talking 'bout your eyes. I mean who you are underneath."

She shook out a pair of my underwear—ugly cotton briefs that came all the way up to my neck, or so it seemed—and started to pin them up.

"Not these!" I snatched them from her. "Especially where the whole world can see them!"

She looked around. "Whole world? What whole world? I don't see nothing but trees and water and—oh! There goes Mister Tony into his house. You worried 'bout Mister Tony seeing your drawers, Miss Kady?" She gave me a little smirk.

"Hardly. It's just that if you have to have your underwear flapping in the breeze like a big flag, it could at least be decent stuff. Those girls Jon hangs out with wear bikini briefs in pastel colors. I see them changing in P.E. and it's embarrassing to be standing next to them in oversized training pants."

"Why, Miss Kady, they're called underwear because they're just that—*under*wear. I don't imagine anybody's paying you much attention while you're dressing."

"Wanna make a bet?"

"Well, you wouldn't catch me in bikini briefs. No, sir. Not Jewel. 'Cause when it comes to underwear my number-one priority is comfort. I ain't bothering with somethin' I got to pull this way and that, no matter how pretty they may look in 'pastel colors'! I like to be covered. Mmm hmm."

I tried not to laugh. Jewel had generous hips, to put it mildly.

"And I'll tell you somethin' else 'bout underwear. If you turn 'em inside out, honey, they're smooth against your skin." Her black eyes sparkled as she pulled up her dress and flashed me a peek of her underwear—an enormous swath of white material, turned inside out.

"I wanna meet this mystery boy before you take off on any boat," Mama informed me Saturday morning, hours before Jon was supposed to pick me up. I hadn't told her or Papa the truth about my date. Only that I was going boating with Jon and some friends. I counted on the fact that the lake was big enough that I'd be able to slip away from her hawklike eyes. At least Papa was away at work, as usual.

"You're a little young to be going on boating outings if you ask me." She snorted. "And you ain't going at all if you don't finish your chores. I need you to fetch a bag of juice oranges for breakfast since your Pa's at work."

Armed with a grocery sack, I stalked past her into the early morning fog that shrouded the trees. I filled the bag with fragrant pineapple oranges, then added a few tangerines that were just beginning to ripen.

I paused by the magnolia tree outside the kitchen window. I'd watched it grow over the years from just a shoot into a tall, stately tree, totally symmetrical even though it was crowded on one side by the Rosados' bamboo, which kept creeping into our yard. Its leaves were so brilliantly green that it looked out of place against the softer, muted colors of the Florida scrub country, like a bright penny surrounded by tarnished coins. It was Rosy's favorite shade spot and looked lonely without her plopped down under it.

A shrill noise jarred me and I turned to see Rooster standing on top of an overturned whiskey barrel that had somehow made its way into our yard.

"GAG-A-GAGAGAGAGAG-GAAAA!" he cried as he flapped his arms and jumped.

I gasped when I saw his purse swing up, then swing back down by his side with a thud as his bare feet hit the ground.

Rooster pulled the gosling out of his purse a moment later, his cheeks flushed. "Wasn't th-th-that f-f-fun, Dandy? You—You—You got wings, you know. These th-things that p-p-oke out right h-h-here. You can fly, all b-b-b-by yourself." He placed Dandy—who was cheeping loudly—on top of the barrel.

Spying me, he hollered, "*¡Madrina!* Watch Dandy!" Then he began chirping "Gag-a-gag-a-gag" to the gosling.

I was amazed how well he'd learned to imitate a gosling after imitating hens for years.

"Kady! Where are them oranges?" Mama hollered from the screen door. "Grampsie's about to have a fit. She will require some orange juice!" She started to slam the screen door shut when she spied Rooster. Her hand froze on the latch and she said in the sweetest of voices, "That's a nice-looking gosling you got there, Rooster."

"*Madrina* g-g-get oranges l-later!" he shouted to Mama, startling us both with the firmness of his demand. *"Madrina* g-g-gonna watch D-Dandy *f-fly!"*

Mama's hand began twitching on the latch and I could tell she was furious. But she managed to nod at Rooster with the faintest of smiles, then call out tersely to me, "Five minutes."

In those five minutes, all Dandy managed to do was flutter his wings and use the top of that whiskey barrel to do his business. But having witnessed Rooster boss Mama around was worth every glorious minute.

For the next few hours I cleaned the house, then decided it was a hopeless situation. No matter how hard I scrubbed, polished and straightened up, the place looked dingy and cluttered. I gave up and got myself ready.

I slipped on the shimmering green bikini I'd worn when I'd met Jon, and was combing out the snarls in my hair when Mama came into my room carrying a wrench.

"I need you to help me unclog the sink."

"Mama, I've got a date!"

"I've got a mess on my hands! And your father's at work."

"So what else is new? Get Wendell to help you."

"I've been hollering for him, but he's nowhere to be found. I need you and I need you now!"

"Honestly, Mama, you were young once," I reminded her as I continued to work out my snarls.

She toyed with the wrench, opening and shutting the mouth as she shook her head. "Don't think I was. I was picking cotton when I was your age. Ain't nothing worse than stooping over from sunup till sunset among the heat and gnats, with someone thumping you on the back with a cotton stalk if'n you don't work fast enough. Them hard, green bolls hurt like the dickens."

"I know, Mama. I used to pick it, too."

She looked at me sharply, as if she'd forgotten I'd been seven when I'd picked cotton alongside her. "By the time I was seventeen, I was working in the muck farms around Lake Apopka, where I met your Pa. Don't think I ever worried about my hair. It was always chopped short like it is now. He didn't mind." She tapped the wrench into the palm of her hand. "If this boy you're about to go gallivanting around with is worth his salt—"

"We're not going 'gallivanting' around, Mama! We're going boating!"

"Well, if he's worth his salt, he won't care how your hair looks, either."

"Hopefully, I won't marry a guy who'd rather look at oranges than me!"

Her eyes narrowed and she was silent for a moment. "If you want to go at all, you'll watch your tongue, miss! Now, I want to meet that boy when he gets here."

"So you say. But I'm not about to bring him in the house with the sink all clogged up!"

"Then you'd better get hopping! Because you're not going

anywhere until it's unclog—"

"Why, Mama . . ." I looked into her eyes, blinking with disbelief. I don't think I'd ever gotten as close to her face as I was now, except to observe those little beads of sweat on her eyebrows. Her eyes were swallowed up by her puffy jowls, so I'd never really noticed the color before, the pink flecks mixed in with the blue. "I can't believe this, but you have violet eyes, too."

"What's gotten into you?" she snorted as she yanked away. She smelled like rotten potatoes.

"I just never realized. . . ."

"I don't have time for this foolishness!" And with a Humph! and another snort, she left the room, muttering she'd find Minnie instead.

I hurried down to the dock to wait for Jon before Mama changed her mind. The last thing I needed was for him to come up to our house with the contents of the kitchen sink cabinets sprawled all over the floor—the canisters of Crisco, the rusted cookie sheets, the box of broken dinner plates that Mama always meant to glue back together but never got around to—while Mama's legs, mapped with varicose veins, stuck out from under our clogged-up sink.

Thankfully, the cattails that grew along the shore obscured most of our house from view. I tried to relax, but when I sat down, the bottom of my bathing suit snagged on a splinter poking up from the weathered boards of the dock. If it wasn't one thing it was another!

I was pulling out the splinter when I spotted Jon's boat cutting across the lake. My heart started to pound as I stood up and waved.

I probably could've made a quick getaway if Wendell, Rooster, and Sammy hadn't rushed up to me with silly grins on their faces.

Wendell thrust a small box under my nose. "Wanna see a dead man's finger? Since you're my sister, I'll only charge ya a buck."

"Go away."

"Once in a lifetime chance. Fresh from the morgue. That right, guys?"

Rooster nodded stupidly.

"Nobody has a real dead man's finger," I muttered, my eyes fixed on the approaching boat. "Bug off!"

"I don't think she has the stomach for it," Wendell sneered. He looked up and regarded the approaching boat. "Expecting someone?" His eyes twinkled with a wicked gleam.

"Mama's looking for you in the kitchen. She's gonna be mad if you don't go there right now," I insisted through clenched teeth.

The boat slowed down as it approached the dock. Jon waved. He was dressed simply in denim cutoffs and a T-shirt, which seemed to accentuate his tan.

"That guy has the whitest T-shirt I've ever seen," Sammy marveled. "Who is he?"

"He m-must use Tide," Rooster remarked. "It m-m-makes clothes th-th-their *whitest!*"

"Shut up, jerk!" Wendell cried, and bonked him lightly on the head.

"Shut up, j-j-jerk!" Rooster laughed back, and bonked Wendell on the head.

"Gag-a-gag-a-gag!" Dandy squawked.

"He's a friend of mine," I explained to Sammy.

"Her boyfriend!" Wendell practically hollered. I was grateful for the loudness of the boat's motor, which kept Jon from hearing him.

"*¡N-Novio!*" Rooster yelled.

I flashed Jon my most dazzling smile as I muttered to Wendell that if he didn't leave this very instant, I'd knock his block off.

"Since you're my sister, I'll show it to you for free," he continued, unfazed, as he pulled off the lid. "See?"

Nestled on a bed of cotton was a human finger, most definitely real. The flesh was pale gray with black-and-blue bruises, and blood oozed out the end, saturating the cotton bed. I was on the verge of screaming when I realized what was going on. Wendell's eyes were too bright, too expectant.

It wasn't a finger from the morgue lying on that bed of cotton. It was Wendell's own finger poking through a hole he'd cut in the bottom of the box, surrounded by ketchup. He was trying to make me look like a fool in front of Jon.

As much as I wanted to kill him, a greater desire to flee overtook me.

The second the boat bumped against the dock, I leaped aboard and pushed it away.

"So!" I said brightly to Jon. "Let's go!"

From the corner of my eye I saw Mama bounding down the

dock, shaking the entire structure with her weight. She'd covered her shirt with a checkered apron that made her look like a walking picnic table. *Was that my destiny? To look like her? So much for having violet eyes!*

"Mama, this is Jon," I called across the water as we puttered away, "and Jon, this is my mother. See ya later!" The wrench she still carried in her hand dropped a little as she gave me an astonished look.

"Don't worry, I'll have her back by dark," Jon called out cheerfully.

As the retreating boat shrunk Mama and the boys smaller and smaller, I fell back with relief. I was free!

The longer I could put off Jon meeting my family the better. Just the other night, Minnie had invited a friend over for dinner and Mama had brought out her Surprise Dish. The Surprise Dish was a regular feature whenever she got unlabeled cans from the bargain bin at the supermarket. She liked to serve whatever they contained along with dinner—unless, of course, there was dog food inside, which had happened once. That time Rosy got the surprise.

The Surprise Dish the night Minnie's friend came over turned out to be hominy. Sammy, who'd never seen hominy, screamed that Mama was serving us horse teeth. Minnie's friend looked at Mama gravely and asked, "Mrs. Palmer, are you really gonna make us eat horse teeth?"

The boat sped across the water, mercifully shrinking my family into oblivion.

13

Rock music blasted from a parked van as we turned into the inlet and puttered upstream. When we pulled into the spring, I noticed a dozen or so colorfully clad sunbathers dotting the sandy shore like exotic flowers. They were clumped together in the few bright spots of sun. There were several parked cars and vans lining a dirt road that led off to the side.

The road was barely wider than a trail, and partly overgrown with potato vines. More vines grew thickly in the trees surrounding the clearing, twisting in loopy arcs. I could hardly believe this was the same wilderness area where Tony, Rooster, Wendell, and I had once chased a family of opossums. Yet the potato vines were familiar. I remembered harvesting the hard brown "potatoes" and using them as ammunition when the palm seeds had run out.

All eyes seemed to fall upon me as we approached, and I self-consciously hugged my towel around my shoulders. It was a faded strip of terry cloth that had been the "special prize" inside a detergent box.

Jon switched off the engine when we were a few yards from shore, then tossed out the anchor. I followed him in the ankle-deep water to the shore as the very ground seemed to vibrate. There was thunderous applause from the sound track, then the next song floated through the air as mystically as smoke from Papa's pipe:

> . . . *And I dreamed I saw the bombers*
> *Riding shotgun in the sky,*
> *And they were turning into butterflies*
> *Above our nation . . .*

"What's that music from?" I asked him. "It's nice."

He looked at me, surprised. "Don't you know?"

I shook my head.

"Woodstock."

"Oh, from the concert they held at that farm in New York last month."

"Yeah. Would've given anything to have been there. Can you imagine Joni Mitchell, The Grateful Dead, Canned Heat, and The Who all in one place?"

I nodded, even though I hadn't a clue who most of these groups were. My meager collection of 45s consisted of The Monkees and Herman's Hermits, as well as a scratched-up recording of *Who's Afraid of the Big Bad Wolf?*

"If I were a little older I would've driven up there," he said as he looked around for our own patch of sun. "But I just got my license last week."

My scanty knowledge of the Woodstock concert flashed through my mind: *"Look at those half-naked fools standing under a piece of plywood in the rain!"* Mama had shouted to the TV and Grampsie had told her to shut up or she'd scare off Dear Walty.

Several people waved at Jon and he nodded back. I caught a whiff of marijuana, but when I looked around I didn't see a joint anywhere. I wouldn't be surprised if somebody was smoking, though. A lot of kids snuck into the bathrooms between classes at school and took a few puffs before flushing joints down the toilets. Some had been caught and suspended.

"Of course, if I were much older I'd probably be in Nam," he went on ruefully.

"What a thought."

"Did you see the *Laugh-In* show where Nixon said, 'Sock It to Me?'"

"No, but I heard it was funny." Grampsie got an eyeful of Goldie Hawn's wiggling bellybutton one night when the variety show was turned on and refused to let us watch it again. That was before she got the notion that Walter Cronkite was paying her a personal visit. Now she probably wouldn't care if Goldie danced in the nude.

"He's the one we're gonna sock it to if he doesn't pull us out of there," he said with surprising anger.

"I take it you're against the war."

He blinked at me in amazement. "Aren't you?"

The truth was, I was quicker to turn to *Charlie Brown* in the comic section of the paper than read the headlines. "Of course, I don't like war," I said. "But—"

"Fighting is so stupid! I mean, here you have all these kids on that farm in Woodstock for three days and not one incidence of violence. Yet the politicians think they know all the answers." He shook his head bitterly. "Let *their* sons come home in body bags."

"Well . . ."

"And for what?" His eyes blazed. "For a war we can't even win!"

Was this the same smiling guy I'd met on the lake? "You don't think we'll win?"

"Guerrilla warfare in a strange country? Shoot . . ."

"Maybe not," I said lamely, not sure how to follow all the twists and turns of the conversation. He wasn't the only one I'd known, though, who had very strong feelings about the war. Lots of people did. Especially guys who would be up for the draft in a few years. There were war protests staged all over the place, with people carrying signs with slogans such as: Make Love Not War, Hell No, We Won't Go! and War Isn't Healthy for Children and Other Living Things. The thought of Jon possibly being drafted chilled me.

He threw up his hands. "Why can't we all be doves, Kady? I don't want to fight anybody."

"Me either," I quickly agreed.

"I just want to live and let live, you know?"

I nodded. I'd heard that expression a lot lately.

His intense expression transformed into a grin. "I sound all heated up, don't I?"

"Yeah," I admitted.

"It's just that my dad and I get into these discussions—if you can call them that—all the time. He thinks the world's 'going to hell in a handbag' and it's the fault of kids who'd rather smoke dope than get their act together."

"Sounds like he and my mother would get along great," I remarked as I helped him spread out his towel. "You don't know how wonderful it is for me to be here, to just sit down for a while," I said as I plopped down. The towel was luxuriously soft and smelled like Downy fabric softener. We didn't have a dryer, and our towels smelled like damp grass and were as scratchy as sandpaper from drying on the clothesline.

A cute guy with a mass of curls tapped Jon with a Frisbee. His hair was held back by a sweatband with a peace sign drawn on the front in uneven black marker. "So, bud, who's your new girl?" he asked, looking at me.

Jon introduced me to the guy, Parker. He started to nod at me, then did a double take, his eyes going from the curves of my calves to the curves of my eyebrows in an unsettling way. "You new in town?"

"No, I've—uh—lived here most of my life."

He looked at me curiously. "I can't believe I haven't seen you around."

I shrugged.

He playfully nudged Jon as he continued to stare at me. "So how'd this animal find you?"

"Animal!" Jon protested in mock anger as he nudged him back.

"This animal's boat nearly ran over me, actually," I grinned.

"Oh, so you're the *mermaid* Mark was telling everyone about." He gave a low, appreciative whistle. "Some chicken of the sea!"

"Cut it out, man, you're embarrassing her," Jon said.

"It's okay," I laughed.

Parker tossed the Frisbee straight up in the air and reached up and caught it. "So how 'bout it, buddy?"

I looked at Jon quizzically. "How 'bout what?"

"Oh. We usually mess around with the Frisbee for a while."

I nodded. "That sounds fun." I started to get up.

"Guy stuff. You don't mind, do you?"

I gave him a wide-eyed stare as I slowly sat back down, stunned that he would even consider leaving me alone after we'd just arrived.

"We have an ongoing game," he added, flushing slightly as I continued to stare at him with a how-can-you-leave-me look. I glanced around and realized I didn't know a soul here, except for Charlotte, who sat nearby in an itsy-bitsy red-and-purple tie-dyed bikini, eating junk food with some friends. I marveled that she kept herself so thin.

"Come on, let me introduce you around first," he said to me, then turned to Parker. "I'll be right there, man."

He took me by the hand and introduced me to his friends, the ones I'd seen from a distance at school but had been afraid to approach. I smiled brightly at everyone, maybe too brightly to make up for my nervousness. The guys seemed a lot friendlier than the girls, who regarded me with detached curiosity. Junk food was being passed around—I got a handful of brazil nuts and some Fritos. The brightly colored wrappers were scattered about like Christmas morning. There was a cooler filled with Coke and beer.

Then I came face-to-face with Charlotte, whose jaw fell at the sight of me. "Kady Palmer!" she practically spit out my name. I felt my face turn bloodred, my worst fears realized. "What are *you* doing here?"

"She's my friend, Lotto," Jon said as his arm coiled around my waist. "What's the problem?"

She stared at me for another incredulous moment, then held the palm of her hand up like a stop sign, her splayed fingers orange with Cheetos: "No problem!" She got up and sauntered away, her fingertips curving inside her bikini bottoms and pulling them over the crescent of her exposed buttocks as if she were in the privacy of her own room, staining her butt a bright Cheeto-orange.

"Don't let her get to you," Jon said as he led me back to our towel. "She's mad at me."

"What for?"

"It's a long story. One that I'm sure would bore you. Just relax and listen to the music and I'll be back before you know it. Okay?"

"Okay." I managed to smile. "How did you find this place?"

"A fishing buddy, believe it or not. He followed the inlet that led to the spring. Said it was like stumbling on the Garden of Eden. And it is, too. Just have a look around." He started to run off, then stopped. "Oh, and if you need to—you know—use the bathroom, there's a portable toilet in Mark's van—it's the blue one with the Sock It To Me bumper sticker."

"Thanks," I replied, embarrassed.

"There's plenty of leaves around for toilet paper," he added, then waited for my mouth to drop open, which of course it did. "Only kidding!" he laughed. "Well, have fun."

I settled back uneasily on my towel as the girls surrounding me sunbathed, chatted, or sang along with the music. My nose quivered at the smell of sour cream 'n' onion potato chips. I'd never gotten around to lunch, and the few brazil nuts and Fritos I'd eaten only made me hungrier. Yet nobody offered me anything now that Jon was gone.

I decided not to worry about it and lay back down under a patch of sunlight streaming through the trees. It seemed an incredible luxury to get a suntan by lying down instead of weeding.

I'd nearly fallen asleep when I felt something sticky hit me on the side of my head. I sat up and pulled it out of my hair. It was a Milk Dud, slimy with spit.

I glanced around to see who'd thrown it, but the only unusual thing I saw was a girl leaning against Charlotte's shoulder. She was wearing a swimsuit covered with silver sequins, and was laughing so hard they shook, glimmering in the sun. She was the same girl I'd seen at school wearing that weird paisley turban.

My eyes narrowed as I caught her glancing at me, then laughing even harder. But she just chirped "Hey there!" in that inane way Charlotte always said it.

I stared at her a moment longer, nearly certain she'd thrown that Milk Dud spitball at me, but the smile didn't fade from her lips. It was as if it was painted on. I wiped my hands in the grass and remained sitting, not sure what to do.

I was glad when Jon returned and we went for a swim. The water was cool and silent, a world apart from the one on the surface. I wished I could stay there forever, to really be Katerina, Goddess of Lake Pomelo. It was fun to kick and splash, to turn somersaults and to go down so deep the water turned ice-cold. There was no noise or confusion under-water—just blue-green tranquillity.

After we got out and dried off, Jon pulled a huge Tupperware container of brownies from a grocery sack he'd brought along and offered me one.

"You must really like chocolate," I remarked. "You had brownies on the boat, too."

"You liked those, didn't you?"

"Yeah."

He nodded, smiling. "I thought you were the brownies type."

Everyone else sitting nearby seemed to be the brownies type, too, and within minutes they were all gone. One girl—who took three—went so far as to say she wouldn't even bother going to the spring if it weren't for Jon's brownies.

As we ate, I kept glancing at the girl in the silver-sequined suit who seemed to be staring at me with huge, unblinking cat eyes. She was very striking, with hair the bleached whiteness of Florida sand—whiter even than Jon's—in startling contrast to her deeply tanned face. Her features were too sharp to be considered pretty, and yet she was beautiful in a riveting sort of way. Her swimsuit was equally riveting, covered with those sequins that glinted with every breath she took. I'd never seen anything like it and wondered if they would fall off if she tried to swim in it. I could picture them floating on the surface like tiny silver dollars.

"Who's that girl?" I finally asked Jon, nodding at her.

"That's Madison. Why? Did she give you a hard time?"

I decided not to mention the Milk Dud, although my curiosity was aroused. "Why would she?"

"Because, well, she used to be my girlfriend"—kissing me on the tip of my nose—"until you took over that position."

His words stunned me. "What?"

His mouth pulled into a grin. "You don't mind, do you, Katerina? Being my girlfriend?"

I was amazed. "I barely know you."

"Tell me you don't like me," he said, kissing me this time tenderly on the mouth. "God, I've been dreaming of doing that."

My face flushed. "Of course, I like you." He started to kiss me again and my heart started racing like crazy, the same way it had on the boat. It took everything in me to break away. "So what happened between you and—and—"

"Madison?"

I nodded weakly, my heart still pounding.

He shrugged. "I broke up with her."

I wasn't sure what to say, so I made the intelligent remark of "Oh."

"She two-timed me," he added after a moment.

"Oh," I said again. "I'm really sorry."

"Yeah, well. I should've known what kind of a girl she was." He glanced over to where she sat regally atop her fluffy towel throne. "I mean, who in their right mind would sunbathe in a dance recital costume?"

"A what?"

"She performed 'Diamonds Are a Girl's Best Friend' in that little number. You can only imagine how many other best friends she's had," he added with a knowing look.

"She's very pretty," I observed.

"If you're into peroxide. She was a brunette last year. A *dark* brunette. Don't look too closely at the roots."

"Honestly, Jon!" I gave a sudden, unexpected laugh.

He shook his head. "You don't know the half of it. But I'll tell you what. I'll take a sweetie like you any day over Madison Madison. That's her name, you know. Same first name as last."

"Weird." I glanced over at Charlotte, who was still sitting next to her. "How does Charlotte fit into this?"

"Charlotte's her best friend. Need I say more? Come here," he said, offering his hand.

"Where are we going?"

"On a walk." He clasped my hand firmly in his and brought me to my feet, which were surprisingly unsteady. "This place is beautiful."

Joni Mitchell's melodious voice wafted through the leaves again and I strained to catch the words:

We are stardust
We are golden
And we've got to get ourselves
Back to the garden . . .

I felt light-headed and dizzy as we walked along the stream, Jon's pulse quickening in my hand. Jon stopped and picked me a wild orchid. Its delicate and softly fragrant petals were snowy white, streaked with dark purple. He was laughing as he handed it to me, even though neither of us had said anything funny. I laughed back, feeling strangely euphoric. *Was this what love was all about?*

> *. . . Then can I walk beside you?*
> *I have come here to lose the smog*
> *And I feel to be a cog in something turning*
> *Well maybe it's the time of year,*
> *Or maybe it's the time of man,*
> *I don't know who I am*
> *But life's for learning.*

The leaves in all their many sizes and shapes seemed to turn brilliant shades of green before my eyes. I'd never really looked at nature so closely and now every fragment of dust floating in the air seemed caught by the sun like golden glitter, like stardust. It was as if my senses were coming alive, the way they had that day when Jon and I met. As I kept staring at those golden specks of dust, I felt so unbelievably light. And even though I had both feet on the ground, I felt as if I were floating, spinning . . . as if *I* were stardust.

I laughed again and Jon turned to me, his eyes bright and shiny. "Here," he said, handing me something.

"What's this?" My voice seemed to come from a great distance, as if it belonged to someone else.

"Look through it." His voice suddenly sounded so close it startled me.

"Oh," I said, and brought it to my eye.

"No, the other way," he said, and turned it around.

I laughed at my foolishness, then tried to look through it again. I saw a leaf split into dozens of leaves, the golden glitter increase a hundred fold, the peace sign on Parker's headband multiply into dozens of peace signs. Everybody—including Madison Madison, whose silver-sequined suit studded the prism with light—looked happy. I began to feel connected to these people, to feel as if I were a cog in something turning.

"You felt like a 'cog in something turning?' Come on, Kady! You were stoned!" Tony exclaimed the following night when I told him about my date.

"Stoned?"

"Stoned."

We were sitting on the plywood table slapping mosquitoes and finishing our Monopoly game as darkness was falling. Señor Rosado had dumped about two hundred cartons of "Bear's Milk" on us to sell that week. Bear's Milk was this powdered substance exploding with nutrients that was supposed to give you boundless energy, make roses bloom in your cheeks, and basically change your life. So far, we had no takers.

"Shut up, Tony! I wasn't either!"

"*¡Mira!*" He looked at me intently in that macho Cuban way of his. "Look at me."

"Okay, so I smelled marijuana. But I didn't see any joints being passed around. And I didn't smoke anything. Do you think I need Mama giving me more hell than she already does?"

"What did you eat?"

I shrugged. "Hardly anything. Exactly three brazil nuts, five Fritos, and two fudge brownies, if you must know."

Tony nearly fell off the table, laughing. "Three brazil nuts, five Fritos and two fudge brownies!"

I wrinkled my nose and stared at him. "What's your problem?"

"You're so naive! Those brownies had marijuana in them!"

I looked at him, stricken. "You're wrong."

"Is a sneaky way to get high. I know kids who eat marijuana brownies during lunch. Then they sit through class glassy-eyed, not having a clue what's going on. They think they're getting away with something."

"Jon would've told me."

"Well, he didn't. You were stoned and didn't even know it!"

"I wasn't, either!"

"First you tell me these girls are throwing Milk Duds at you—"

"Just one girl, and I'm not even sure—"

"—and the next thing you're saying is that you felt like a 'cog in something turning.'" He shook his head in disbelief as he landed his token—a Hot Wheels school bus—on Baltic Avenue.

"Double rent!"

"Since when?"

"Since I bought Mediterranean last time."

Tony tossed eight one-dollar bills my way as if they were confetti and called me a Capitalist.

I grabbed the money from the air, put it in the bank, and plopped down a gleaming green house on Baltic. "I will *EEEE*-rect a house in your honor."

"Just remember," he said, "people smile when they're high the same way babies smile when they fart. It doesn't mean anything."

"Don't tell me my feelings don't mean anything!"

"Fine! So you felt great being high!"

"How 'bout I felt great, period?" I took a swig of Blazin' Berries, a ghastly purple punch that tasted like liquified dog biscuits. Señor Rosado had boxes filled with gallon jugs of the stuff stacked everywhere. Rats were beginning to gnaw their way through the plastic caps, so Tony said we had to drink it up.

"I wouldn't want someone slipping me something," he went on. "Aside from screwing up your mind, what if your parents had found out? They'd never let you out of the house again."

"Nobody slipped me anything!" I insisted, although I was beginning to wonder. I *had* felt unusually giddy both times.

"And what if you'd had to drive?"

"You know I don't drive yet! I had a great time. And even if there was pot in those brownies—and I'm not saying there was—I could've eaten oatmeal cookies and felt the same way. High on life!"

"*¡Qué cosa!*" he hooted.

"*¡Qué cosa!*" I mimicked. "I'm going inside if you don't stop fighting with me."

His eyes widened in surprise. "This isn't fighting. This is the way we usually talk."

"Well, some people are starting to realize how stupid fighting is," I went on loftily. "Like those kids at that Woodstock concert. A half million of them crowded together for three days, and there wasn't one incidence of violence. And yet our politicians—"

"Who fights when they're stoned? Or even thinks?"

"You can't tell me all of them were stoned!"

"Okay. Maybe one or two of them weren't stoned."

"Honestly Tony, there's a *peace movement* going on in this country! Yet here we are fighting a war we can't even win."

He blinked at me in astonishment. "Since when did you care about the Vietnam War? You're too busy dreaming your head away."

"Well, I'm starting to care about a lot of things." I landed on Community Chest and picked up the card. As soon as I read it—a tax assessment on every house and hotel you owned!—I tossed it aside. We never bothered with that one. I picked up the next card: "PAY HOSPITAL $100." That was worse! I tossed that aside as well, and picked up a third card: "BANK ERROR IN YOUR FAVOR. COLLECT $200." Much better. I took two-hundred dollars out of the bank. Tony was so caught up in what he was saying that he didn't even notice.

"Everybody thinks winning is the important issue. The 'war hawks' want to escalate the war so we can *win* it faster. The 'peace doves' want to pull out because we can't *win* anyway—"

"What's wrong with that? Jon and I are doves."

Tony started to snicker.

"What's so funny?"

"Of course, Jonny Boy is a dove!"

"You don't even know Jon! And what's wrong with being against the war?"

"You can bet when he turns eighteen he'll be flying to Canada on his little dove wings so he won't get his butt shot off."

"Why do you have to be so cynical about everything? Why can't you just learn how to live and let live?"

"*¡Ay, ay, ay!* Don't tell me you're one of those people going around saying Live and Let Live! When are you going to start thinking for yourself?"

"I *am* thinking for myself!"

"If you were, then you'd realize the real problem with the war is that nobody seems to be questioning the 'why' of it. Are we really helping the South Vietnamese? Are we really listening to what they want?"

"I don't know."

"Those are the questions we should be asking. Because some wars should be fought, just as others should be avoided." He fell silent for a moment as he flipped his token back and forth. "José Marti said that a government must come from the makeup of the people and I believe that. I think the American government has forgotten that in South Vietnam. And for that reason, I think the war will fail just as the Battle of Giron failed in Cuba.

"That battle might've succeeded if the Americans had listened to the Cuban exiles when they made their plans to invade. They would've known the Bay of Pigs was Fidel's favorite fishing hole. He knew every inch of it! Another blunder was the inflatable boats they insisted on using to bring the soldiers ashore. The exiles told them about the coral reefs lurking under the surface, but they didn't listen. No wonder their boats were ripped to shreds! They also failed to realize that a lot of the fishermen around the bay *liked* Fidel. He was, in many ways, an improvement over Batista."

He tugged at a splinter in the plywood, pulling it loose. "In spite of all that, it still might've succeeded if the Americans hadn't stopped the air strikes barely after they'd begun them. Now Fidel is the tyrannical king of his island castle, surrounded by a ninety-mile-wide moat. And those still trapped inside those castle walls are his captives."

"I'm sorry. You never told me all this."

His eyes were hard and shiny. "That was a war that should've been fought but wasn't because too many people refused to get involved. I'm sure they were all doves, too."

He fell silent after that as we concentrated on the game. But his foot kept knocking against the sawhorse, jangling the little plastic motels. Finally, the mosquitoes descended in hordes and we scrapped the game.

That night, Jon called me and asked me to meet him in front of the school in the morning, on the path between the two grapefruit trees. He said it would be the perfect place for us to meet every day. I was so excited that I couldn't sleep. Instead, I lay in bed for hours, staring at the bamboo outside my window, watching the slender stalks dance against the sky.

When morning came, I had nothing to wear! Spying the dark red shift that made me look like a giant hot dog, I yanked it out of my side of the closet and put it into Minnie's. Something she could look forward to when she grew a little taller. I ended up wearing the same embroidered dress I'd worn the first day. Tony didn't help matters any as we walked to school. He was still in a bad mood from the night before and didn't say much.

When I got there, I found Jon waiting for me. He took the books from my arms, stacked them next to his on a bench, and taking my hand into his, pulled me into his circle of friends.

After a few awkward attempts at trying to enter into the conversation—which bounced from the latest Beatle album (which I didn't have) to makeup (which I didn't wear) to movie stars (which I rarely went to the movies to see) to pain-in-the-butt-teachers-to-favorite-pig-out-foods-to-sports-cars-to-who-was-seeing-who—I didn't feel so much like that cog in something turning anymore. I just felt tired.

My eyes drifted down to everyone's feet. Most of the girls were wearing white T-strap sandals that showed off their freshly painted toenails. I also noticed a pair of red eyelet tie shoes, a pair of fuchsia clunky-heeled slip-ons, and a pair of glittery gold sandals with straps that criss-crossed all the way up the calves. (Those belonged to—wouldn't you know it—Madison Madison, who regarded me as if I were a piece of lint on Jon's shirt.) I learned exactly where the scuff marks were on each pair of shoes, and how worn down the heels were. Jon had little tassels on his loafers, with the ends slightly frayed. When he was telling a joke, his ankles had a funny way of rocking from side to side, which made the tassels shake.

I, too, was wearing white T-strap sandals, much to my satisfaction. They just happened to be of different sizes, the left sandal a somewhat snug size five and the right sandal a roomy size six-and-a-half, thanks to Mama and her bargain buys. I discreetly placed one foot behind the other so nobody would notice. But then I was concerned about the ankle hairs I'd missed while shaving. Nobody else had missed theirs! I was relieved when the first bell rang, even though it meant letting go of Jon's hand.

For the rest of the week I followed the same routine: trying on half a dozen outfits until I found something to wear, then dashing off to school in a nervous huff until Jon took my hand in his. After trying to enter the conversation, my hand would grow sweaty in Jon's palm as I waited for the bell to ring. Sometimes Jon would whisper something nice, such as how good I smelled (I wore Orange Blossom perfume that Papa had given me for Christmas); or how pretty my long, strawberry blonde hair looked (I set it on Coke cans, which I'd overheard the girls say was the best way to get lots of body); but mostly, I didn't know what to say to anybody. Even to Jon. I began wishing we didn't have to hang around his friends.

Then on Thursday night, Jon called and asked me to go to the spring again the following Saturday. This time, my parents insisted that he pick me up at the house to be properly introduced.

I spent every spare minute I had fixing the place up: vacuuming the living room rug—a nauseating blend of brown, green and gold that Mama had selected because it wouldn't show food stains; restuffing our sagging couch with old towels because I couldn't find anything else to stuff it with; varnishing the indentations of Grampsie's tree-climbing boots on the hardwood floors (thank God she didn't wear those anymore!) and then going into a tantrum because nothing I did made a difference. It didn't help matters when Rooster and Dandy burst into the house and Dandy left a trail of gosling droppings!

Just before Jon showed up, I couldn't find my flip-flops, so I was running through the house on a rampage as Papa was ushering Jon in through that ripped screen door. "Hello, young man!" Papa exclaimed as he pumped Jon's hand with an overly long handshake.

Suddenly we were all staring at one another, Papa with his company smile, Mama with her hands covered with flour—only Mama would pick this time to make biscuits—me scurrying around searching for my flip-flops, and Jon, startled by the squalid surroundings.

Mama wiped her hand on the back of her housedress and insisted on shaking his hand the same hearty way Papa did. Even she couldn't help but notice how he backed up to the dollhouse afterwards and brushed his hand on the green towel that served as the yard, staining it white with flour.

Papa asked him several questions about what he planned to do when he got out of high school. Jon said he wasn't sure yet. I wondered if he would tell Papa about his father being a developer and all, but he didn't. As they talked, I could see Jon looking around, taking in the sagging armchair with the spring poking out that Tony called the abortion chair, the puke yellow chipped linoleum floor peeking from the kitchen, the piles of clutter filling every imaginable space, and the spiders that resided in the upper corners of the ceiling that Mama refused to let anyone mess with, insisting that no home should be without spiders because they ate the cockroaches. Papa sounded stiff and overly formal, and there were gaps in the conversation that Mama filled in with a brittle laugh that didn't sound like Mama at all.

Then, when Mama offered Jon a bottle of Coke—a "Company Only" beverage that she kept under lock and key—Papa found his voice. Did Jon know that the Coca-Cola Company was one of the largest buyers of citrus by-products? And that the smell clinging to the very bottle he was drinking was from lemon peel oil? He told Jon he ought to consider a career in the citrus business, that citrus was used in everything from cattle feed—which his plant happened to produce—to medicine.

Jon chugged down his Coke, marveled at the lemony smell, then turned to me with a tight smile. "Are you ready?"

"After you see my dollhouse," I replied, as I still couldn't find my flip-flops.

"She spent the whole summer making it," Mama said with a touch of pride. That was a surprise! Mama usually complained about the time I spent on the dollhouse, never missing a chance to grouch about the chores not getting done.

Papa went to fetch us some tangerines for our boat ride,

while Mama surprised me again by insisting on taking our picture. I was about to suggest that she take it in front of the dollhouse when she cried out cheerily, "Say cheese!" and half blinded us with the huge flash attachment on her camera that was embarrassingly old-fashioned. Jon and I blinked at each other, seeing stars, as Mama excused herself.

Jon knelt down to peer inside the dollhouse. "You made this?" He looked at me with admiration.

I nodded proudly as I started picking up the latest clutter dumped on the yard, more of Wendell's stupid Creepy Crawlers.

He inspected the window boxes—still blinking from the flash—the gabled roof, all the details I'd worked so painstakingly on. "The house you wished you lived in, huh?"

My hand froze on the tiny doorknob.

"I mean . . . I'm sorry, Kady."

"It's okay," I said as I glanced down at my feet.

"What I mean is, this dollhouse is so nice that anybody would want to live in it. Including me."

"I'll start getting some people next," I told him as I nervously opened and shut the tiny front door.

"What's this?" he asked, sliding my china doll's coffinlike box out of the attic and opening it. Then he saw her broken face oddly glued together. "What happened here?"

"She—umm—got dropped."

"Too bad. She's got a beautiful gown, though. I didn't realize they could make such tiny ruffles."

"Yeah, I know," I smiled.

"And look," he went on, peering even closer. "Look at how it shimmers in the light. What is this stuff?"

"Sateen, I believe."

I spied my flip-flops under the abortion chair and slipped them on with great relief. "We can go now." I clamped down the lid of the china doll's box and sped toward the door.

We were halfway across the lake when Jon brought the boat to a stop, reached under his seat and pulled out a present. It was a beautifully wrapped box with a pink-and-gold satin bow. I was so astonished I couldn't speak.

"Go ahead, open it."

"But . . . what's it for? It's not my birthday, it's not Christmas."

"Can't I just give you a present because I want to? Go on, open it."

I couldn't imagine even opening such a package. My parents used the comic strips for wrapping paper and told us that it didn't matter what the paper looked like as long as it covered the present. But with Jon's insistence, I carefully untaped the wrapping and pulled out a dress nestled on a bed of tissue paper.

It was a pink peasant dress, with bouquets of violets embroidered on the bodice, a full skirt, and gathered sleeves. There were delicate pink T-strap sandals to go with it, both the same size five.

"I guessed at the sizes, so if anything doesn't fit let me know."

The flowers began to waver as tears welled up in my eyes.

"What's wrong, don't you like it?"

"I love it," I managed to say, "but it's too much."

"Don't worry about the money, Katerina. I can get anything I want wholesale through Mom's shop. She even helped me pick it out. Oh, and by the way, she wants to meet you sometime."

"Really?" The thought made me nervous.

"I told her how pretty you are. Even with your peeling nose," he said as he kissed the tip of it. "It just makes you more ap-peeling."

"You have an ap-peeling nose, too," I laughed as I shyly kissed the tip of his nose.

"Here, slip this over your bathing suit."

"In the middle of the lake?"

"Sure. Why not?"

I glanced toward the distant shores, then slipped the dress on and strapped the sandals onto my feet. The sandals were a little small and hurt when I walked around the boat, but they made my feet look so dainty that I didn't have the heart to tell him. And besides, all new shoes hurt, didn't they? I would get used to them. But the dress! I felt as if I'd been planted in the middle of a flower garden. The violets swirled when I moved and the cottony fabric seemed to breathe against my skin.

He smiled at me with admiration. "I knew you were special from the moment I saw you in the water."

I glanced down. "I don't know how you can say that. After you came to my house."

"Actually, it was interesting going to your house, seeing the pig in the side yard and thinking for a minute that you really were Circe and had changed someone into a pig. And wondering who the poor guy was."

My mouth curved into a smile.

"And seeing that doll that was so much like you."

"Like me?"

"Yeah."

I tugged self-consciously at the neckline of my new dress. "How like me?"

"Well, because you're both . . . let's see . . . pretty . . . sweet . . . unspoiled."

"Unspoiled?" My face flushed. "You mean because I haven't had a boyfriend before?"

"So, I am your first."

"Yeah."

"I thought so. . . . I'm glad."

"Why?"

"Oh because"—shrugging—"I guess because I want to mean something to you."

I felt a rush of tenderness toward him. "Of course you mean something to me. You mean everything to me."

"Really?"

"Yeah." I popped a strand of hair into my mouth and nervously chewed on it without realizing what I was doing. He slowly drew it out. "Your hair is too pretty to chew on."

"I do that sometimes when I'm nervous."

"You're not nervous around me, are you?"

I nodded.

"Don't be." He pulled me against him and kissed me. "There's so much I want to show you, so much I want to give you."

I started to kiss him back, then thought about what Tony had said about the brownies. *I had to know.* "Like brownies with marijuana in them?"

He looked at me, stunned. "I thought you knew."

I stared at the water sloshing against the side of the boat.

"You really didn't?" he pressed.

I shook my head.

"Remember when I told you I put all my secret ingredients in them? I thought . . ."

"I just thought you meant some special kind of chocolate."

"I'm sorry," he sighed, "I wasn't trying to be sneaky with you because, like I said, I thought you knew. I just don't want anyone finding out. Especially my dad. He's not cool about stuff like that. But you don't have to eat 'em if you don't want to. I mean that, Kady."

Yet when he brought out the brownies at the spring, I took

a little crumb. I couldn't tell any difference in how I felt, so I took another. Several crumbs later when I felt a mellowness come over me, I began to wonder if the brownies were such a big deal. Señor Rosado got drunk and nobody put him in jail. Then I started thinking, what if Mama were to start eating them? I couldn't imagine anything better than a smiling mom to come home to. Imagine sharing brownies and milk with *that* mom after school. We would chatter like chipmunks and dance about the room! I fell back on the grass, laughing.

"What's so funny?" Jon asked.

His eyes sparkled like a kaleidoscope, mesmerizing me. He was so cute. . . . I was so lucky. . . .

The cooler days of November brought the first blush of color to the fruit. The oranges began to glow like lanterns against the emerald leaves. Birds arrived from the north and Papa set up a feeder outside the kitchen window. Every morning we watched them fight over food. There were soft gray mourning doves, bright red cardinals, pushy bluejays, mischievous thrashers, and hummingbirds no bigger than your finger. All of them overjoyed Rooster, who treated them like long-lost cousins. A handful of coots showed up on the lake, too, as well as some mallards.

Rooster and Dandy were inseparable. They spent hours on the lake, Rooster propped up on a Styrofoam boogie board, paddling in front of Dandy as if he were his mama. And when Dandy would "tip up" to get submerged food, Rooster would tip up, too, then come up sputtering and laughing. He didn't mind that the water was getting chilly. Or that the rest of us made fun of him.

It was funny to hear the two of them talking. Dandy would peep, "Bib-bib-bib!" (I am here, where are you?) and Rooster would reply, "Bee-bee-bee!" (Right here! Never fear!) Dandy didn't look a bit like a dandelion anymore. He was soft gray, with long, sturdy legs. His tail and wing feathers had already grown in. He'd follow Rooster's great running strides, then fly in little hops about the yard. Rooster was delighted to see him rise so easily and would follow him on the ground, flapping his own arms. But whenever Dandy disappeared for the briefest of moments, Rooster would nervously shout, *"GAG-A-GAG-AGAG!"* until the gosling reappeared.

He still carried his red purse for when Dandy got "tired." Sometimes he would chase Dandy on all fours and Dandy would come after him, wings outstretched, mouth wide open, and bite him on the neck. Rooster would playfully bite him back.

Now that Rooster was Dandy's O Mighty Protector, he didn't spend as much time following me around, although he did continue to dump gifts in my dollhouse. More punk bark PEE PULL, crudely woven grass rugs, weeds planted in shampoo caps. He couldn't stand the place empty. "*Papi* fill up house, y-y-yard, everything!"

I explained that the stuff I wanted was worth waiting for, unlike the junk his father hauled in. I might as well have talked to a tree.

One afternoon, I found Rooster's school picture Scotch-taped to the wall of my dollhouse living room. It was the dumbest picture imaginable: his hair plastered to his head and a studious look that didn't resemble the real Rooster at all.

I started to throw it away, but then, on a whim, cut a circle around his head and taped his picture in the middle of the rotary dialer on our phone. I figured he'd like the idea of his face spinning around every time someone dialed.

The next day the same picture was back on the wall! I wondered if some sort of Mary Poppins magic had glued the corners back. Then I realized Rooster had taped a duplicate picture of himself. He probably had a five-year supply of his pictures on hand, since most kids traded their pictures with their friends, but who wanted a picture of this nut?

I didn't have the heart to take it down after that, so I left it on the wall where my Greek *Venus de Milo* statue would eventually go.

Jon continued to meet me before school every day. Some mornings he'd slip me a present as soon as we met under the grapefruit trees; usually, it was a dress, which he would coax me to wear right away. Then I would go on and on about how he shouldn't have, but secretly I'd be thrilled. Once, he gave me a box of chocolates, which Rooster got ahold of and ate in one sitting, except for the ones with either pink or orange insides, which he spit out. Mama said she didn't think I should accept so many presents from a boy, but I just laughed as I marveled at the new girl emerging in my mirror.

At the same time that I felt myself begin to blend in with Jon's friends, Madison's outfits becoming more outrageous. She would show up in flowered hats, men's boots, vests and ties, plaid shirts over paisley skirts, brightly colored turbans, clunky jewelry, anything, it seemed, that struck her fancy. One chilly morning, she even showed up wearing oven mitts!

On the day she wore safety pins for earrings "just because," it was Jon who noticed them first. He couldn't stop going on and on about how stupid she looked.

Bathing suits of summer gave way to peasant dresses, bell-bottom jeans and halter tops as the spring remained a popular hang-out. As the word spread about its isolated location, even more kids started showing up.

My parents, however, only allowed me to go "boating" on Saturday afternoons because of all the chores I had to do.

Then came the day Mama almost kept me from going at all.

"Rags! Rags! Rags!" she exploded as I walked into the kitchen after school. She tossed one article of clothing at me after another. All of them had pink blotches on them.

"What's wrong?" I asked as my stomach did a flip-flop.

She pulled a stick of lipstick from her pocket and tossed it on top of the heap. "It's yours."

"Oops! I must've forgotten to take it out of my pocket before I tossed my jeans into the washing machine."

"Ruined! The whole dang load!"

"I really thought I'd checked my pockets. But don't worry. They've got these amazing stain cleaners—"

"I ain't seed nothing that really works, so you might as well kiss these clothes good-bye!"

"I'll bet Jewel can think of something."

Mama glared at me.

"Look, I'm sorry."

"Humph! Girl falls in love and the whole world goes to pot."

I laughed to myself at her choice of words.

"Last week, I asked you to dig up the tomatoes. Well, you did such a mighty fine job that you dug up all my parsley! Then, I asked you to scour the bathroom floor. You didn't tell me you poured *bleach* on it and didn't even bother to mop it up. So you can understand my amazement when I dropped my drawers while using the commode, and saw white spots appear on 'em right before my eyes! I'd just bought that pair of pants—a nice brown polyester for only two-fifty on account of a tiny run—and now I look like an Appaloosa horse in 'em!"

I almost started laughing in spite of the trouble I was in, as I pictured bleach spots on Mama's rear end.

She gave a long sigh that sounded like a kettle that had been abandoned on a burner. "What you don't understand is that we don't have money to waste! Every penny counts. And when you ruin a pair of good pants, or rip out a garden, you set the whole family back."

"I'll try to be more careful."

"You certainly will, since you're gonna pay for every one of these clothes."

"What!"

"Every single one."

"But there's a whole load! Grampsie's blouses, Papa's shirts, your 'Old Fart' T-shirt—surely, you don't want another of those!" Tears stung my eyes. "I don't have that kind of money." Fortunately, my new dresses weren't among the casualties, since I took the extra time to wash those by hand.

"You'll need to drum up some baby-sitting jobs lickety-split and start using your earnings to replace everything. I saw a notice on the church bulletin board just last Sunday that a Mrs. Nichols is looking for someone to watch her children while she gives piano lessons. Wasn't she your Sunday school teacher a few years back?"

I nodded sullenly, thinking of Mrs. Nichols's five unruly kids.

"Well, good. Why don't you give her a call right now? I think she needs someone three afternoons a week and Saturdays. I'll allow you to baby-sit after school instead of helping me here until you get these items replaced. And that's a mighty big concession on my part."

"But on Saturdays I go boating with Jon."

"Not anymore you don't. Not until you've replaced every single article of clothing you've destroyed!"

"Be reasonable! It was an accident! Anybody could've done it."

"Your excuses ain't gonna wash with me." She stormed over to the phone and picked up the receiver. "Call her right now."

"But I don't even know her number."

"Then call information first!"

Grampsie poked her head into the kitchen. "Anybody seen my choppers?"

Mama paused. "I beg your pardon, Ma?"

"My choppers," she said, gumming her mouth. "They're missing."

"Check the bathroom cup where you usually keep them," Mama suggested, her voice distracted.

"Not there. Not anywhere! How am I going to see Dear Walty without my teeth? News will be on in a few hours and I won't be respectable!"

"Just a minute, Ma. I'm right in the middle of something," Mama replied irritably, then thrust the receiver into my hand. "Call—now!"

I reluctantly did as she told me. To my dismay, Mrs. Nichols was not only glad I called, but she hired me right over the phone! She remembered me as the girl who always volunteered to serve the punch and cookies at the end of Sunday school class (my way of getting a few extra Lorna Doones). In the background, I could hear a child shrieking.

I spent the rest of the afternoon sullenly doing my chores. I didn't want to give Mama any more excuses to yell, and things were relatively quiet until we all sat down to supper. I was just about to pass Papa a plate of biscuits, when Grampsie showed up for dinner. Her hair was unkempt, her eyes wild, and her mouth clamped so tight it looked as if it had rusted shut. It barely yielded when she slurped down the entire contents of the can of chicken broth that had been the Surprise Dish.

Grampsie had barricaded herself in her room at the time I was supposed to do her hair, but I was in such a rotten mood that I had barely noticed.

"What's her problem?" Wendell whispered as he passed me the carrot salad.

I whispered back that she'd misplaced her teeth, and was horrified that Dear Walty would see her toothless.

Grampsie, watching this exchange, pointed an accusing finger at me. "You took 'em! You ruined my favorite blouse and now you've taken my teeth! Don't think I don't see you sashaying around in them fancy new clothes! You're after Dear Walty!"

My eyes widened in disbelief. "What?"

She slammed her bony fist down, rattling plates, cups, and silverware. "I won't have it! The TV's off from now on. Off! Off! Off! And if Dear Walty comes to the door, we won't answer it!"

"You're a *lunatic*," Wendell muttered under his breath as I yelled back at her, "I don't have your teeth and as for Walter the Walrus, you can have him!"

"Let's all calm down," Papa demanded, then turned to his mother and carefully explained, "Ma, stop this nonsense. Kady doesn't have your teeth. I'm sure you've just misplaced them."

"She has them, I know she does! Wants Dear Walty for herself!"

I turned to Papa and blurted out, "I'm not responsible for every little thing that goes wrong around here! And Wendell's right, she's a lunatic!"

"GREAT SPIRIT!" Papa bellowed, stopping me cold.

When I told Jon the next morning that I had to start baby-sitting, he was angrier about it than I was. "They can't do that!" he cried, taking my books from me with surprising force and tossing them on the bench so that half of them fell to the pavement.

I blinked at my scattered books. "Yes, they can."

"But when can I see you, Kady? They already make it almost impossible for us to be together. You're the only girl I know who has chores after school. I mean, who besides you has to clean out a hog pen—"

"Don't remind me," I cut him off as I stared down at my shoes, mortified.

"—and now you can't see me on Saturdays, either? I might as well just—"

His tone of voice startled me. He'd never been short with me before. Or insulting. "Just—just what?" My cheeks flushed. *Not see me anymore? Was that what he was about to say?* I bit down on my thumb, scraping my bottom teeth against my nail as I waited for his response. The pale pink polish I'd painted it with was bitter on my tongue.

He looked at me with such a pained expression that for a moment I thought that was exactly what he was going to say. Then he squeezed my left hand and said, "Nothing. We'll figure a way."

By that afternoon he *had* figured a way. He told me to call Mrs. Nichols back and tell her I wouldn't be able to baby-sit after all.

"But I can't do that!"

"Sure you can," he said smoothly. "I'll give you the money to replace the clothes and your mother will never have to know."

"But you can't just—just *give* me money!"

"Awww," he said with a wave of his hand, "I get twenty dollars a week for allowance. I usually blow it, anyway."

I blinked in shock.

"It's really not a big deal."

"Maybe not to you."

"Listen," he said, "my parents are never around, so they give me money. The consolation prize."

"But it's still your money. I can't let you do this."

"I'll take you around to thrift shops so it won't cost much, if that'll make you feel better. I don't think anyone in your family cares, do you?"

My face turned red. "Oh, well . . . I guess not."

"I mean, it's sort of the thing these days to shop at thrift stores," he quickly added.

"Still, giving me money isn't right," I said.

"I want to be with you, Katerina. Every single minute I can."

"I want the same thing. But—"

He held his finger to my lips. "No buts. This way you'll be able to be with me during the week when your parents will think you're baby-sitting."

I was stunned by his cleverness. Such an idea never would've occurred to me. "But what if they find out?"

"Do they know this Mrs. Nichols?"

"Not really."

"Then what's the harm? Your family gets new clothes, and you and I get more time together."

"Yeah, well . . ." I let the words hang.

The next afternoon, instead of heading to Mrs. Nichols's house on the bike—the one Wendell refused to ride—I rode to the spring.

It had been a hard phone call to make, especially when I heard the disappointment in Mrs. Nichols's voice. But as soon as the background shrill of children's voices dissolved into the dull hum of dead wire, I felt liberated. Just because Mama had worked her entire life didn't mean I had to follow her dreary footsteps. Why should I have to replace a whole load of clothes because of one careless mistake?

I quickly fell into the habit of hanging out with Jon at the spring three blissful afternoons a week, then all day on Saturdays. I'd never realized the joy of doing absolutely nothing. And all the while, Mama thought I was wiping snotty noses and slapping peanut butter on bread!

As soon as I arrived on the bike, I would help myself to a brownie, or maybe take a few drags on a joint, if one happened to be passing around. The first time I did this, I started coughing violently. Then Jon showed me how to let the smoke slowly fill my lungs, hold it in for a moment, and slowly let it out. Within minutes I began to feel light-headed and relaxed.

Sometimes Jon would play Frisbee for a while and leave me to myself. But most of the time I nestled in the crook of his arm in drowsy, joyous contentment. He was cute and funny and I would tell him so with kisses and soft words.

One afternoon, Madison sauntered up to me as I was hiding my bike behind some bushes. She had a pretzel looped through her finger, which she was twirling around. A smirk formed on her lips as soon as she saw me.

"Aren't you getting sick of those flowery peasant dresses?" she asked as she brought the pretzel to her mouth and licked the salt.

I felt the blood rush to my face as I stared at her, dumbfounded. "What do you care what I wear? You throw on anything you please!"

"Exactly," she said smugly.

"I like my dresses."

"Really? Somehow you don't strike me as the sweet and cutesy type. Jon may think you're that kind of girl, especially when he keeps you stoned—"

"What?"

"—but I know better. He did, after all, buy you those dresses, did he not? I mean, it's pretty obvious you didn't buy them," she went on as she licked the salt on the loops of the pretzel with her reptilian tongue. "You, with the dirt under your nails and muscular calves—*thick* muscular calves. You're hardly the feminine kind."

"Shut up!"

"Hey!" she said, throwing up her arms in mock despair, the pretzel hooked by her finger, "don't take it so *personally;* I'm simply pointing out the unusualness of a girl like you wearing dresses like that. In fact, I'll let you in on a little secret"—she moved closer to me, her doughy breath in my face—"my kick of the day is watching you whiz up that sandy trail in those sugar sweet dresses and waiting to see if the hem gets caught in the spokes. Charlotte and I have a bet going. If you spin out, I owe her a bag of peanut butter cups. If you don't, she owes me a box of Milk Duds. My guess is that you're too much of a tomboy to—"

The way she said Milk Duds with a gleam in her eye made me so angry I wanted to rip the safety pins right out of her ear lobes. "No wonder Jon broke up with you!" I cried. "You're a bitch!"

She leveled those enormous cat eyes at me and calmly replied, "Jon broke up with me because he couldn't contain me. He never realized that was one of my better qualities."

"Couldn't contain you? You two-timed him!"

She rolled her eyes. "Sharing one dance while waiting for Charlotte to find her dumb nail?"

Charlotte, who was standing nearby working her way through the bag of pretzels, spoke up. "Hey, what are you talking about?"

"Last summer you were into Lee's Press-On Nails, remember?"

"Oh, yeah," Charlotte nodded, "what of it?"

"And somebody slammed into you at the Sweatshop and broke off one of your nails?"

Charlotte nodded. "So?"

"I was telling Kady how Jon broke up with me because of that night—"

"Oh, yeah. When you danced with Jerry Harrison. Anybody would've wanted to dance with him, but of course he picked you because"—playfully rumpling Madison Madison's hair—"you get everybody."

"It wasn't like that at all! I hardly knew the guy. The band started to play 'I Wanna Be Free' and my feet just went—well—crazy."

"Then Jon comes along and has a fit." Charlotte shook her head. "How I do remember that little scene. How everybody in the entire club remembers that little scene!"

"All because I wanted to dance!" Madison exclaimed. "Next thing I know he shows up here with"—tapping me with her pretzel—"Miss Subsidized Lunch."

My ears burned. It was true I qualified for free lunches. Once a month, I was issued these little red tickets, which I hid in the palm of my hand as I waited in line.

"It's disgusting watching you drape yourself all over him," Charlotte picked up, "and smile at him so adoringly." She batted her eyes and gave an impression of me: "Why, I'd never dream of dancing with anyone but you, Prince Charming! I'll do *anything* to live in your castle!"

I whirled around, my face flushed with rage. "What'd I ever do to you, except help you that one time?" I snarled. "You remember. You'd started your period in English class and were so afraid someone might laugh at you."

Charlotte drew back.

"Maybe the truth is that Jon and I have something really special that you two wouldn't understand!"

"Oh, I understand plenty. And the way I see it, Jon two-timed me!" Madison piped up. "But guess what? I'm not angry anymore. I'm glad I'm over a guy who thinks he can own me."

"Jon doesn't own me!" I scoffed. "You're just too selfish to understand love."

"Don't you get it? You're nothing but Play-Doh."

"Bull!"

"His own little toy to worship and adore him. As long as you're pretty—and yes, you're amazingly pretty for someone who could never even afford braces—he doesn't care where you come from. In fact, he *likes* it that you come from a deprived background. It makes you more adoring!"

"You've got a helluva lot of nerve—"

"It's not a relationship, Kady," she cut me off. "Because it's only about him."

My face fell even though I tried to stare at her impassively.

"Don't get me wrong about Jon. I don't hate him. We grew up together."

"Or at least one of you did," Charlotte corrected her.

Madison nodded, grinning. "That's just it, Kady. Jon's still a kid inside. And if you don't believe me, just wait until you step on a crack or color outside of the lines."

I glared at her.

"Just wait until you don't 'Obey.'"

"Shut up, Madison. Just shut up."

*   *   *

Soon after, Madison began showing up at the spring with different guys, all older, and most with some form of hair on their faces: a guitar player, a philosophy major from a local college, and a telephone lineman. Jon told me he should've realized she was the kind of girl who collects guys like charms on a bracelet, then jangles them in everyone's face to show off her "life experiences." He said if I had any sense, I'd stay away from her. I was more than glad to.

But as time went on, I began to wonder why he continued to hang out with the same crowd she did, even if they did live in the same neighborhood. I looked forward to late afternoons when Jon and I would go on a walk alone.

We'd usually follow a path along the water's edge until we came to a tangle of huge elephant ears. And there, half hidden from the world, we'd either talk or make out.

One afternoon, after we'd gotten higher than usual, I watched a spider build its web in the crotch of an elephant ear. For some silly reason I began to recite, "Itsy-bitsy spider went up the waterspout." Jon joined in and we began to recite one nursery rhyme after another, laughing uproariously. It felt so good to collapse in the dark shade of those giant plants, my body soft and loose like a puddle of jelly.

We'd run out of rhymes when I remembered another and began to recite: "Georgie Porgie Puddin' Pie, kissed the girls and made them cry."

All of a sudden, tears welled up in Jon's eyes and he began to cry.

Thinking he was joking, I told him that Georgie made the girls cry, not the boys. Yet, as I nudged him, his head fell to his hands and he began to sob so hard his shoulders shook. I stared at him, baffled. There was such a wad in my head that nothing seemed to connect. Finally, the simple words came to me: "What's wrong?" My voice sounded tinny and faraway.

"Oh," he said, struggling to regain his composure. There were smears of dirt on his cheek where he'd tried to wipe his eyes. "Rosa . . ."

"Rosa?"

"Our maid. She was taking care of my little sister, Julie, when Julie died—"

"When she . . . *died?*"

"It wasn't Rosa's fault. It was an accident. But my parents never forgave her." The little muscle in his jaw knotted.

My head reeled. "Wait a minute, now. . . . I had no idea you had a sister." Then, I remembered him once telling me there were only "three of us, now." I remember asking him about it, thinking maybe he had an older brother or sister who'd gone off to college, and how he hadn't answered my question.

"Yeah, well, I wasn't ready to talk about her." He brought his fist to his mouth and bit down on his forefinger. "She died when she was just a baby. I barely . . . barely remember her. She was beautiful, though . . . oh, man . . ."—breaking into a smile—"she had these big circles of curls on her head that I could poke my finger through. . . ."

"What happened to her?"

He squeezed his eyes shut and it was a long time before he spoke. "Rosa was giving her a bath in the kitchen sink when Julie reached over and grabbed the prong that went into the electric skillet and put it in her mouth. It happened so *fast*. . . . I was standing right beside the sink playing with my Hot Wheels cars."

I screwed up my face, trying to follow what he was saying. "The prong from the skillet . . ."

"Rosa, see, had pulled the plug from the skillet but had forgotten to unplug the other end . . . you know, the electrical cord it's connected to, from the wall outlet. Julie was"—fresh tears welling up in his eyes—"electrocuted."

My heart raced. "Oh my God . . ."

Jon yanked at the grass growing in sparse clumps under the elephant ears and shredded it. "Mom never got over it. . . . She fired Rosa, who I"—his voice cracking—"loved."

"How old were you?"

"Oh . . . let's see . . . four . . . almost five."

"I'm really sorry." The world seemed to be spinning as if I were trapped inside a washing machine. I had to put both hands firmly planted on the ground to keep my bearings. *I couldn't be hearing him right. . . . This was so sad!*

"Sometimes . . . even after all these years, Mom'll go into Julie's room and stay there for hours. . . ." he went on after a while. His voice seemed to be in slow motion, now.

"What's in there now?"

"It's a guest room . . . but a lot of Julie's things are still there, her clothes, toys, all just sitting in a chest of drawers as if she might use them at any time. . . . I've caught Mom fitting little stars, rectangles and circles into slots on this Tupperware toy. It's . . . weird."

"Yeah . . . weird," I echoed, not knowing what to say.

"I thought Mom'd stay home after Julie died to take care of me since I was the only one left and all, but instead she put in even more hours. . . . She wouldn't even look at me, Kady. Dad became more driven, too, to the point they began calling him 'The Bulldozer' at work. . . . I started calling him that, too, behind his back. . . . Now, I say it to his face."

"How's he like a bulldozer?"

His glassy eyes flickered with fire. "Knocks down everyone who doesn't see things his way—the *only* way! He flattens them! He's got no sensitivity whatsoever, Kady."

"Oh . . .," I said, startled by his sudden anger. I brought my hand to my forehead and massaged my temple. He was telling me so much, and I had to pay attention. But it was so hard . . . so very hard . . . to remember what he said from one minute to the next. . . .

"He's perfect for the building business where concrete rules," he went on, his words beginning to slur together. "Because in his way of thinking there's nothing a good slab of concrete can't fix, pour it on thick enough and you never have to worry about cracks. . . .

"I don't think he ever cried over Julie, just gets this fixed look on his face if you even mention her name. . . . Nobody crosses him in the business world, either. . . . Nobody . . . Nobody has the guts. . . . He'll own this state before you know it and it won't be a pretty sight. . . . Nope . . ."—shaking his head—". . . not a pretty sight at all, a solid slab of concrete stretching from coast to coast with his name carved on it, HAMILTON ENTERPRISES—BUILDER OF DREAMS . . . Ha!"

I looked at him, confused. "I thought you like what he builds."

He clamped his eyes shut and shook his head. "My father's a machine. Cut him open and there's no blood . . . just mechanical parts. . . ."

"And you say he started getting like that after Julie died?"

"He was always like that. He just got worse. . . . Fortunately, he wasn't around very much after the accident. The only time he thought about me was when they needed a baby-sitter. . . . He and my mom must've gone through a dozen—some real kooks, too. There was Lucy who stole a ham and hid it in the dryer; Hattie, who burned a hole in Mom's silk pajamas; and . . . oh, what was her name? The one with the false teeth that clacked together when she ate?"

He stared at me, his eyes red and glazed over, as if he expected me to know the answer. "Oh, man . . . I'm so high I can't think straight. . . . Opal! That's it. Opal with the opal teeth."

I imagined a mouthful of iridescent teeth and I burst into laughter. Try as I could, I couldn't shake the picture from my mind.

I laughed so hard I began to cry, tears streaming down my cheeks, smearing my makeup. The silly, nonsense words started floating through my mind, *"Georgie, Porgie, puddin' pie, kissed the girls and made them cry. . . ."* I began singing the verses as I wondered: *Had Jon kissed me? Was that why I was crying?* I couldn't remember.

Jon, hearing me sing, whispered, "Rosa used to sing that while she made the beds and washed out the tub. . . . I love that song."

" . . . oh, yeah," I remembered now. He was telling me about Rosa, his favorite maid and how she'd been replaced by Pearl with the pearly teeth. . . . No, Opal with the opal teeth . . .

I was about to burst into fresh laughter, when all at once he was holding me so tightly under the elephant ears that I could scarcely breathe. "You mean the world to me, you know that?" His eyes sparkled unnaturally, and held mine fiercely, as if he were afraid to even blink for fear I might leave him, too.

The following afternoon, Jon took me to the Salvation Army to buy some replacement clothes. I'd just started through the racks when he placed a red motorcycle helmet with a decal of a fire-breathing dragon on my head. I snatched up a lacy French coif and put it on his head. Before we knew it we were trying on hat after hat as we roared with laughter. It was good to find things to laugh about after all the crying we'd done.

Finally, under the stern gaze of the manager, we settled down to business. I picked a white blouse with daisies embroidered on the collar to replace Grampsie's favorite blouse.

It was a very nice blouse, even though slightly frayed, and I was shocked when she threw it at my feet later that day. "What's the point?" she railed at me. "I'm not respectable!"

Since she'd lost her teeth, she'd lost all interest in her appearance. Thick hairs had begun to sprout from her chin, and she wouldn't let Mama pluck them out. She'd sometimes show up with her bra over her blouse instead of under it, and she'd developed an odor—an awful smell of moldy cheese. Most of the time she stayed in her room, rocking back and forth in her rocking chair, which set the whole house creaking ominously.

Mama arranged for the dentist to come to the house to fit new dentures, but Grampsie went berserk when he showed up. She screamed that he was a cold-blooded murderer and that she wasn't going to die at his hands like Leopold Baines Palmer had. When he tried to convince her that her husband's heart attack wasn't his fault, she bit him with her gums. He left in a huff, swearing that hell would freeze over before he came back.

An even worse episode occurred when Papa brought out a social worker to talk to her. Grampsie was convinced she was another dentist in disguise. She kicked the lady squarely in the chin and Papa had to rush the woman to the emergency room. She received twelve stitches and Papa received a hefty bill.

Afterwards, Mama suggested they have Grampsie put in a special home. I heard them talking about it on the front porch one night while I was doing the dishes and turned off the faucet so I could listen in.

"Hold your horses, Mattie. She's always been unusual. But life's been hard on her. Especially when she lived with Pa."

"Who's she gonna kick next?"

"Ahh," he said, with a wave of his hand, "she's not the violent type. Just had a hard life with Pa. He never liked work of any kind, and she always held things together. What's the harm in letting an old dame have a few delusions? It's not like we have the money for a home, anyway."

Mama puckered her cheeks, but in the end let it go.

"Is Grampsie gonna die?" Sammy asked Mama one night as we prepared dinner.

"Certainly not," she replied, as she handed him the silverware to set the table. "She's just going through a difficult time. You can help by being especially nice."

"Then why does she look so awful? Wendell thinks so, too, don't you, Wen?"

"If I were Dear Walty, I'd run for the hills!" Wendell laughed.

Papa set down the paper he was slowly reading. "Stop it, both of you!"

"That's it!" Wendell pointed to an ad in the newspaper Papa had just set down. "The sale I've been waiting for!"

"I mean it, boys," Papa glared at them. "Not one more word against your grandmother."

"Okay," they both agreed.

"Wendell, I need you to get the drinks on the table," Mama said as she set down the Surprise Dish, a steaming bowl of green goo.

"In a minute!" Wendell cried impatiently, then turned back to Papa. "You've GOT to lend me the money for this bike! It's got ten gears, the newest thing—"

"Like I said before, son, you're gonna have to earn the money," Papa said firmly.

"But with a sale like this, I don't need that much. And by the time I earn it, it'll be over."

"Well, that's the way it goes. But I'm sure another sale will come along."

Papa set aside the paper as Mama set down a plate of hot biscuits. I was starving and snitched one. It seemed as if supper would never be ready. I'd already done my share of the work, peeling and mashing a whole mess of potatoes, and making a nice milk gravy for the fried chicken Mama had made from a store-bought chicken.

Minnie snatched the biscuit out of my hand. "Wait for dinner!"

I snatched it back, and we started to fight.

"I really need this bike!" Wendell insisted.

"I really need drinks on this table!" Mama retorted.

She'd no more spoken than a deafening blast shook the house. All at once, the floor shook beneath us, the electricity flickered, and plates and silverware rattled about. The very walls shuddered, and Grampsie's nearby rocking chair rocked by itself! We were so stunned that for a moment all we could do was grope around to find something to hold onto.

"What the devil?!" Papa hoarsely cried out when an even

louder crash came from the kitchen.

Minnie screamed in terror and grabbed my arm. "It's an earthquake!" she gasped, and burst into tears.

I managed to wrap my arm protectively around her, even though I was so scared and confused that my teeth were chattering. *Florida didn't have earthquakes . . . did it?* I wondered.

Dust littered the air and my nose pricked at the smell of fresh sawdust and plaster, mixed in with Mama's cooking. We made our way to the doorway of the kitchen and saw sunlight pouring in through a gaping hole in the ceiling. A tangled mess of bamboo, magnolia branches, plaster, and twisted tin filled the room. We stared at it in shock.

"Watch it!" Papa hollered as he held us back. "Stuff's still falling." He carefully made his way to the window and peered outside. "It's Rosado! The damn fool's dynamited his bamboo!"

"Without telling us?!" Mama cried.

"Not the bamboo!" I shrieked.

"It's taken the magnolia tree with it! That's what's fallen through our roof. Could've killed us!" He picked his way back into the dining room. "Come on, Wendell, let's check it out."

"I'm coming, too!" Sammy shouted, following them.

"Make sure Rooster wasn't nearby!" Mama hollered after them.

A moment after they left, Minnie yelled, "The kitchen's on fire!"

I watched in horror as orange tongues quickly spread from the pilot light inside the stove to consume the oozy glop from a grease jar that had overturned on the burners.

"GET SOME WET TOWELS! CALL THE FIRE DEPARTMENT!" Mama bellowed as she watched the blaze spread to a dented box of Lucky Charms next to the stove. She threw the box to the floor (fortunately she was still wearing her oven mitt) and stomped on it until the flames went out.

The cabinets had started to burn by then—everything was happening so fast—and I helped her beat them with hand towels dipped in a pitcher of iced tea.

Minnie rushed to the phone and told us a moment later that the fire trucks were on their way.

"Good! Now get out! And make sure everyone stays out!" Mama ordered as smoke began to sting our eyes.

"What about Grampsie?" Minnie asked as she headed out with her cat.

"Good grief!" Mama cried.

We dropped the hand towels and rushed to her room.

We found her sitting in her rocker with her hands clapped over her ears. "A lot of racket going on. A body can't get no rest!" she complained. She was dressed in pajamas and her spiked boots, which I'd thought she'd quit wearing. The hairs growing out of her chin were quite long now and gave her the appearance of a wild boar.

"The house is on fire, Ma. You have to come outside with us," Mama explained in as calm a voice as she could muster.

Grampsie looked at us, horrified. "You've brought another dentist! That's what this ruckus is all about! Send him away!"

"The house is on fire," Mama repeated.

"I'll not die at the hands of a cold-blooded murderer! No, siree!" She began to briskly rock back and forth.

"We gotta get outside before we burn up!" I cried. "There's a fire!"

Grampsie's eyes widened with incredulity. "Fire?"

"Yes, FIRE," I repeated. "We have to get OUTSIDE."

Her face clouded over. "Why . . . I can't go outside . . . I'm not . . . not respectable."

Mama pulled Grampsie to her feet. "I've no time to argue with you."

I ran to help support her, as she had trouble standing up on those ridiculous boots.

"Get away!" Grampsie shrieked, kicking me in the shin with the pointed end of her boot. "I won't be tricked! There's a DENTIST out there, I heard his drill! So loud the whole house shook!"

I thought I was going to pass out from the pain. "Stop it! There's NO DENTIST!"

Mama grabbed Grampsie (as she nearly fell over backwards from kicking me), heaved her bony frame over her shoulder, and carried her toward the door.

"I won't be tricked!" Grampsie screamed as drool foamed from her mouth and dribbled down the back of Mama's dress.

Papa banged on the window. "Smoke's everywhere; get out here!"

I opened up the jalousies and pulled the screen off with shaking hands while Papa and Señor Rosado loosened the metal casings and slid out the panes of glass one by one. I don't know why anyone had designed such silly windows as jalousies. Dozens of panes in ugly metal casings. If we burned up, I was gonna haunt Mr. Jalousie, whoever he was.

"Hurry!" Mama cried. She could hardly hold Grampsie, who managed to kick her as well with those horrid boots. "Those boots have got to go, Ma!" Mama muttered through clenched teeth. "They are lethal weapons!"

"Oh no, not OUTSIDE!" Grampsie hollered as Mama forced her through the narrow opening. I went next, then Mama, whose stomach got stuck, so they had to pull out two more panes of glass.

Grampsie's jaw slackened when she saw flames of fire darting out of the kitchen windows. "Lordy," she gasped, "there really *is* a fire."

Señor Rosado insisted on taking Grampsie to a grassy spot away from the flames. To everyone's surprise, she slumped down on the grass, limp as a ragdoll, and gazed with childlike wonder at the fire. She barely noticed the blanket Señor Rosado draped around her thin shoulders. He gave more blankets to Mama and me—ragged army blankets that smelled like mothballs—and tried to get us to sit down as he apologized profusely. "I try to clear space is all! I mean no harm!"

"Where's Rooster?" Mama interrupted.

"In house. He fine," Señor Rosado insisted.

"I can't believe you'd destroy the only decent thing about your property just so you could store more junk on it!" I yelled at him.

"I blast *mucho* cane in my time, *sí?*, and never have this happen. *No comprendo* . . ." He made a sweeping gesture toward the fire.

I could smell the liquor on his breath. "You're drunk! That's why! You could've killed us!"

His eyes widened and he backed away. *"Ebrio?* . . . Noooo . . ."

"I can smell it on your breath!"

He held up his hands. "I mean no harm! *Lo siento.*"

"What's going on here?" Tony cried, rushing up to us. He was breathing so hard he started coughing. "I saw the fire from the highway and—" His eyes lingered on mine another split second before Papa hollered for him to help put out the fire.

"Your drunk father just about killed us all!" I yelled after him.

"We've got a fire to put out!" Mama screamed in my ear as she brushed past me toward Rosy's trough. There she dipped the blanket Señor Rosado had given her in the murky water, then rushed to the kitchen window and beat at the flames Papa and Wendell were feverishly trying to put out. "DIE! DIE! DIE!" she screeched.

I numbly did the same thing with my blanket. Tony had managed to climb up to the roof. I could barely see him behind a shroud of smoke, steam, and the fiery branches of the fallen magnolia tree.

A few minutes later two fire trucks pulled into our yard, their sirens wailing.

Mama pounced on them. "What took you so long?"

"Tricky driveway, ma'am," one of the firefighters said.

I thought they'd never get their pumps connected to the lake and the fire would take the whole house, but to my amazement, they had the hoses spraying the roof in minutes, sending up hissing clouds of smoke and steam.

After the smoke had cleared, they went through the house for what seemed hours, inspecting it. We waited outside, listening to the scratchy reports blasting on the truck radios as we tried to absorb what had just happened. The blaze had been so intense, it had gutted the kitchen and could have easily taken the whole house with it, but our fast work had saved it, so they said. They wanted to take everyone to the hospital to be checked for smoke inhalation, but Mama told them we'd been through enough without having to endure "high-priced doctors poking our bones."

After they left, I walked around in a daze. My eyes stung from smoke as I stared at the twisted roots of my beloved bamboo. Never again would I watch the moon rise through the dancing stalks or hear Rooster yell about the "Land of the Free" during a rainstorm.

I'd be able to see straight into the Rosados' yard now, the rusted appliances scattered like corpses under the cruel eye of the sun; the dilapidated house and garage, swathed in that peeling pink paint. I wandered into their yard to get away from the smoke and sat down on the plywood table where Tony and I played Monopoly.

Through blurred tears, I saw Tony standing in front of me.

"Go away!" I snarled.

"Kady, I know how much you're gonna miss the bamboo. I'm really sorry. I—"

"Sorry is right!" I was enraged that he had figured out the real reason I was crying when everyone else was upset about the house. "Your whole family is nothing but sorry!"

"I wasn't even here! If I'd had any idea *Papi* was gonna do something *loco,* I would've stopped him."

"Till the next time you go off somewhere and he keeps company with a bottle? Face it, Tony, he's nothing but an old drunk!"

He flinched and looked away.

I felt a pang of guilt, for I knew it wasn't Tony's fault who his father was. He'd probably suffered more because of it than anyone, except maybe Rooster. My voice dropped. "Look, I'm sorry. It's not your fault."

He struggled to regain his composure. "I'll miss it as much as you will. It was one of the few things that grew"—kicking a rusty fan at his feet in a burst of anger—"on this damn junkyard!"

I gave the fan a good swift kick of my own. I hurt my big toe and fell back on the plywood table in pain.

"You hurt it bad?" He leaned over to have a look.

"Never mind my toe!" I cried, pushing him away. "Never mind anything! Just leave me alone!"

"Oh, Kady," he murmured as he pulled me into his arms on that sagging, splintery table. I demanded that he let me go as tears welled up in my eyes. But he just held me firmly until my body finally relaxed. "Bamboo is a very stubborn plant," he said as he wiped away my tears, "one, they say, grows the most after a storm. A good rain may bring it back yet." Then he kissed me softly on the mouth.

I looked up at him, startled by his kiss. But he was smiling at me so tenderly that I gently kissed him back. We'd been friends, after all, for a long time. The next thing I knew the Monopoly game board slid to the ground as he began kissing me wildly. His shirt was made of soft flannel and I slipped my arms around him, held him close. I could taste the gum in his mouth . . . Doublemint.

"Oh, Kady, *querida amiga mía* . . ."

All at once his tongue shot into my mouth, stunning me.

"Stop it!" I cried, slapping him. "What do you think you're *doing!*"

He drew back, speechless.

"Why can't you just leave me alone like I asked you to!"

His shoulders slumped as he turned away.

I wandered around aimlessly after that, and eventually slipped inside the sanctuary of the widowmaker tree. Darkness was beginning to fall when Rooster squeezed in beside me.

"H-H-House okay now," he said reassuringly. "*Papi* say so."

I knew he'd be giving me that dopey smile of his if I looked over at him, so I buried my head in my arms.

He pressed something into my hand. "Rooster m-m-make m-more PEE PULL."

"Geez," I groaned.

He thrust it under my nose, forcing me to look at it. I glimpsed at the arms, jaggedly torn from the papery soft punk bark, completely out of proportion. "Wow," I said, feeling a well of meanness rise in me, "you made a *loco* one like yourself."

"Oh . . .," he said, the concept taking root in his mind and clearly delighting him. He began to nod vigorously. *"Rooster* PEE PULL!" He began to play with the doll, making weird honking noises. He'd been around Dandy for so long that he was beginning to sound just like him.

This was more than I could stand. "SHUT UP!"

Rooster's head jerked backwards as he sucked in his breath and stared at me. Then his eyes slowly clouded over and his face screwed up the way it did before he started to cry. A wad of pink gum fell from his mouth in a puddle of drool as his arms reached out for me. *"¡M-M-Madrina!"* he sobbed, *"¡Madrina!"*

His hands, wet with snot and saliva, roped around my neck in the tight space of the hollowed tree, and I reluctantly held him until his shrieking sobs slowly subsided.

✲   ✲   ✲

After finally eating our dinner of stone-cold biscuits, stone-cold mashed potatoes, congealed milk gravy and stone-cold green goo (the fried chicken was in the kitchen when the fire broke out), Mama marched up to Señor Rosado and informed him in a steely voice that if he didn't restore the kitchen, we'd "SUE THE LIVING DAYLIGHTS OUT OF HIM!"

He had the workers start three days later.

Even so, he tried to cheat us by replacing the stove and sink with his worthless junk until Tony made him buy new ones. I don't know where he got the money from, as his only steady source of income appeared to be refugee relief checks. At any rate, when the work was finished, we had a kitchen far nicer than it had ever been, complete with a garbage disposal that terrified Mama the first time she used it. After that, she was so impressed with its efficiency that she went out of her way to find things to grind up.

The bitter smoke lingered on, permeating the furniture, our clothing, the very walls. We washed and scrubbed until we thought we'd drop, but it just hung around like a bad cold. Yet as the weeks went by, we realized the dynamite had taken its toll in a far worse way. The widowmaker tree, which grew at the edge of the bamboo thicket, was beginning a slow decline. The leaves were turning shades of yellow and brown, and instead of dropping to the ground as they did with the subtle change of season, they clung to the branches in a death grip.

Wendell flew into the yard on a new ten-speed bicycle one sunny afternoon in late November. "Hey, everybody! Come see my new bike!"

I looked out the kitchen window from where I was hurriedly peeling potatoes, anxious to be on my way to my "baby-sitting job," and saw him doing catwalks in the front yard.

Mama—who was having a wonderful time grinding up the peelings in her new garbage disposal—was shocked. "Where'd he get a bike like that?"

"Stop putting those peelings in the disposal! You know Rosy likes them," I told her. Until the garbage disposal had been installed, she'd never wasted a morsel of food. Now her passion was to take a whole dinner plate of leftovers and stuff it into the grinding mouth of the disposal. I nodded toward Wendell. "He probably stole it."

"I don't raise my kids to be thieves," she said as she reluctantly put the rest of the peelings into a bowl. "Come, let's see."

When we got outside, Jewel was laughing uproariously as Wendell was coaxing her to take a spin on his handlebars. "Why, you know I can't fit on those handlebars!" she cried, slapping him with a pillowcase.

I'd never seen him so happy. His cheeks were flushed and his eyes shone like sapphires. "Then you try it, Mama," he teased.

Mama gave him one of her no-nonsense looks. "So, where'd you get it?"

"Bought it with my own money," he said proudly.

"I didn't think you had any money."

"I raised it by going around the neighborhood like Papa told me to do," Wendell replied as he rubbed a speck of dirt off the handlebars. "Aren't you gonna congratulate me?"

"I don't know why you needed a new one," she said, shaking her head, "but it's right sporty."

I eyed him suspiciously. "You're too lazy to raise a wooden nickel."

"Heck, Kady, you don't give me credit for anything."

Rooster came running up to Wendell. "R-R-Rooster ride!"

"Sure, kid. Hop right up here on the handlebars."

"Rooster, be careful!" Mama cried as Rooster managed to scramble on top of the handlebars and balance himself.

"Ahh, Mama, he's fine," Wendell shrugged her off.

"Rooster f-f-fine!" Rooster reassured her.

"Well, keep both hands on the handlebars!" she told him.

Wendell took off down the driveway, kicking up sand and dodging potholes as Rooster, perched on the handlebars—one hand gripped to the handlebars while the other arm flapped—honked with delight.

"Rooster!" Mama cried out. "Keep *both* hands—"

"Lookee m-m-me, *M-M-Mami* Palmer!" Rooster cried out. "GAGA-GAGA-GAGGGG!"

"GAGA-GAGA-GAGGGG!" Dandy echoed as he flew in hops beside the bike.

"—on the handlebars," Mama muttered to herself as she watched them disappear around a bend. Then she turned to Jewel. "Honestly, Jewel, that boy doesn't have a lick of sense."

"Who, Rooster?"

"No! Wendell. What's he driving so carelessly for?"

I decided to hightail it out of there before she found fault with me, too. Only Rooster never did anything wrong.

A few minutes later, I rode past Wendell and Rooster on the old bike Wendell refused to ride.

"Having fun?" I called out to Rooster, who was still cackling like a goose.

"H-Having f-fun!"

"When you're finished replacing all those clothes maybe you'll start saving for a bike, too!" Wendell shouted at me, then laughed as he sped past me in a burst of speed, kicking up sand. Rooster laughed, too, for the pure thrill of it.

I pretended not to hear them, reminding myself that if it wasn't for the old bike, I'd be walking to the spring. Or worse yet, Mama would insist on driving me the three miles to Mrs. Nichols's zoo.

When I got to the spring Jon was having an Oreos attack. "We smoked a joint before you got here, and it made us ravenous," he said with a sheepish grin. "Ate up everything in sight. Let's make a run to the store."

"Are you okay to drive?" I asked as I looked into his eyes. They were glazed over.

"Of course," he assured me with a bright smile.

As soon as the word spread that we were going to the store, coins poured into Jon's hands like gumballs spilling out of a machine. Everybody, it seemed, wanted us to pick up something. It amazed me how much cash these kids carried.

Jon had to write everything down so he wouldn't forget: sour cream 'n' onion potato chips for Charlotte, Fritos for Mark, pretzels for Madison, and so forth. Parker decided he might as well come with us because he couldn't decide what he wanted. He just knew he was starving.

When a green-eyed girl wearing bell-bottoms and an orange tie-dyed shirt named Gretta asked me what I was getting, I was about to tell her Lorna Doones when Jon told her he'd be sharing his Oreos with me.

Jon finished writing out the list and the three of us drove to the store.

We went inside, and Jon told me to get the chips while he went over to the cookie aisle. Parker remained up front at the candy display, scratching his curly mop of hair in bewilderment.

I was grabbing the Fritos and Madison's pretzels (I don't know why I bothered) when I saw Rooster.

He was standing quietly at the postcard rack looking at the pictures when he looked up and clapped his hand over his mouth in amazement. *"Madrina* in st-st-store?" He rushed up to me.

"Heck, Rooster, I go to stores, too."

"Rooster in store, *M-M-Madrina* in store!" He jumped up and down with excitement, the red purse on his shoulder swinging wildly.

"Where's Dandy?"

"D-Dandy in Tony's car."

"Then why are you carrying that purse around?"

"Because—Because—" He spied the Fritos in my hand. "For m-*m-me?*"

"Sorry, Rooster, but these are for a friend."

He grabbed another bag off the shelf. *"These* for me?"

"Ask Tony to buy you some. He brought you here." I'd seen him under the hood of his father's old pickup as we pulled into the parking lot. My cheeks had turned red with embarrassment at the sight of him, remembering how he kissed me the day the house caught fire. He hadn't noticed me as we piled out of Jon's car, which suited me just fine. I'd been going out of my way to avoid him. I still couldn't *believe* he'd kissed me like that. Not Tony, my friend! It was too weird to even think about.

The back of his pickup was piled high with plastic gnomes, the kind you saw in front of cheap motels. I couldn't imagine the gnomes selling any better than the cookie presses had and could now look forward to seeing dozens of grinning midgets where the bamboo had reigned.

Jon had burst out laughing when he saw all the gnomes in the parking lot, but I'd just groaned.

Rooster thrust the bag under my nose. "Tony a-a-always s-s-say nooooo!"

"Put it back," I demanded. Of all the people to run into!

He grabbed me with a sticky hand that smelled like tar. I wondered what he'd picked up in the parking lot. An old piece of gum maybe? "P-P-PLEASE!"

I pulled free of him and explained with annoyance, "This stuff isn't for me. I didn't bring my own money."

Jon and Parker approached me. "Ready?" Jon asked.

Rooster's eyes lit up when he saw all the brightly colored packages they were carrying.

"Yes," I said, anxious to leave. I turned to Rooster. "These are my friends, I gotta go now."

"*Rooster* is—is—your friend," he pointed out.

"I got us two bags of Oreos," Jon said, holding them up to me.

"Lorna Doones are pretty good. Maybe we could get a bag of each," I suggested.

"Oh, but Kady"—Jon shook his head reproachfully as he smiled at me—"you just can't beat an Oreo."

Rooster pulled a Fritos bag off the shelf. "R-R-Rooster want—"

"Please put that back," I hissed as I followed Jon and Parker to the cashier.

"R-R-ROOSTER WANT!!!!" he screamed with insistence as he clutched the bag and followed me.

I yanked the bag away from him and put it back on the nearest shelf, among some jars of baby food. "Enough, Rooster! This isn't my money!" I muttered through clenched teeth. "Don't you get it? Don't you get *anything?*"

Several people turned to stare. Jon looked back at Rooster and me with a funny smile. "Kady, who's this kid?" I noticed that he called me Kady whenever he seemed annoyed with me.

"Ummm," I hedged, "just Rooster."

"Rooster?" Parker repeated with a smirk. "What kind of a name is that?"

"A nickname."

They both took note of his mop of unruly hair, his mis-buttoned shirt, the shredded wad of Kleenex falling out of his pant's pocket, and his red purse with goose droppings splattered on the side of it.

"Does he think he's a girl?" Parker asked.

"No! That's not a purse, exactly. It's a carrying case."

"For what? His Barbies?" Jon snickered.

Rooster stamped his foot and cried out, *"ROOSTER!! WANT!! CHIPS!!"*

Jon laughed uneasily. "Go tell your dad, kid. I'm sure he'll get them for you."

"Nooooo," Rooster said, shaking his head. "N-N-Not here. And-And Tony *N-N-NEVER!* But—But—But *M-M-Madrina CAN! Madrina* can do ANY-ANYTHING!"

"Sorry, Rooster, but we gotta go!"

As we made our way to the cashier, Jon turned to me with a quizzical expression. "I've never seen that weirdo before. Where do you know him from?"

"He—umm—lives next door."

"In that house with all the junk?"

I nodded, not wanting to say too much. Not wanting to even *think* about Rooster. *Why did Tony's pickup have to break down here?* And yet, looking at Rooster now as he kicked at the bottom of the postcard rack, regarding me forlornly, made me wonder why we couldn't go ahead and give him something. He wouldn't have made such a scene if I hadn't shown up in the first place. He'd still be staring quietly at the postcards. Rooster could look at pictures for hours.

"What's his problem?" Jon asked.

"Problem?" I cleared my throat. "His mother had a—umm—difficult birth. He's a little slow."

"Slow isn't the word," Parker said as he unloaded a bag of Fritos, a bag of pork rinds, a Pay Day, and a package of jaw

breakers on the counter. "Birdbrain is more like it."

"He won't hurt you guys or anything," I said. "He just doesn't understand why we can't buy the Fritos for him." I turned to Jon as the cashier bagged Parker's stuff, then started ringing up ours. "Do you think that maybe"—I bit down on my lip—"we could?"

"Seriously?"

"Well . . . yeah," I said, skirting his penetrating gaze. "They're only what? Twenty cents?" My voice came out small, apologetic.

Jon handed the cashier a pile of crumpled bills and coins, then took his change and jiggled it in his hand, frowning. "Shouldn't he be living in some kind of a home instead of hanging around regular people? I don't know if we should encourage a guy like that."

Parker nudged me. "Don't look now, but your buddy doesn't look too happy. He's about to topple the postcard rack." He turned to Rooster and hollered, "Hey, Birdbrain!"

Rooster looked up.

Parker held up the bag of Fritos he'd just purchased. "Want some chips?"

Rooster stopped kicking the postcard rack. "Y-Yeah!"

"Here!" Parker showered him with several handfuls that got caught in Rooster's curls and fell at his feet.

Rooster was momentarily dazed by the onslaught, then stooped down, picked a chip up from the floor and slowly brought it to his mouth.

"Hey, you!" the cashier cried out angrily to Parker.

"Don't worry, sir," Parker replied politely, "it'll be cleaned up in no time flat." He pointed to Rooster, who began stuffing the chips into his mouth while laughing uproariously at his good fortune.

My eyes widened in horror. "Parker!"

"Hey"—he shrugged—"he said he wanted chips, didn't he?"

"Yeah, but—"

"Well, by golly, I gave him chips," he smirked. He tossed a few into his mouth, then held out the bag for me.

"No," I said, pushing the bag away.

"My God!" Jon exclaimed. "He's *eating* them right off the floor!" He stared in amazement at the black-and-white linoleum squares littered with cigarette butts, gum wrappers and dusty footprints. Many of the chips had smashed on impact and Rooster, who had already gobbled up the bigger pieces, was now licking his fingertip and using it to pick up the crumbs. "Right off the dirty floor!" he repeated, staring.

"Oh, what's the big deal? As far as he's concerned, I made his day," Parker said. He called out to Rooster, "Hey, Birdbrain! Why don't you take some home in that cute purse of yours?"

Then he showered him with another handful of chips.

"Let's just get out of here," I said, anxious to get as far away from Rooster, from this whole scene, as possible. I nearly collided with Tony as I headed out the door.

"Kady," he said, as startled to see me face-to-face as I was to see him. "What are you doing here?" His eyes twinkled mischievously. "Stocking up on Doublemint?" A grimy hand attempted to wipe a smudge of grease from his nose, yet only succeeded in making it worse.

My face flushed like a stove burner turned on high.

"I'm—uh—leaving," I struggled to say.

I didn't turn around to see if Tony figured out what had happened. I just got into that shiny, cherry red Mustang and slammed the door shut.

Darkness was falling when I got home. I could see everyone sitting down for supper through the dining room window as I put the bike away. I'd gotten too high, laughed too hard, and time had slipped by.

"What kept you so long?" Mama asked as I slid into my seat.

I told her that Mrs. Nichols had to do a make-up lesson and had asked me to stay late. I said it easily, and was amazed at what a good liar I was becoming. I'd been going to the spring for a month now, and Mama still hadn't figured it out.

I dug into a mountain of mashed potatoes without the slightest feeling of remorse as the phone rang. Mama got up to answer it.

Grampsie started nibbling at the meat loaf, mashing it with her gums, which made a loud clacking sound. Then she saw peas in it—which she detested—and complained of stomach pains. She got up from the table and demanded that a bottle of

Pepto Bismol be sent to her room along with a tablespoon—not a teaspoon.

A look of concern swept Mama's face and she motioned for everyone to be quiet.

". . . Flowers? Why, Wanda, there must be some mistake. . . . "

I thought that Rosy had gotten into Miz Sanders's garden and spoke up, "Don't let her shoot our pig!"

". . . she's been sick, but—certainly not—"

"Rosy's not sick!" I interjected. "She eats like a pig."

"She eats like a pig!" Sammy howled.

"Hush up!" Papa silenced Sammy. "Your Mama's on the phone. What is it, Mattie?"

". . . Well, I should know!" Mama's eyes fell on Wendell, who had stopped eating and began circling the rim of his milk glass with his forefinger until it squeaked.

I kicked him under the table. "Rosy's life's at stake. Stop it!" That was when I noticed how peculiar he looked, as ashen as dirty soap.

". . . Yes, he'll be there first thing in the morning—I'll make mighty sure of it," Mama said as she glared at Wendell. "Thanks for calling."

I looked at Wendell sharply as he started squirming in his seat. If the phone call wasn't about Rosy, what was it about?

Mama's nostrils flared as she slowly walked back to the table. "That was Wanda Sanders," she began with a forced smile, then paused until she heard Grampsie shut her bedroom door behind her.

"She wanted to extend her sympathy to Grampsie, who she learned through our dear boy, Wendell"—her smile sickeningly sweet now—"is gravely ill."

Papa was stricken. "What!"

"'One shake away from her Maker,' is the way her 'pneumonia' was described by Dear Wendell," she continued with that same sickeningly sweet smile plastered on her face.

"Why you little jerk!" I cried. "What were you thinking?"

Sammy began to cry. "But Grampsie's not dying . . . is she? I asked you before and you said she wasn't!"

"Of course she's not," Mama assured him, then turned to Wendell. "She especially wanted to thank you for your thoughtfulness in taking up a collection for flowers for her"—her eyes blazed—"HOSPITAL STAY!"

Minnie sputtered a mouthful of milk all over the table.

"So that's how you got the money for the bike!" I pounced. "I'll bet you canvassed the entire neighborhood and collected a small fortune. You WORM!"

"It's a good thing your grandmother just left the table. It'd break her heart to hear this," Papa said.

Wendell smiled sheepishly. "It isn't that big of a whopper. I mean, she *is* gravely ill"—circling his finger around his ear and leveling his eyes at Papa—"up here."

He met Papa's granite expression.

"Guys!" his voice squeaked with sudden nervousness. "You never buy anything new! You won't even get Jewel a clothes dryer!

She uses that stupid wringer that belongs in a history museum! I don't know why she even comes here anymore!"

Papa rose from the table, tapping his belt buckle. Wendell excused himself and fled down the hall, brushing past Grampsie who was slowly making her way back to the kitchen.

"I heard yelling," she mumbled, her eyes wide with fright. "Where's the fire?"

"There's no fire, everything's just fine," Mama said soothingly as she led her back to her room.

"I'll need some Pepto Bismol and a *table*spoon, not a *tea*spoon."

She looked fragile as she padded around in her bedroom slippers, older and thinner than ever, with dark veins protruding from her hands.

After Grampsie had been given her Pepto Bismol and settled back in her room, Papa went to Wendell's room. I went outside, not wanting to hear anything. I knew Wendell would be sitting on an air cushion for the next week or so.

Wendell rode the new bike for the last time the following morning—back to the bike store. Then, Mama ordered him to return the money to every neighbor he'd taken it from.

"You'll tell the truth to every one of 'em, ya hear?" Mama insisted. She was standing in front of the living room mirror, tying a bow on her best church dress. It was an oversized bow, the ridiculous kind often featured on maternity clothes. She wore that dress to all inescapable public functions and rushed to get out of it the minute she returned home.

Wendell looked at her in horror as it dawned on him what was about to happen. "*You're* not going with me!"

"I most certainly am."

"But nobody is seen with their mother! I'll give the money back, every single dime, I promise!"

Mama didn't say anything as she tugged and pulled at the silly bow. Her callused fingers couldn't get it to lie flat, and it occurred to me as I watched her struggle with it that the reason she was going along had nothing to do with giving the money back.

Squares of white and black flashed through my mind, and I squeezed my eyes shut to block out the memory of Rooster's hands reaching, grabbing, and stuffing all those chips into his mouth. And his foolish laugh of pleasure.

20

January came and the leaves began to fall, painting the world brown. The brightest color around was Rooster, who flew about the trees like a leaf from another land, with Dandy fluttering alongside him. Mama had given him red flannel shirts on Three Kings Day, the day his family exchanged gifts. I myself didn't look so drab, either, thanks to all the new dresses, plus tie-dyed shirts and dangling earrings Jon gave me for Christmas. Mama, who got a nice but boring sweater from Papa, looked like an oversized house sparrow. She clucked her disapproval every time I sashayed about in my pretty new clothes.

Papa agreed with Mama that I shouldn't have accepted so many Christmas presents from Jon, but admitted that I looked "mighty purty." (All I'd been able to afford to give Jon was the photo Mama had taken the day he'd come to the house, matted in a nice frame. It wasn't even that good of me—I had a surprised look on my face, as if I'd swallowed a bug!)

I loved the fresh smell of the new clothes Jon gave me, and the way they felt so crisp in my hands, as if they had a life of their own. I discovered that when I wore my new clothes to school or to the spring, I didn't hold Jon's hand so tightly when we gathered with his friends. Sometimes, I didn't even hold it at all as I talked to the girls—everyone but Madison.

The falling leaves floated on the water of the spring like tiny boats, then slowly sank, turning the water the color of cream soda. Maybe that's why nobody saw the alligator on that Friday afternoon we were hanging out.

Charlotte and Madison were wading in the chilly stream throwing junk food to a family of raccoons, their bell-bottoms rolled up to their knees. The raccoons had moved under the roots of a cypress tree that grew on a little island a short distance from shore. Normally nocturnal, they had started coming out during the day to feast on the junk food we left behind. Gretta, and a wide-eyed brunette named Jean, who had a neon flower painted on her cheek, were right behind them. They'd all just finished painting their nails with some glittery polish Madison had brought along, and their toenails shimmered through the water like rose petals. I trailed after them, amazed by the bold raccoons. Soon we were all laughing as the playful creatures snatched up food with their humanlike hands and raced under the cypress roots to eat it.

"Look! A baby!" Gretta laughed, her green eyes dancing. "Isn't he cute?"

"Oh yeah. Especially with those big eyes! I could fall in love with that guy," Madison said.

"Who couldn't you fall in love with?" Charlotte groaned.

"Here, baby!" Madison coaxed, as she held out a handful of raisins. "Come see Maddy!" She looked around. "Anybody have any more raisins?"

"No, but I've got some potato chips," Jean said, and tossed him a few. Jean reminded me of a doe with her big brown eyes and soft-spoken voice. She seemed like a nice girl, although unusually shy for this group. She was always adjusting her clothes, poking in her bra strap, tightening her belt, or brushing off the leaves. It seemed to disturb her, too, to use the portable toilet in Mark's van, for she would come out holding her nose and making a terrible face.

"Do you think he should be eating junk food like that?" I asked. "He's a wild animal. One that normally only comes out at night."

Jean shrugged.

"Look! He's taking one!" Gretta pointed excitedly.

Madison waded deeper toward the baby with more chips. "Come on, baby! Meet some girls!"

Then, I noticed something on the far side of the inlet moving toward us. At first I thought it was an otter, eager to share the potato chips, but then I saw the pair of slitty eyes emerge. A chilling horror spread through my body, and for a moment, I could scarcely breathe.

"Alligator!" I cried hoarsely as I grabbed hair, T-shirts, and arms. The girls pulled away from me as if I were crazy.

"Stop it, Kady!" Charlotte cried as she slapped my hand.

"ALLIGATOR!" I screamed. "GET *OUT!*"

Their faces registered incredulity, then panic. "WHERE?!" they cried as they raced from the water.

My hand trembled as I pointed to the concentric circles radiating outward from where the eyes had been.

Madison, who had managed to evade my grasping hands, had waded even farther into the stream, the water now lapping against her rolled-up jeans. "You've been had, fools!" she laughed heartily.

"GET OUT!" I hollered.

She waved her hand dismissively. "I'm not about to be made a fool of by Miss Subsidized Lunch!"

"YOU'RE THE ONE ABOUT TO BE THE LUNCH!"

She leisurely reached her hands over her head and stretched while letting out an enormous yawn.

"Oh-mi-God," Jean moaned as she wrung her hands together. "Oh-mi-God! Madison, maybe you should lis—"

"DO YOU THINK I REALLY EVEN CARE?" I yelled.

When she still refused to come in, I muttered under my breath, "I don't know why I'm doing this," and went in after her.

"I think—I think I saw something, too, Madison!" Gretta cried out with a nervous laugh. "Who wants to risk ending up gator bait, ya know? Both of you get back here!"

"COME ON, you guys!" Charlotte chimed in.

"Yes, come on!" Jean echoed.

"Honestly," Madison sniffed as I dragged her by the arm back to shore, "all this racket is giving me an *excruciating* headache!" She shook loose of me, plopped herself on a dirty stretch of sand at the water's edge, and glared.

I quickly moved away from the shore and stood with the other girls. It was extremely rare for an alligator to attack a human, I told them, but who wanted to take that chance? They all nodded in agreement, their eyes big, their lips trembling.

It wasn't two minutes later that the jaws of the alligator exploded from the water, then snapped shut on the baby raccoon who stood apart from his family, watching us. He didn't have time to even whimper as the flashing teeth dragged him under.

In the horrifying calm that followed—like the tranquillity of the sea after a ship has sunk—we blinked as if our eyes had played a trick on us. Then Jean let out a bloodcurdling scream and the guys came running.

Madison slowly turned to stare at me.

"An alligator ate a raccoon!" Charlotte shrieked.

"A what?" Mark cried as he rushed up to Gretta.

"An ALLIGATOR—"

Jon's jaw dropped. "For real?"

"He's still there." She pointed with a shaky finger.

"Cool!" Parker exclaimed.

"Shit, Parker, it could've—could've—been—" Jean began to cry.

Jon went over to her. "You okay?"

She nodded through tears.

He awkwardly massaged her shoulder. "Everybody else okay?" He looked around anxiously, until he saw Madison. I watched him relax at the sight of her, then tense up again as her face slowly went ashen. His hand stopped massaging Jean's shoulders, and for an unbearable moment I thought he might rush over to Madison, take her in his arms, and—

He had to say my name twice before I realized he was talking to me. "You okay?" He was wiping a stray hair from my face as his eyes kindly looked into mine.

I gave him a shaky smile.

Madison slowly walked toward us, trancelike. "I didn't believe you," she said breathlessly as she let out a little laugh. There was no light in her eyes, just dull gold. The thin bones in her hands stood out as she clutched her arms. "I've been coming here since summer and never—" Her voice caught and her teeth started to chatter.

"I was pretty shocked to see one so bold, coming right at us in daylight," I said. "They usually only come out at night and rarely bother anybody. But then, with all the junk food and the raccoons out, too—"

"Thanks," she said, looking me squarely in the eye.

She walked past us to her blanket, and, pulling up the sides, wrapped herself up in it like an Egyptian mummy.

"What was she thanking you for?" Jon asked.

"For making her get out," Gretta explained. "Kady started yelling 'Alligator!' and everyone got out except for Madison who, as usual, does exactly as she pleases. She didn't even care that her jeans got wet! She thought Kady was playing a joke on her until I started yelling that I saw something, too. I wasn't sure what I saw—I didn't really think there was an alligator—but if Madison hadn't got out when she did, it could've been her instead of the raccoon."

Jon raked the hair back from his forehead, resting his hand on the top of his head as he took in her flood of words. "Really?"

"You should've seen the way it shot out of the water!"

Jon looked uneasily at the stream.

I was so exhausted by the adrenaline rush that I sat down right where I was standing.

Jon yanked me back up. "Don't sit here! You're too close to the shore! Last year, a girl in Coral Gables was making sand castles in her backyard—I guess her family lived on a canal or something—and her mother called her to supper and she didn't answer. They found her mangled body a week la—"

"Stop it!" I cried.

"I'm sorry. I wasn't thinking."

"What's that over there?" Mark asked, pointing excitedly. Several people peered at the water.

"Just a stick," Parker finally said, disappointed. "Let's find that sucker before he gets away."

Jon and several others nodded in agreement.

I looked at Jon incredulously. "What are you going to do if you find him?"

"Kill him with our bare hands, of course," he growled, then broke into a grin. "Actually, I was thinking of making an alligator purse out of his hide just for you."

"You'll be arrested for poaching," I said dryly.

Several of the guys began combing the shoreline and throwing rocks in the water, but those of us who had seen the alligator attack couldn't calm down. Before long, we had inched our towels and blankets so close together they were overlapping. Then we terrorized one another with horror stories. Some were familiar, such as the one about the man with a golden arm who murdered young couples while they were making out in parked cars. Others knotted our stomachs with revulsion, especially the one Madison told about the python that lived in the walls of an old house and ate the newborn baby of the unsuspecting tenants. They found the snake in the crib with a huge lump in its stomach. "It's true," she insisted as we demanded that she shut up in a tone of voice that really meant "*Tell us more!*"

It was right after Charlotte told us about an unsolved mystery—an ax murderer still at large in central Florida and last seen in a desolate area—that Mark burst through the trees, shouting, "There's a weirdo running around the woods!"

We all stared at him, stunned. Finally, Madison laughed shakily and said, "Quit it, willya? I've had enough scares for one day."

"I'm not kidding," Mark said flatly as he removed his tinted sunglasses and massaged his eyes. "Where's Jon and the rest of the guys?"

"I thought they were with you," I said.

"We split up. Damn!" he muttered as he started off again. "He'd know what to do."

Gretta noted the worried look on my face and said, "They'll be back before you know it."

"How can you be sure? The world's full of crazies, like that freaky Manson guy and that monster who murdered those eight student nurses," Charlotte piped up in a wobbly voice.

"Richard Speck. I get sick every time I see his picture on the news," Jean moaned. "He looks so normal."

"I know it," Charlotte agreed as she ripped open a bag of Reese's peanut butter cups and passed them out. To my amazement, she gave me two. "He just rang the doorbell and one of the nurses let him in the apartment." She pulled the brown paper off her peanut butter cup and circled her fingertip around the chocolate ridges, unable to eat it.

"Didn't one of them get away by rolling under a bed?" Madison asked as she bit into her own stash of Milk Duds.

"Yeah, I think so," Gretta said.

"Can you imagine what she felt like hiding there, listening to him butcher her friends one by one and not sure if he realized she was missing?" Charlotte said breathlessly. "Under the bed is the first place they look."

"She never would've gotten away with it under my bed," I

remarked. "There's so many dust bunnies she would've started sneezing."

"I would've *died* the moment I saw his face peering under the bed, the moment he knew he had me," Jean shuddered. "Does anyone have a joint? This is making me crazy."

"I don't think it's a good time to light up," Gretta cautioned. "You never know who might show up with this gator business."

"Have a brownie instead," Charlotte suggested.

Jean looked around for the brownies, then screamed as Rooster leapt right in front of her.

The rest of us screamed, too, as if Richard Speck himself had appeared.

I pressed my hand to my chest to slow my pounding heart. It was only Rooster after all. He looked terrible, with a mud-streaked face, rumpled shirt, and leaves and sticks clinging to his hair.

"Birdbrain?!" Parker exclaimed as he came into the clearing along with the rest of the guys he'd rounded up upon hearing our screams. "Hey, man, what are you doing here?"

Rooster turned to him with a dazed smile.

"That's the guy!" Mark exclaimed.

Jon did a double take. "*That's* who you're afraid of?" He started to laugh.

Everyone laughed with him, relieved that the weirdo had turned out to be the "birdbrain idiot" Parker had told them about who'd eaten smashed Fritos off the floor of the convenience store. I found myself gulping down a brownie, wishing Rooster would *disappear altogether*. It was getting so there was no place I could go without him showing up, no place I could find a life separate from his.

"Are you sure you're not Richard Speck?" Charlotte asked him, poker faced.

"Nooooo," the boy gravely replied.

More laughter broke out.

"Charles Manson, then?" Mark asked.

"Noooo. *R-R-Rooster!*" He nodded his head affirmatively.

"Rooster, is it? As in 'cock-a-doodle-do'?" Gretta asked.

The group howled. Rooster shrunk back, confused by the loudness of the laughter. Then he saw me and ran over to where I was sitting.

"D-Dandy fl-fl-fly away!" he exclaimed, pointing at the sky. "GONE!" His eyes shone with tears.

"So?"

His eyes widened in disbelief. "So!"

"He flies a lot now, Roos! He's not a gosling anymore. He's a big white goose."

"*Sí,* but—but—he *usually* c-c-comes back right away! I j-j-just *honk* for h-him and—and— there he is!"

"I'm sure he's fine, Roos."

He kicked at the dirt. "No! *N-Not* fine. He's—He's disa . . . disa . . . PPEARED—" He looked straight up into the clouds, pointing.

"Please don't worry about him, Rooster. He'll come back when he's ready to!" I snapped at him. *I couldn't believe he'd found his way all the way out here to my sanctuary!*

"NOOOOOO!" he shrieked. "Rooster O-M-M-Mighty Pro-Protector! L-L-Lions and-and tigers and-and-and bears and oh-mys m-might *g-get* him!" He grabbed my hand so hard he nearly broke the bones. "*¡V-Vamos, Madrina!* You hafta—hafta help me!"

"Ouch!" I yanked my hand away as my temper flared. "Rooster, go home! He's probably back there already!"

He was about to start shrieking again when Parker walked right past him.

"Chips!" he called out.

"So you remember me, do you? The chips man," Parker sidled up to him with a crooked smile.

The boy smiled shyly and nodded his head. "Rooster l-likes chips." His face suddenly lit up. "And D-D-D-Dandy, *h-h-he* likes . . . likes . . ." He looked skyward again as his voice trailed off.

Parker grinned slyly. "Got every single crumb off the floor of that store, didn't you?"

Rooster looked back down as he kicked the dirt. "T-Tony made me—m-made me go."

Parker feigned horror. "He made you leave all those chips BEHIND?"

Rooster nodded sadly.

"I bet you wanted to put them in that cute red purse of yours, didn't you?"

He nodded again.

"Where is that cute red purse, anyway? You wouldn't want to be without your Barbies now, would you?"

"Oh, Parker, give the kid a break," Madison spoke up. She turned to Rooster and spoke loudly enough for everyone to hear: "We've got plenty of food around here, kid. Help yourself to anything you want."

To show him she meant what she said, she handed him a box of Milk Duds. I looked at her warily, but she shrugged me off with a smile.

Things calmed down after that. Rooster, overwhelmed by all the junk food, forgot about Dandy for a while as he roamed from towel to towel and sampled everything. Someone turned the music back on and we tried to forget the horror that had taken place earlier.

I ate two more brownies. Double fudge to mask the extra marijuana Jon had been putting in them lately—some pure "gold" a friend of his had started supplying him with. I'd come to realize that Jon used most of his allowance to buy marijuana. The brownies tasted like chocolate, but were so mushy they stuck to the roof of my mouth. I didn't care. I just wanted that mind-numbing happiness to fill me up.

"There's a Valentine's dance coming up and I was wondering if you'd go with me," Jon said as he squeezed my hand.

I leaned over and kissed him. "Why, I'd love to."

"Wow," he murmured, kissing me back. "Is it me or the brownies?"

"You, of course," I replied, giggling. The brownies were already making me so light-headed I felt as if I were floating.

"There's this gown in the window of Mom's shop that would look perfect on you."

"Oh, Jon, you can't keep giving me clothes! Especially a gown." I giggled again. I watched a leaf spin toward the ground. I had no idea leaves were so brilliantly white when caught by the sun. . . .

"But I can see you in it. Especially this particular gown. I had to stop and catch my breath when I saw it."

"What?" I asked, captivated by the spinning leaf. It was so alive in its hour of death . . . so carefree. . . .

"The *gown.* I had to stop and catch my breath when I saw it."

"Why's that?"

He shrugged. "Because it's so . . . I don't know . . . perfect for you."

"And how did you know this?" I fell back into his arms as the whole world started to reel. A smile crept to my face. No wonder they called it marijuana "gold."

"That's the part I can't tell you . . . the surprise . . ."

He seemed to be speaking very slowly, as if coming from a radio low on batteries.

"Surprise?"

"Yeah . . . I mean, there's something about this gown that's got your name written all over it. . . . You'll know what I'm talking about when you see it."

"Oh, I will . . . will I?" I giggled again.

"Yeah," he said, kissing me again.

"Can't you give me a hint?"

"Nope . . . But what I can tell you is that I've already ordered it . . . so when you get a package in the mail . . . don't be surprised."

He sucked in the air as if it were drenched in sugar as he traced the contours of my face, then my neck and collarbone. His touch sent shivers down my spine. "I can just see you in this gown . . . just picture us together on that dance floor . . . swirling like a top until the colors are one. . . ."

"Swirling?" I giggled again as I pictured us both as dancing leaves. . . .

Rooster ran past us, his arms outstretched and his head thrown back. "GAGGGAGAGAGAGAGAGAGGGGG!" he honked joyously.

"Ooo-wee! The Birdbrain flies!" Parker hooted.

"OOOOOO—*WEEEEEEEEE!*" Rooster echoed and began flapping his arms as if he were about to take flight. "*GAG-A-GAG-A-GAGAGAGAGAGGGGG-A-GAG-A-GAG-A-GAGAGAGAGAGGGGGGAG-A-GAG-A-GAGAGAGAGAGGGGG!*"

Laughter broke out.

"Looks like he's gotten into the brownies. . . ." Jon said. "Kid's high as a kite."

I saw the dark crumbs around his mouth. "Oh no . . ."

Jon shook his head and laughed. "He hasn't a clue, not a clue!"

Rooster climbed onto the low branches of a live oak and leapt off, screaming with exhilaration. "*OOOOOO—WEEEEEEEEE!*"

"*Go, Birdbrain!*" Parker cried.

"*G-G-GO, BIRD!*" Rooster echoed. "*OOOOOO—WEEEEE EEEE! OOOOOO—WEEEEEEEEE!*"

I closed my eyes and shook the image of Rooster from my mind like an Etch-A-Sketch drawing. When I opened them again, Rooster was a splotch of bloodred—a leaf from another land. . . .

"I got my dog high once," Jon said, his eyes as shiny as newly minted coins. "Funniest thing you ever saw. . . . An ambulance went down the road with its siren on and he started to sing. . . . Wouldn't shut up for hours. . . . They could've stuck *him* on top of the ambulance!"

"Oh . . . yeah?" I started to giggle and couldn't stop.

"Oh, God, Kady . . . you should've been there." He doubled over in laughter. "Mom finally came out on the patio and asked, 'What's wrong with Moon?' . . . That's his name. . . . And I . . . and I just shrugged. . . . It's never occurred to her I smoke pot. . . . Man, is she ever naive. . . ."

I lay back on the fluffy towel and stared up through the trees, at the kaleidoscope of leaves changing patterns with the shifting wind.

*   *   *

My bike felt like an airship floating through space as I whizzed home along the dirt trails later that afternoon. When I turned onto the highway and saw an ambulance race by, I started to laugh, thinking of how that drugged dog must've howled. Even the potholes didn't jar me back to reality as I jounced over them on my driveway. It wasn't until I'd propped the bike against the solid wall of the garage that I realized something terrible had happened.

Mama was sobbing as Papa led her out of the house and Sammy was screaming, "No!" as he trailed behind them. Tears were rolling down Minnie's cheeks as she chased after Sammy to comfort him, but he just shoved her away.

Wendell pointed to me as he whispered to Papa, "Kady's back from her job." He seemed afraid to approach me, which wasn't like him at all.

Then I saw the most surprising thing of all. Jewel was standing behind our kitchen window, her eyes squeezed shut, her hands clasped under her chin in prayer. *What was she praying for? And where was everyone going?*

I was afraid to move forward for fear I'd fall off a cliff.

"Kady," Papa said levelly, "there's been an accident. Rooster"—his voice cracked—"it doesn't look good."

I stared at him numbly. His words made no sense. "Rooster?"

He nodded.

I started to laugh. "Oh no, Rooster's fine! I just saw him dancing around—"

"When?" he pressed.

I tried to think, but I couldn't remember how long ago it had been. Had he left before I had? Then I remembered I was supposed to be baby-sitting. How could I explain having seen Rooster? My head began to reel. "Oh—I don't know." I shrugged. From the corner of my eye, I saw Jewel spit into the sink three times in a row, then cross herself six times.

"They just took him in an ambulance to Pomelo General," Papa explained. "Tony and his father went with him. He fell out of Miz Sander's live oak, the one overlooking the lake. Looks like he broke his neck."

"Broke his *neck*?" I was so high I had to be hallucinating. *Oh, wake me up! Wake me up!*

"Come on, if you're going with us." He gently tugged me toward the car. "Jewel's gonna stay with Grampsie."

My legs nearly collapsed as I struggled into the back seat next to my siblings.

On the way to the hospital, Mama told us what Miz Sanders had told her: She noticed Rooster out in her backyard because he was wearing a red shirt that caught her eye. He'd been climbing an oak tree along her shore to retrieve Dandy, who had lit upon the top branches. But just before he reached the goose, it took off again. Instead of climbing back down, though, the boy did something very peculiar—even for Rooster. He honked at the top of his lungs and leaped out of the tree. It was as if he truly thought he was a goose, too! she'd told Mama. Not just because of the sound of his honking—why she had to look twice to make sure the honk wasn't coming from the goose!—but the way his arms lifted majestically into the air. That was the very word Miz Sanders used, Mama emphasized—majestically. Strangest thing she'd ever seen him do, and she'd seen him do plenty of strange things over the years, from going around hollering about oh mys to dragging around that ridiculous suitcase of shoes.

Then her blood froze when she saw him fall straight down like an arrow, his little body ripping right through leaves and small branches. Next thing she heard was a sickening thud sound. She tore out of the house and found him ankle-deep in lake water. The water had softened the impact of his fall, but not by much.

Mama blew her nose as she finished telling Miz Sander's story, then added as she dabbed her eyes with her wadded ball of Kleenex, "He's right lucky he hit that water. Coulda just as easily hit her dock."

"Are you sure he *leapt* out of the tree, Mama?" I asked, alarmed.

She cradled her forehead in her hand. "I dunno. I just dunno."

"That's just what she said, Kady, that he leapt out of the tree, 'his arms lifted majestically into the air'," Papa said as he looked at me through the rearview mirror.

Wendell shook his head. "I don't believe it. Even Rooster's not that stupid! And everybody knows Wanda Sanders is nothing but a crazy coot! If it weren't for her, why—"

"Now, boy, just because she caught you in a lie doesn't mean you can go around calling her a crazy coot!" Papa exclaimed.

"She *is* a crazy coot! And it has nothing to do with that business over the flowers. Rooster was just trying to get Dandy to come to him and lost his balance!"

"But Rooster thinks he's a bird, too," Sammy pointed out.

"He doesn't really," Minnie said. "It's just his way of taking care of Dandy. Wendell's right. He never would've jumped. Everybody loses their balance sometimes."

I rolled down my window and let the air roar in my ears to block out the conversation. I closed my eyes and saw Rooster climbing onto the low branches of a live oak and leaping off, screaming with exhilaration.

"OOOOOO—WEEEEEEEEE!"

"Go, Birdbrain!" Parker cried.

"G-G-GO, BIRD!" Rooster echoed.

Oh, God! Why hadn't I realized it? After eating those marijuana brownies, he thought he could fly just like Dandy. He'd leapt off that tree to show his goose the way home! When he'd run past me with his arms outstretched, shrieking with delight, I'd tuned him out. Even after I'd seen the dark crumbs around his mouth—those crumbs that make you forget who you really are for a while—I'd tuned him out. *If Rooster died, it would be my fault.*

When we arrived at the hospital, we found Tony pacing the floor of the waiting room. Señor Rosado sat in a chair, his face without expression. But his knuckles were white as he gripped a small card in his hands. It had a picture of *La Virgen de la Caridad* on it. Tony rushed up to us the second he saw us.

"This can't be happening," he moaned. "The whole way in the ambulance Rooster was so still, not like Rooster at all."

Mama steered Tony toward a chair and made him sit down.

"*¡Dios mío!*" he cried, bringing his hands to his face. "The doctors are operating on his neck. There are two or three spots where it's broken."

I walked to a window, reeling with dizziness. I needed a joint to make this all go away! Maybe if I called Jon, he'd bring me one. But I was afraid to call him, afraid that everyone would find out what had happened. And what was I thinking, anyway? The last thing I needed was a joint!

After a while, Tony came up beside me and stared out the window with a stoic expression. I wanted to turn to him and comfort him, yet was afraid he'd see my guilty expression. Tears stung my eyes and I fled to the restroom. I stayed there for a long time, letting the water gush from the faucet as I washed my face compulsively with the gritty soap that came from the dispenser.

I glanced up at the mirror over the sink. There was nothing pretty about the bloodshot eyes that stared back at me, the blotched skin, or the red nose that needed a Kleenex. I dabbed my nose with a scratchy paper towel, then forced myself to go back to the waiting room.

Tony was still staring out the window, while Mama and Papa drank coffee with Señor Rosado. I walked over to the nurse's station and asked if they had any news about Rooster. The nurse told me kindly that the surgery was very delicate and might take hours. I nodded and started aimlessly pacing the floor.

"*¡Qué horror!*" Señor Rosado cried, as he spat out his coffee, startling everyone in the waiting room. Then he turned to my parents who were sitting beside him, and went into a rampage. He said there was nothing in the world he hated more than *Americano* coffee. That his beloved wife, Angelina, would be outraged if she were here. And that he'd give anything now for a cup of her *café*. He dissolved into tears, burying his face in his hands. "*¡Ay,* Angelina, *mi amor!*"

Mama turned nervously to Papa, not sure what to do. Papa shifted his feet, not certain what to do, either, so Mama gently leaned over and stroked Señor Rosado's back. He didn't recoil from her touch, so she continued, digging her bitten-back nails through his shirt awkwardly, yet steadily.

Meanwhile, Wendell, Minnie, and Sammy watched *Gilligan's Island* on a black-and-white TV, their eyes glazed over and unblinking, their mouths curled in frowns.

Someone had recently scrubbed the linoleum floors with ammonia, and the smell nauseated me. I slumped into a vinyl chair that stuck to the back of my thighs like melted cheese and stared at the idiotic grin of Alfred E. Neuman on a copy of *Mad* magazine. I finally flipped it over because it reminded me so much of Rooster's idiotic grin. An hour passed, then two. I thought I'd go crazy staring at the walls, at the floor, at the stupid TV. But at least when I looked at the walls, I could avoid Tony; avoid Señor Rosado, who was pouring out his life story of heartache to Mama and Papa, his words all slurred together; avoid everybody. The longer the surgery dragged on, the worse I felt.

Tony started tugging at the cord on the blinds over the window, a gesture that reminded me of Rooster's constant fidgeting. Papa walked over to him, and they started talking. I overheard Tony tell Papa how worried he was about Rooster's spinal cord, how it might've been injured. I shuddered at the thought of Rooster as a vegetable for the rest of his life, unable to move his arms or legs. Maybe even unable to breathe on his own. *Would he still call me his* Madrina *then?* The thought filled me with horror.

Finally, two doctors, dressed in green surgical gowns, stepped into the room. I bolted up as did everyone else, except for Señor Rosado, who slowly raised his head.

The doctors looked questioningly at Papa. "Mr. Rosado?"

Papa gestured toward Rooster's father.

Señor Rosado slowly rose to his feet. Tony stood next to him, gripping one of his shoulders with white-knuckled fingers. He asked that Papa stay with them.

My heart was pounding so hard I thought I would pass out. "He's out of surgery," one of the doctors said, "but he may not come to for a while."

"What do you mean?" Tony asked.

The voices dropped low, which scared me. Both doctors were frowning and cupping their chins in their hands. Tony nodded intently as his fingers dug into his father's shoulders. Señor Rosado stared straight ahead as if he wasn't even listening.

It wasn't until the doctors escorted Tony and his father down the hall that I found out from Papa what was going on. I knew it was something terrible, because Mama had collapsed on a chair and was sobbing. Papa told me that Rooster had broken two vertebrae in the lower part of his neck. He'd come through the surgery successfully, with no apparent damage to his spinal cord. That was the "Good News."

"Thank God!" I cried with relief.

"But," Papa went on, his face grave, "he also suffered a concussion in the fall and has slipped into a coma."

My mouth went dry. "A *coma?* But why?"

Papa shrugged as he pulled me into a hug. "There was trauma to his brain when he fell—"

"To his *brain!* But that means—"

"Not necessarily. The tissues have swollen and unfortunately in the brain, there's no place for the swelling to go. But they're giving him medications right now to draw the fluids back out."

I nodded numbly, my head limp against my father's shoulder.

"The doctors say it doesn't appear to be a serious concussion," Papa went on as he drew his arm around me, "although with any brain injury, the swelling often gets worse during the first day or two. So they're gonna have to keep a real close watch on him."

I burst into tears and fled to the restroom, this time barely reaching the toilet before I lost the contents of my stomach.

When Tony came out of Rooster's recovery room a while later, he told us he'd put us on the list of immediate family and that we could see him as soon as they transferred him to intensive care, but only for a few minutes.

When I was finally able to see him, nothing prepared me for how frail he looked stretched out on that bed. There were tubes running out of his nose, arms, back, and legs, and machines that made whirring noises, in sharp contrast to the utter stillness of his body. Most of his head and upper body were encased in white bandages, and except for that little gap between his front teeth, you couldn't tell it was Rooster under all that.

I lay awake in bed for hours that night, bracing myself for the shrill ring of the phone. It would be followed by Mama's anguished cry as Tony told Papa the bad news. *Rooster had died during the night.*

I longed for the familiar creak of the bamboo to comfort me, but it was only a memory now. Instead, all I could hear was the rattling of the widowmaker's dying leaves as the wind of an approaching storm tore through them. It had gotten so there was scarcely a green leaf left on it. Papa wanted to take the tree out before it lived up to its name, but Mama wouldn't hear of it.

During the night, the storm took its toll on the old tree. In the morning, a heavy limb fell, just missing the chicken coop and the house. I woke up to the sound of my parents arguing bitterly outside my bedroom window.

The branch had already rotted before it had fallen, and broke into several pieces on impact. When I came outside, Papa was studying the wood.

"It's Rooster's tree," Mama insisted. "He'd be heartbroken."

"If I don't cut it, it'll come down on its own anyway," he retorted, his pipe bobbing up and down in his mouth.

"I'll not have you taking down that tree and that's final!"

"I'm getting my chain saw, Mattie!" he insisted. "The tree is going to hurt someone!"

"You're getting dressed is what you're doing. So we can go back to the hospital!"

The phone rang, interrupting them. They fell silent as Wendell yelled from the kitchen, "I'll get it!" I ran back to my bedroom and threw a pillow over my head to block out what I feared was bad news.

But just a moment later, Minnie yanked the pillow away from me and told me that Tony had called to report that Rooster had made it through the night.

I fell back with relief. Then I decided to call Jon and tell him what had happened.

I went out to the kitchen to make the call, but froze when I saw Rooster's goofy school picture still taped to the front of the rotary dialer. *If a picture drops from the wall for no apparent cause, someone will die,* Jewel's voice came to me. I jammed my finger down hard on the picture to make sure it was held securely, all the while telling myself that I didn't believe in Jewel's crazy superstitions. Then I dialed. When Jon picked up on the second ring, my voice came out all wobbly as I told him about Rooster's accident and that it was my fault.

"Kady, there's no way you could've known he'd do something crazy like that. Normal people don't leap out of trees."

"Well, Rooster isn't normal, and I should've known better than to let him get into those brownies!"

"You didn't let him get into those brownies—he helped himself."

"He wouldn't have if they hadn't been sitting out. They were in that Tupperware container. And nobody thought twice about it.

He had no idea what he was eating! I didn't know, either, the first time you gave them to me."

"Stop beating yourself up, Kady. You'll drive yourself nuts." There was a pause, followed by a long sigh. "You want me to come over?"

"Thanks, but I'm going back to the hospital. He's made it through one night, but that doesn't mean . . ." I started to cry.

"Kady, don't talk like that. I'll meet you at the hospital later, okay?"

I spent the remainder of the morning in Rooster's room, and when
my family finally left for a late lunch, I told them I needed to stay.
Señor Rosado sat nearby in a rocking chair with his eyes half-
closed, and his hands still clutching that small card he'd held in the
waiting room. He had some rosary beads, too. Tony hovered over
Rooster's bed like a clucking hen, unable to keep his eyes off the
various monitors attached to his brother's body. I asked the doctor
dozens of questions when he showed up, and was reassured that
even though Rooster was still in a coma, the swelling in his brain
hadn't gotten any worse and was, in fact, going down.

"Will he suffer permanent brain damage?" Tony asked.

I could tell it was a really hard question for Tony to ask,
because he had trouble looking the doctor in the eye.

"The fact that the swelling is going down is a good sign," the
doctor replied with a tight smile, "but we won't know the extent
of his injuries until he wakes up."

His evasive answer only seemed to upset Tony more. He
began vigilantly watching the monitors for any sign of change.

Then, when a tiny air bubble from the IV drip bag found its way into the tube leading to Rooster's arm a short time later, he frantically rang for the nurse. He'd heard that air trapped in IV tubes can stop a person's heart.

"A little bubble's not going to hurt him," the nurse told him. "It'd take a long line of air to stop his heart."

"I don't care how small the bubble is!" Tony barked. "I don't want *any* air in that tube!"

"Mr. Rosado, you must calm down or I'll be forced to ask you to leave," the nurse replied sternly.

"Come on, Tony," I found myself saying as I took him by the arm. "Let's get a Coke."

We went down to the second floor where the vending machines were and dug nickels and dimes out of our pockets. The Coke machine ate my money without giving me my soda, and in a burst of anger, I started kicking it.

"Miss Palmer, you must calm down or I'll be forced to ask you to leave," Tony replied in a voice that imitated the nurse's. Then he pointed to the red circle on the machine. "It's empty, see?"

I felt like a fool. "Oh."

He pushed the metal coin release and a shower of nickels and dimes fell to the little slot at the bottom. He put the money in another machine and handed me a cold can. "You need this Coke as badly as I do."

"Thanks," I said as I plopped down on a metal chair.

He got himself an Orange Crush, then sat next to me.

"When I filled out the admission form, I put his name down as 'Rooster.' The lady thought I was *loco*. She wondered why I was filling out the form in the first place when I'm only his brother." He traced the water beads that clung to the outside of his can and sighed. "I don't think *Papi* gives a damn if he lives or dies."

"Don't say that."

"Why not? He hasn't cared about anything since *Mami* died."

"Well, at least he's here. That's something."

"One little crumb. *¡Ay, caramba!*"

"Then why's he clutching that card so tightly if he doesn't care? The one with the picture of the Virgin Mary?"

"Did you see what's printed on it?"

I shook my head.

"*'Devuélvenos a Cuba.'* It means 'Return Cuba to us.' I'd give anything in the world for that to happen, but"—shaking his head—"I'm a realist. *Papi*, though, lives in the past. Even before the *Revolución* he was like that. I think that's why he's never accepted Rooster, because he's never let go of the boy he was supposed to be. He doesn't even know the boy buried under all those tubes."

He shook his head bitterly. "*Ay*, Kady, if it weren't for your family, I don't think I could get through this."

A wave of guilt washed over me.

"Listen," he went on awkwardly. "I know you don't see our relationship going the same way I do and that's okay.

I'm sorry about the kiss. I didn't mean to scare you or anything. I'm not even sure myself what came over me, except that the way you kissed me back made me think, well—" He pushed the hair from his face as he gave me that intense Cuban stare of his.

I dropped my eyes to the floor. I couldn't speak to him, couldn't even look at him or I knew I'd start to cry. There was no way he'd ever forgive me for what I'd done.

My mind raced. *If I didn't mention the brownies, he'd probably never find out the real reason Rooster had fallen. And neither would anyone else, because I was certain Jon and his friends wouldn't say anything. I would simply make the vow to myself to be Tony's friend—a real friend—from this point on. And if Rooster didn't make it, then I would devote the rest of my life to secretly making it up to Tony.*

But would I ever be able to look him squarely in the eye again without flinching? Without knowing that I was a coward and, worse yet, a traitor to everything he believed in? And to everything I believed in? For as much as I hadn't wanted to be Rooster's Madrina, *he'd picked me.*

"Don't worry," he went on with a little laugh. Then he gingerly touched the side of his jaw as if it still hurt where I'd slapped him. "I won't be grabbing you on any more plywood tables." His voice grew serious. "But we were friends first and that means a lot to me, especially now. *Aquellos son ricos que tienen amigos.*"

He was gently lifting my chin so that he could look straight at me as he spoke, with eyes wide and trusting. I'd never known him to be so tender. I felt a lump grow so big in my throat that I could hardly swallow.

"As for Rooster, why, he adores you. No matter what happens, you must remember that. It's why he calls you *Madrina.*"

I couldn't stand it anymore and burst into tears.

"STOP IT!" I cried. "I'm not his *Madrina,* okay? I never have been!"

But he still didn't catch on, still didn't realize what a traitor I was! His arm encircled my shoulder as he murmured, "*Ay, Kady, querida amiga mía*, we will get through this, you and—"

I yanked away from him and blurted out, "Rooster didn't fall out of a tree, Tony. He *leapt,* and it's . . . my fault."

He raked back his hair with a confused look. "Noooo, he fell out of a tree."

I shook my head. "No! He leapt just like Miz Sanders said. He was trying to catch Dandy and thought that he could—"

"You know Rooster has more sense than that! He would never *leap* out of a tree, especially one that far off the ground. He had to have been twenty feet up."

I rocked the Coke can uneasily on the table. "He would," I went on slowly as my heart began to pound, "if he thought he could fly."

"Fly!" He snorted with laughter. "Rooster isn't a fool!" His eyes narrowed. "Why are you saying these ridiculous things?"

"Well, because, because"—I bit down hard on my lip to steady myself—"I don't think it's such a farfetched idea under the circumstances."

"What circumstances?"

I squeezed my eyes shut. "That he was high."

"I know that."

I blinked at him, startled. "You do?"

"*Sí,*" he said with a wave of his hand. "About twenty feet. Miz Sanders even pointed out the branch from where he fell."

"No, no." My stomach turned to lead. "High as in *stoned.*"

"What?"

I forced myself to look straight at him. "He'd been eating brownies that had pot in them."

His face turned chalky white.

"You remember when I told you I felt like a 'cog in something turning' and you said I was stoned? You remember the brownies?" I went on slowly.

"*Sí.*"

"Well, you were right, you know. They did have pot in them."

He blinked at me in horror. "And Rooster ate some of those?"

I nodded.

His voice shot up an octave. "You *gave* him some!"

"Not exactly."

"Not exactly! What is 'not exactly!'?" He was on his feet now, staring down at me with eyes lit with fire.

I tried to keep my voice steady. "Well, Rooster showed up at the spring yesterday. You know, that place where we built those forts that summer?"

"Sí." He motioned for me to go on.

"I go there a lot these days"—I nervously bit my fingernail—"when Mama thinks I'm baby-sitting. Lots of kids hang out there."

"What kind of kids?"

"You know, from school."

"Since when?"

"Since the summer, I guess. It's just somewhere to go. And Rooster showed up yesterday. Maybe he heard the music coming from the car stereos, maybe he remembered it from when we used to go there, I don't know. But I think he was just looking for Dandy and stumbled upon it."

"And?"

"Well, he was upset because Dandy had flown off. He was afraid he was lost. Then some guy named Parker started teasing him—"

"Parker *Burton?*"

"You know him?"

"He's in my physics class. He was at the Stop 'n' Go with you the other day."

"That's right. He gave Rooster some chips."

He looked at me askance. "Kady, there were chips all over the floor when I found Rooster."

"Okay, so Parker threw them at him. I didn't like it, okay?"

He looked at me as if I'd stabbed him.

"Anyway," I went on as my voice started to wobble, "Rooster recognized him as the Chips Man. But Parker said he didn't have any more, so this girl named Madison felt sorry for him and told him to help himself to anything. There's always food lying around—when you're high you're starving all the time. It didn't occur to me, or to anyone else, that he'd get into the brownies. When he did, when I saw those crumbs around his mouth, I just—just—" I closed my eyes and shuddered.

"*¡Mira!*" he demanded.

I kept my eyes shut.

"Oh, I get it! You did the same thing you did at the store when Parker threw chips at him—*nada!*"

I forced my eyes to meet his.

"You were out of that store so fast. I figured you'd given him a handful of chips and he'd dropped them. I never would've thought you'd let something so humiliating happen to Rooster! And now you're telling me you got him high?"

"The brownies were lying around. He found them and ate them like the rest of us did. We were all high!"

"With one big difference. You knew you were high. He didn't!" he cried as he reduced his Orange Crush can to a wad of foil.

I brought my hands to my face. "I never thought anything bad would happen."

He looked at me as if I were the biggest idiot on earth. "*¿ESTÁS LOCO?* THIS IS ROOSTER WE'RE TALKING ABOUT!"

"I know, I know!" I nodded through sobs. "I wasn't thinking, okay? But it's making me crazy knowing I have a lot to do with him being here, and I thought you should know the truth."

"*¡La verdad!*" he wailed as he spun away from me. He walked around the room in a daze. Then suddenly he was right in front of me, eyes blazing. "Who brought the brownies to the spring?"

From the corner of my eye, I saw Jon walking through the doorway. I tried to turn so he wouldn't see me, but it was too late. His face lit into a sympathetic smile as he headed straight toward me. He was carrying an extravagant assortment of helium balloons, which splashed the stark room with color.

Tony, spying Jon the same time I did, whispered hoarsely, "It was him, wasn't it? The same *gusano* who got you high for the first time without your knowing it."

My face went pale.

Tony leapt in front of Jon. "*¡Gusano!*"

"Excuse me?"

"*¡GUSANO!*"

"What's your problem?" Jon demanded as he shifted the balloons from one hand to the other.

"You gave my brother your damn brownies!"

"Brownies?" he repeated nervously.

"You got him high the same way you got her high"—pointing to me—"without him even knowing it!"

"I didn't *personally* give him anythin—"

"*I'LL KILL YOU!*" Tony exploded as he slammed his fist into Jon's nose.

Jon fell to the floor, yelping in pain as the balloons scattered.

"TONY!" I screamed. I jumped in front of him before he hit Jon again.

Tony backed away, his hands still clenched. "Nobody messes with my brother! You got that?" He yanked a wad of napkins out of a dispenser on a nearby table and threw them at Jon, then stalked away.

"WHAT KIND OF A MANIAC ARE YOU!" Jon yelled after him as he cupped his hand over his nose. Blood streamed between his fingers, staining his white cotton shirt. "I CAME HERE TO SEE HOW THE KID WAS DOING, DAMMIT!"

With shaky hands, I began dabbing Jon's nose. "You're gonna have to hold your head back until the bleeding stops."

He jerked away from me. "What the hell did you say to him?"

"Just that—that—" I was shaking so hard I could barely speak, "—that Rooster got into the brownies."

He realized he was drawing a crowd and snarled, "Whatcha staring at? I'm fine, okay?" He waved everyone away. "Go on! Get!" Then, turning back to me, he said, "Why'd you mention the brownies?"

I swallowed hard. "I thought Tony should know the truth."

"The truth is that the kid fell out of a tree. It was an accident, Kady. An *accident!*"

I squeezed my eyes tight, wanting desperately to believe he

was right. That Rooster had simply lost his balance and fallen out of that tree. But I couldn't keep that image of him leaping into the air out of my mind, how he'd imagined the air rushing up to greet him, his arms like wings; how he'd truly thought he was Dandy's O Mighty Protector. *There was no way he would've leapt if he hadn't eaten those brownies!*

"Rooster didn't realize what he was doing eating those brownies any more than your baby sister realized what she was doing when she put that prong in her mouth," I blurted out.

He just stared at me.

"She was a baby, Jon, a baby!" I went on, even though my hands started to shake as his eyes burned into mine. "She needed protection."

"Don't say anything against Rosa," he warned as he tried to sit up.

"I only meant that if Rosa had been more careful—"

"That was an accident, too, Kady! And because of it, I lost the only person who ever gave a damn about me." He stared at me, red-faced, blinking back tears. A wad of blood-stained napkins dropped to the floor and blood began oozing again from his nose.

"I'm sorry about what happened to Rosa," I went on carefully, "I don't think she was a terrible person. I don't think we're terrible, either. Just careless! And because of it Rooster got into those brownies and—"

"The *brownies!* The *brownies!* The *brownies!* Why don't

you tell the whole damn world about Jon Hamilton's marijuana brownies!"

"I only told Tony," I said quietly.

"And you don't think he'll tell the whole world?"

"I wasn't thinking about that. I just thought he should know the whole story."

"What good does it do? These balloons could've been in the kid's room right now, but instead they're scattered to the four winds and I'm lying on some damn floor with a bloody nose! Where are your *priorities?* You ought to be using your energy helping the kid get better, not digging up muck!" He shook his head in disbelief. "All this time I thought you truly cared about me and were loyal to me. Now I know you're nothing but a backstabber!"

My eyes widened in shock. "How can you say that! I'm just trying to tell the truth, like I already told you. And the truth hurts me more than you! Because *I'm* the one Rooster trusted and *I'm* the one who let him down!"

"Well, you can bet your bottom dollar your little news about the brownies will spread like wildfire. And God help me when my old man catches wind of it." He glared at me. "I can't believe you're doing this to me. To *us.*"

"I'm not trying to hurt you!" My eyes filled with tears as I gave him a meaningful look. "I'm just trying to—"

"To *us!*" he sneered. "What a joke. I don't know who you are, Kady. Maybe I never did."

"Maybe I don't know who you are, either," I found myself saying.

He blinked at me painfully, the way someone blinks at a harsh light, before he managed to straighten himself up. Then he walked away, leaving behind bright drops of blood on the glossy linoleum floor.

I had an impulse to run after him, to tell him I was sorry. But in the end I just sat down in a metal chair and stared numbly at a balloon that had nudged against a fluorescent light. I wondered how close it would get before it popped.

"Is it true?" Mama asked, her face suddenly looming over me.

I was still in the cafeteria, staring numbly at the balloons, and jumped up, startled. "Mama, you scared me!"

"Is it true?" she repeated, her voice high-pitched and brittle. A protruding vein in her forehead pulsed with blood as she stared at me point-blank, and I knew that Tony had told her everything. I couldn't bear the way she was looking at me, and began absently gathering up the stray balloons, my hands shaking violently.

"Yeah, Mama, it's true." I swallowed, my throat closing with fear. "I'm really, really sorry."

Mama's eyes narrowed into slits. For a long, terrible moment, she didn't say a word. The gesture unnerved me even more than if she'd started yelling at me. Then she drew her car keys out of her pocket and jangled them in her hand. "I'm driving you home."

"Driving me home! Mama, I can't leave Rooster!"

I stormed toward the elevator and jammed my finger on the "UP" button. Mama stormed after me and jammed her finger on the "DOWN" button. Then, as the white "UP" light above the elevator lit up and the doors opened, Mama blocked my way.

"Mama! Get out of my way!" I cried as I tried to step around her.

An elderly man, who was also trying to get on the elevator, cleared his throat and said, "Excuse me." But Mama didn't budge.

"Mama! I need to see Rooster!"

The man mumbled something about the staircase and ambled away.

"Do you really think Señor Rosado or Tony want to see your lying face today, or ever again, for that matter?" Mama lashed out at me.

I felt my insides cave in.

"I don't have much use for you, either," she went on, her voice like ice water running down my spine. I stood there, unable to move as the doors shut behind her.

When the red "DOWN" light lit up a moment later—a triangular devil's pitchfork—I let go of the silly balloons and numbly followed her inside the elevator and on down to the parking lot.

We drove home in silence, Mama's hands clenched so tightly to the wheel that her knuckles gleamed. She jounced down the bumpy driveway, stopping long enough to deposit me at the front door, and without a backward glance whirled the car around—the tires grinding into sand and gravel—and headed back to town. I watched the taillights glowering at me as I stood in the growing darkness.

Jewel flipped on the porch light and peered into the twilight.

"What happened, Miss Kady? Is Roos—"

The sight of her warm brown eyes was too much for me. I threw myself into her arms, sobbing, "Jewel, Jewel, it's all my fault!"

At first her body was stiff with surprise, but then she drew my head to her shoulder and held me close. My tears soaked the cotton of her dress as she patted my hair, murmuring, "It's all right, Miss Kady. Everything's gonna be all right. . . ." She smelled of fried onions and laundry soap, familiar, comforting smells. For some reason that only made me cry harder.

Jewel just went on holding me and patting my hair.

Finally, I dried my eyes and told her everything. I was grateful she didn't say anything, just listened. Then, Grampsie poked her head out the screen door, demanding her supper. We went inside and for the next half hour I pushed my food around my plate, unable to eat a bite, while Grampsie gummed down two servings of mashed potatoes and redeye gravy. She had a wide-eyed, vacant stare and I knew she hadn't a clue what was going on. Afterwards, I helped Jewel put her to bed, and was about to crawl under my blankets myself when the station wagon chugged into the driveway.

I half-expected everyone to burst through the door, bickering as usual, but tonight they filed into the house like they'd come from a funeral.

"How's our boy?" Jewel asked, and Mama burst into tears. Wendell spoke up and said he was still in a coma. My mouth went dry when I saw the wounded look in Papa's eyes as they slowly met mine.

He motioned for me to come out to the front porch, where he told me how bitterly disappointed he and Mama were in me. "I can forgive you for a lot of things, Kady, but you lied to us." His voice shook as though he was trying to keep from crying, or yelling, I couldn't tell which. I expected Mama's anger, but the hurt in Papa's voice tore into me. I couldn't bear looking at him and buried my face in my hands.

As he spoke, Mama came outside and started screaming at me. I was too upset to hear what she said; all I caught were snatches— "liar," "pothead," "irresponsible" . . . I didn't know what to say to her. Every word was true.

It took Papa to finally calm her down enough to speak to me without screaming. By then, it didn't matter. I'd screwed up so badly that I didn't think anything was ever going to be okay again. And it wasn't over yet—Rooster was *still* unconscious, over a day now, after his surgery! I sat there with my face in my hands as they told me my punishment—a list of chores that made my head spin.

In addition, I was grounded for six months, which meant I could only go to school and back. Papa said my punishment would've been worse if I hadn't confessed the truth to Tony. It showed that at least I had a conscience. Then Mama cried out that if she ever caught me taking drugs again she'd call the cops on the spot, by golly, and have me hauled off to jail!

Then, barely taking a breath, she told me my first chore was to repaint the detached garage, a job that involved scraping off fifty years' buildup of paint. Papa said there was a lesson behind that particular assignment, something about "fresh starts."

"But I've already learned my lesson!" I broke down crying again. "Can't I at least be allowed to see Rooster?"

Mama was about to say something when the shrill ring of the phone startled us all. For a moment, nobody could move. *Nobody called this late, except in a crisis,* I thought as my heart began to pound. Then Minnie called from inside, "I'll get it!"

Mama told her not to touch it, then went inside and grabbed it herself. ". . . Hello?"

I held my breath, terrified that it was bad news. But a moment later, her face crinkled into a huge grin. "He . . . *did?*"

"Did what?" Papa rushed inside, the screen door banging behind him, shutting me out.

". . . *really?* . . . When?"

"Did what?" Papa repeated.

Mama held her hand over the receiver and said to him, "It's Tony. Rooster just now opened his eyes!"

"Thank God!" I cried, falling back with relief against the rickety railing surrounding the porch.

Mama talked to Tony for a few more minutes, pumping him with questions, before she reluctantly hung up.

Suddenly, I was on my feet, rushing into the house. "I've *got* to go see Rooster! Right now! *Please!*" I begged my parents.

Mama shooed me away, clearly unable to stand the sight of me, and for a moment, I thought Papa was going to do the same thing. But then, as I continued to beg, he finally said, "It's too late for visitors tonight, Kady. But you can ride your bike over to the hospital after school on Monday afternoon and see him. But only for a few minutes."

From the corner of my eye, I could see Mama glaring at him, but she remained silent.

I practically leapt into his arms, hugging him. "Thank you, Papa. Thank you! You'll never be disappointed in me again, I swear!"

"Now, now, you don't have to swear," he said, gently patting my shoulder. Then his face grew serious. "Just because Rooster opened his eyes doesn't mean he's out of danger, Kady. In fact," he sighed, "it's way too soon to get your hopes up."

Rooster's fall made front page news in the *Pomelo Courier* the next day: "Boy in Coma After Fall from Tree." Right under the headline was a huge photo of Rooster's school picture, the awful one with the plastered-down hair and studious smile. Although the article didn't mention anything about drugs, word about Rooster accidentally getting high on Jon's brownies spread like wildfire, and there was a follow-up article describing the spring as a "secluded, woodsy area that had become a popular hang-out for hippies."

It was right after the second article came out that a man dressed in a pinstripe suit showed up at Pomelo High at lunchtime, parked his mammoth Cadillac in the emergency zone, and marched straight into the attendance office. I was outside, sitting by myself, eating a baloney sandwich that had gotten squished in my locker, and stared at him, wondering who he was.

I didn't put together what was going on until after school when, out of the corner of my eye, I saw Charlotte making a beeline straight towards me. Her face was flushed, her fists balled, and the pointy heels of her new shoes bit into the concrete like nails. Trailing behind her were some of Jon's friends.

"Bitch!" she cried, practically spitting at me.

I whirled around to face her. "Excuse me?"

"BITCH!" she cried, loud enough for the whole school to hear.

I stood there stupidly before her, too stunned to move, wearing one of Jon's dresses—orange, with swirls of yellow flowers—while she went on to tell me that if I hadn't opened my big fat mouth and ratted on Jon, his father wouldn't have showed up at the school a while ago and packed him off to boarding school.

"Boarding school?" I cried out hoarsely. "What are you talking about?"

"*Military* boarding school, at that! And it's not even in this state!" she'd cried before stalking away.

It turned out Jon had been sent to Blackwell Academy, a Northeastern military boarding school that Mr. Hamilton himself had once attended. Jon never even called to say good-bye.

As the days went by, Rooster slowly emerged from his coma, moving his fingers and toes, then his arms and legs, and finally turning his head from side to side. He moved deliberately, not like the old Rooster at all. Once, he tugged wildly at his breathing tube, which prompted the staff to tie down his hands. But whenever he opened his eyes, he didn't seem to really see us. He never said a word, either. Only moaned.

I rode that rickety old bicycle to school every day so I could ride over to the hospital afterwards and spend a few minutes with Rooster before I began my marathon list of chores.

On that first afternoon I showed up in Rooster's room, Tony barred me from the door, crying, *"¡Lárguese!"* I didn't even want to know what it meant. Fortunately, there wasn't a nurse around, so I pushed past him. I pulled a metal chair from a hook on the wall and sat down next to the breathing machine with its tubes running every which way.

Much to my disappointment, Rooster was fast asleep. I leaned over him and gently called his name, but it was no use. So I studied the machines and tubes connected to the frail mound of his body: the IV tubes running from his chest and arms, the breathing tube covering his mouth like a scary Halloween mask, the thin feeding tube filled with whitish fluid that ran down his nose, the neck brace that circled his throat like an over-starched collar, the heart monitor that steadily bleeped, the breathing monitor with its sensitive, zigzagging needle that marked each breath of oxygen pumped into his chest, the shunt taped to his hand where they injected medications, some other tube connected to his big toe that I couldn't imagine the purpose of, and the catheter that ran from his hospital gown down the side of his leg and into a bag filled with yellowish red fluid.

The metal chair pressing against my bottom was cold and unyielding. As I sat there uncomfortably, Tony began fiddling with one of Rooster's tubes. There were dark circles under his eyes, his clothes were a wreck, and his hair so unkempt that he bore a striking resemblance to Rooster. I realized that he didn't have the energy to fight me.

Rooster remained in intensive care, with round-the-clock nurses monitoring his care. Mama and Tony became such permanent fixtures in the room that they started looking like furniture. The staff didn't seem to mind their presence, or anyone else's, as long as nobody moved too much, or got too close to Rooster, or, God forbid! yanked loose the electrical cords that ran along the floor and into the wall outlets. Most of the staff didn't even know that Mama wasn't his real mother. Señor Rosado would sometimes be there, but when he was, he was usually more out of it than ever. I'd often have to climb over his outstretched legs and listen to his loud snores in order to take my spot next to Rooster's bed.

Only the whir of the machines and visits by the nursing staff broke up the almost unbearable tension of everyone staring at Rooster's frail form. It was as if he were the centerpiece of a gruesome dinner, the way he lay atop that sheet-draped slab, with our chairs solemnly drawn around him. A sacrifice to a merciless god. Whenever he'd open his eyes and start to move, we'd call out his name and talk to him. I told him not to worry about Dandy, that he'd flown back home and was safe. But he still didn't seem know who any of us were, and we began to worry if he ever would.

One afternoon, when, by chance, I happened to be the only one in the room with Rooster, Madison Madison showed up carrying a huge, stuffed Snoopy dog.

I was so stunned to see her that I abruptly set down the math homework I'd just started. My grades had been slipping since Rooster's fall, especially in math, which I couldn't concentrate on. Its cold logic depressed me.

"Soooo," she said with a doleful smile, "how are you holding up?"

The question surprised me. Most people only asked how Rooster was doing. I gave her a guarded look. "As expected."

She handed me the stuffed dog and added, almost apologetically, "I didn't know what he'd like."

I couldn't help but smile at the dog. Its comical expression reminded me of Rooster. "This is perfect," I said as I put it on a far table so the nurse wouldn't have a fit. Anything brought into the room was supposed to be sterilized so Rooster wouldn't pick up any germs. "But you didn't have to do anything."

I wondered if she saw my hands shaking as I set the dog down. *What are you really here for?* I wondered. *To call me a bitch in front of the whole hospital?*

"Look," she said, as if reading my mind, "I'm sorry about the other day, you know, when Charlotte called you a bitch. She was really out of line." Then, after a beat: "We were all out of line."

I looked down—stunned—not sure whether to trust anything she said.

"The nurse said I could only stay five minutes since I wasn't family," she went on with a little smile. She looked uneasily at all the tubes and machines connected to Rooster. "Oh, God . . . I can't believe that's the same boy!"

"They say he'll put the weight back on pretty quickly," I said. My heart was pounding. She was being so kind, so normal.

"Are you sure that he's gonna . . . you know . . . be okay?"

"Well . . . we can hope."

She picked up a bottle of antiseptic soap and set it back down on the washstand. "I feel so guilty."

My mouth fell open. *Madison Madison felt guilty?!*

"Here I am offering him food when the brownies are sitting right out. I wasn't thinking!" A furrow appeared between her eyebrows and she looked genuinely distressed.

"None of us were," I said slowly.

"Then, later, when we all knew he was high, the way he was running around shrieking, we all thought it was funny." She shook her head with incredulity. "Dear God, Kady, what was wrong with us?"

I swallowed hard as tears of guilt-relief-pain flooded my eyes. "I don't know."

"Well," she said, glancing out the window as if to give me a moment to compose myself, "at least you didn't think it was funny when I was in the water with the alligator. Which is pretty amazing, considering . . ."

"Yeah, well, you hardly deserved getting attacked by an alligator."

She fell quiet as she studied the fluids slowly dripping through the IV tube. Then she said, "I thought you should know that Jean got a letter from Jon yesterday."

"Jean?" I felt a small, stabbing pain in my chest.

"Yeah, Jean." She looked me straight in the eye.

I tried not to show her any expression. I'd written him two letters—mostly nonsensical because I didn't know what to say—but they both came back with RETURN TO SENDER scrawled across the front in angry black marker. "Why her?" I asked as casually as I could muster. An image of Jean's sweet face flashed before my eyes and I knew the answer before Madison even spoke.

She shrugged. "Why you? Why me? I don't know why he picks who he picks. Except that they're always pretty and adoring."

"You were adoring?"

"For a while," she replied in an unusually soft tone of voice, a tone that made me certain that for all her tough-girl talk, she'd really cared about him, too.

I bit down on my lip to stop the trembling that had started there.

"He told Jean that he hates it up there. That it's like living inside a 'dirty Ping-Pong ball,' is I believe how he put it—gray dorms, gray skies, gray trees, gray uniforms, gray food, gray moods, gray-haired professors, an entire gray world you can't break out of." She paused a moment. "I think that's all of the grays he mentioned. Oh—*Grey*hound buses. It's the only way he can get around. His father took away his car."

I smiled in spite of my pain. Jon had always had an interesting way of putting things. "That grim?"

"Well, Jon's always been on the dramatic side. Still, I can't believe the way his father yanked him out of school!" She shook her head. "I didn't even get to say good-bye."

I pulled off a petal that was turning brown on a flower arrangement. "Me, either."

"Yeah," she sighed, "he's really angry . . . Maybe I shouldn't mention this, but he asked Jean if she—and well—if all of us were on his side."

"All of *us?*" I asked sharply.

"As opposed to your side. I thought that you should, well, know."

I nodded, unable to speak.

"She said he trashed you pretty bad in the letter. Blamed you for ruining his life and that sort of thing."

My temper flared. *So that was the real reason she was here. To make me feel worse than I already felt!* "I certainly didn't mean to ruin his life! I mean, who would've guessed his father would pack him off to boarding school!"

"Hey, calm down! I'm not here to give you a hard time."

I stared at her, uncertainly.

"I know you don't believe me, but it's the truth."

"I don't know what to believe anymore, or what's the truth!"

"Look, Kady, I do care about Jon, same as you do, whether you admit it or not. He's hardly the kind of guy you easily forget. And, of course, I hate seeing him getting stuck in boarding school. But this isn't about taking sides. Even though," she bit down on her lip, "some people may think so with the spring off-limits now."

"What do you mean, 'off-limits'?"

She looked at me, surprised. "You don't know?"

I shook my head.

She took a deep breath. "Mr. Hamilton's gone and bought it."

I looked at her in horror. "No!"

"Yep," she nodded. "All fifty-seven acres. He's already got a big sign next to the road: HAMILTON ENTERPRISES—BUILDER OF DREAMS."

After she left, I thought of the magnolia tree before the dynamite had killed it, the way its glossy limbs had grown perfectly evenly, in spite of being crowded on one side by bamboo. Madison was like that tree, not to be compromised by anyone. Rather, she was the type to step on the cracks and color outside of the lines if it suited her. Strange that I would begin to think of her as a friend.

When I came home from the hospital that afternoon, I couldn't believe my eyes. There was Grampsie, waltzing around the living room—or at least attempting to waltz, as her body didn't move like it used to. She was dressed in a stunning gown that shimmered and crinkled when she moved, and had a wide, toothless grin on her face.

The gown looked eerily familiar, with leg-of-mutton sleeves festooned with maroon bows, and a flounced skirt that nearly required a hoop for all its yards of ruffles. The bodice was cut so dangerously low you could see her shriveled breasts hanging like thick ropes against her bony chest. The puffy sleeves were so oversized on her tiny frame that they looked liked wings. Her hair was piled atop her head with a mishmash of bobby pins holding it in place and silly bows were pinned haphazardly about. Her mouth was coated with lipstick that bled clownishly beyond the natural boundaries of her lips.

Mama had finally gotten rid of Grampsie's tree-climbing boots, and bought her three pairs of bedroom slippers.

Grampsie was now wearing a purple slipper on one foot and a pink slipper on the other. On the stereo, Andy Williams was crooning "Never On Sunday" in a hokey Italian accent from the only record album we owned.

I looked at my family huddled about the dining room table, with eyes popping. "What's going on here?" I asked Papa.

"The UPS man showed up about an hour ago with a package while she happened to be in the living room," he said. "She didn't want to get the door because, well, you know, she wasn't respectable. But I called out to her to go ahead and answer it, that it was only the UPS man. I was busy helping your Mama unclog that new disposal she keeps putting too many potato peelings into." Papa glanced at Mama.

"But it's a disposal," Mama piped up. "It's supposed to grind up everything from T-bones to corncobs."

"Corncobs!" Papa cried. "Now, you know better than that, Mattie."

"But it said so on the brochure, Barney."

"Why, you know you can't read a brochure."

"Maybe not all of it. But I can spell corn. C-O-R-N."

"Well then, it probably said corn *husks*. But anyway, Kady, next thing I know, your grandma's sobbing real loud. So we come rushing into the living room thinking she's hurt, and find her huddled under a pile of wrapping paper, clutching this gown to her chest."

"It turns out she was sobbing with joy," Mama explained

without looking directly at me. She was still so angry at me because of Rooster that she never looked directly at me as she spoke—now she was staring vaguely at my hair. "She said the gown was from Dear Walty and that it was a profession of his love for her in spite of her missing teeth. Then she came sashaying out here a while ago all dressed up, announcing she was going to the ball."

"The ball?!"

Papa shook his head wearily. "We did our best, of course, to keep a straight face. It was your mother's idea to turn on the stereo so she could practice her steps until Dear Walty arrived."

"The music hasn't stopped since," Mama sighed. "She's got it on 'repeat.' And I need to get on down to the hospital to check on Rooster."

I started to tell her that he still didn't recognize anybody, then I blinked at the gown. Was it the gown Jon had promised to send me before we broke up? I blinked again. It had to be! "Oh my God, that's my—my—"

Papa gave a stiff nod. "We saw the return address." He stopped without saying more. Jon was a sore subject, to say the least.

I fell into a chair, my head reeling. He'd gotten me a near-replica of my china doll's gown! That had been the surprise.

I nearly burst into tears as I watched my shriveled grandmother waltzing about in my gown.

Had Jon forgotten to cancel the order? Or had he intentionally let the gown come as a cruel reminder of what I'd lost?

I couldn't get over how beautiful it was, with its incredible attention to detail. No wonder Jon said he'd had to stop and catch his breath when he saw it. And yet, there was something strangely odd about it. Something comically out of place. Something that had nothing to do with my foolish grandmother. I envisioned myself fast-dancing to something like "Honky Tonk Woman" in it at the Valentine's Dance and started laughing so hard that I had to excuse myself.

But once outside, as I walked through the grove, glowing with fruit, I remembered how tender Jon had been when he'd told me about my "surprise."

"I can just see you in this gown, just picture us together on that dance floor, swirling like a top until all the colors are one. . . . "

I slumped against the smooth bark of an orange tree, my laughter giving way to tears as I remembered the blissful, drowsy contentment I'd felt in his arms that day. The memory of Jon's laugh, his smile, and the touch of his fingers stroking my cheek seemed so vivid that I was filled with unbearable emptiness.

I went back to my bedroom, slammed the door against Andy Williams's nonstop singing, and stared at a copy of the picture Mama had taken of us until tears blurred the image. After a while, I wrote Jon another letter. This time it was an outpouring of such passion that it made me blush. I was willing to do anything to save our relationship. But by the time I rode my bike to the post office—where I'd planned to mail the letter "Certified" so he'd have it right there in his hands—it seemed such a stupid mess of clichés such as "Love Will Conquer All," and "I Love You Always and Forever" that I ended up going to the convenience store across the street instead and dropping it into the trash can. I then bought the biggest package of Lorna Doones they sold, sat down on a little bench, and gobbled them up all by myself.

The following afternoon, when I got home from the hospital, I saw Jewel hanging up the wash and rushed up to her. For in spite of eating all those cookies and thinking I was over Jon, I'd gone to bed that night missing him all over again. Why was love so confusing? I wasn't exactly sure what I wanted Jewel to say, but I was surprised when she told me that she'd known for a good while that Jon wasn't right for me.

When I asked her how she figured that, she told me about the sign she'd seen. I told her I didn't put much stock in signs, but she told me the whole story anyway. Just days before Rooster's fall, she'd pulled into the Stop 'n' Go and was digging out quarters and dimes from the bottom of her purse to buy gas with, when she saw Jon inside the store. She recognized him from the picture Mama had taken. He was standing in the Paper Goods aisle, staring at the rolls of paper towels as he held a quart of oil. She didn't think much about it, until she happened to notice that the "O" was missing from the sign over his head.

"Huh?" was all I could manage to say.

"One of the 'O's' wasn't there. So instead of reading 'PAPER GOODS,' the sign read, 'PAPER *GODS.*'"

"So?"

"So!" She let out an exasperated sigh. "Did I ever tell you 'bout the time I was fifteen, traveling through Georgia on the back of a hay truck?"

"No," I said as I pulled a pillowcase around my head like a shawl.

"Well," she said as she snatched the pillowcase away from me and pinned it on the line, "my Pa threw me out after he lost his job for the umpteenth time. Never did last long any one place, but that's another story. Anyway, I started walking down the road, didn't know I where I was headed or nothing, just liked the idea of going somewhere. After a while, this hay truck pulled up alongside of me and asked me if I wanted a ride." She paused and shook her head. "Mmmm hmmm, I should've been paying more attention."

"To what?"

"The *sign*, Kady. That truck stopped right next to an old Stuckey's Restaurant billboard that had the last two letters of 'Stuckey's' washed out. So instead of saying 'Stuckey's,' it said 'Stucke' just as plain as the nose on my face. Mmmm, hmmm, I'm a tellin' you. . . . When that truck driver stopped for lunch at one of them roadside eating places, I managed to get me a job fixing hamburger platters and malted milk shakes," she mumbled as a clothespin bobbed up and down in her mouth.

"Well, it was a job, Jewel. Isn't that what you wanted?"

She shook her head firmly. "No ma'am, it was a terrible place. The manager, why, he was plumb crazy. And I was STUCK there for two years!"

"And you think the Stuckey's sign had something to do with it?"

She nodded soberly.

"Oh, Jewel, that's a lot of superstitious bull!"

"That boy now," she went on without paying me a bit of attention, "was standing right under that missing 'O'!"

I shook my head, baffled. "So what? I can't imagine what it meant, if it meant anything at all. Unless that he was STUCK there!" I laughed at my own joke.

"He was standing under a sign that clearly read, 'PAPER GODS'!"

"Well, I guess that means he's some kind of a god then, someone deserving of worship. . . ." My voice softened. "Lord knows there was a time I sure did worship him."

"A god of paper? Humph! What kind of a substance is paper, honey child?"

I shook my head again, irritated by the conversation. Nobody but Jewel could follow Jewel's logic!

"Flimsy!"

I stared at her.

"Guys like Jon only appear strong," she added with a snort as she shook out a pair of my father's boxers.

"Well, I don't guess I'm any stronger than Jon," I said. "I'm responsible for what happened to Rooster more'n anybody, 'cause I know how he is. And I was really ticked when he showed up at the spring because he was his usual drive-everyone-crazy self!"

"And you've been agonizing over it every day, too, haven't you?"

"Well, of course."

She shook out a T-shirt and pinned it on the line. "Then you're stronger."

"Why do you say that?"

"'Cause that's not what Jon's off at that school agonizing over, now is it?"

"I don't know what's going through his mind these days. He won't even answer my letters."

"What do you think that boy's agonizing over?"

I thought about it for a moment. "That I told Tony about the brownies. That I betrayed him."

"And did you?"

I thought about it a little longer, then slowly shook my head. "I don't think so." Then, giving it more thought, I firmly said, "No. Tony needed to know the whole story. Even though he may never speak to me again." As I spoke, I felt as if something very heavy was being lifted from my back. Muscles I hadn't even realized were tense began to relax.

"There you go." She shook out a pillowcase. "You're stronger, see, 'cause you can face the truth. Not shrink from it and pile blame on somebody else. And bein' strong's what helps you get through life intact."

I thought about all that as I pinned up several of the pillowcases. Then I straightened myself a little and said, "You know what I did yesterday?"

She shook her head.

"I ate an entire package of Lorna Doones all by myself."

"Say what?"

"I ate an entire package of Lorna Doones all by myself," I repeated as a grin slowly spread across my face. "I know that sounds stupid, but you know what I just figured out? That's a sign, too."

In the middle of the night, I heard voices outside my window.
At first I thought I was dreaming, but then I distinctly heard
Grampsie's peal of laughter. I stumbled out of bed, peered
through the darkness, and saw her dim form in the moonlight.
I'd thought Mama had hidden the gown away, but Grampsie
was wearing it now as she awkwardly swayed among the new
shoots of bamboo that were pushing up through the ground like
freshly sharpened pencils.

Her bedroom slippers were so thin that I was worried the
bamboo would pierce through them. But she seemed blissfully
unaware as her arms—raised like misplaced wings—embraced
an imaginary dance partner. Dear Walty had finally taken her
to the ball.

I started to go after her when I heard the screen door slam.
Mama and Papa had beat me to it.

"Honestly, Ma, you're lucky you didn't trip on that bamboo.
It's sharp as a razor!" Mama's voice rang out, harsher than I'd

ever heard her speak to Grampsie. "Get back inside before you make a complete fool of yourself!"

"Let me handle this, Mattie," Papa insisted. He nudged Mama away—a gesture I'd never seen before—as he led his mother back inside. Grampsie's face crumpled with disappointment at being led home early. But then, as she got closer to the bright outdoor light, her arm latched onto Papa's and she looked frightened and disoriented.

I went back to bed, and for a long time I lay there, listening to Papa tucking Grampsie back in bed as if she were a small child. I began to toss and turn, wishing he'd tuck me in bed, too, like he used to when I was small. I could almost hear his off-key voice singing to me about playmates climbing apple trees. *Oh, what was the name of that song?* It seemed so long ago and fuzzy now. I had learned so much, grown up so much, in a very short time. What I wanted now was a safe place to come to, but I didn't know if that was even possible anymore.

I flung off the covers and crept down the hall. Grampsie was already sound asleep, her snores already rumbling through the thin walls, and Papa had closed the door to my parents' bedroom.

I wandered outside into the cool moonlight. The chickens were squawking, so I went ahead and fed them. None of us paid attention to them the way Rooster did. As for Dandy, he hovered around Rooster's front porch squawking forlornly.

As I was leaving the coop, I heard a cry coming from the

widowmaker tree. A human cry. The tree was shrouded in darkness. "Who's there?" I called out, fearful of what could be lurking in the darkness.

"Get me out of this confounded tree!" the voice pleaded.

"Mama?" I called out, dumbfounded.

"GET ME OUT!" came the muffled bellow.

Fear gave way to laughter. "Oh my God! You're stuck in the tree!" I leaned down beside the opening and felt a swath of material. It didn't budge.

"Papa may have to cut down the tree to get you out."

"Not in my lifetime," Mama snapped. Her foot emerged, followed by a knee, then another foot, another knee, and feeling a bit like a midwife about to perform a breech birth, I yanked the rest of my mother from the hollowed trunk by her ankles. "It's a live birth!" I cried. "A six-hundred-pound girl!"

"Cut that out!" she groaned as she lay sprawled on the ground. Even in the faint moonlight, I could see that she was covered with the charred markings of the tree.

"What were you doing in there?"

"Oh . . ." she struggled to sit up. "Just praying."

"*You* praying? Since when?"

A tear spilled from her eye.

I strained my eyes to see her better. "Mama? Are you all right?"

She buried her face in her hands and started to cry.

I sat down beside her, among the acrid smell of chicken droppings. "Mama, what's wrong?"

"Your grandmother, we've lost her. She might as well be a ghost dancing among the bamboo."

"Yeah," I sighed, "she's getting worse."

"I don't think, I really don't think I can take any more sadness around here," she went on between sobs.

"Well, at least she's happy like this," I said.

Mama pulled out a hankie she kept crammed inside her bra, and blew her nose in a hard honk that set the chickens squawking. "If only you'd known her when she was younger. She grew up in the scrub country. Never had any luxuries like flush toilets or air-conditioning until she came to stay with us."

I blinked. "Since when did we have air-conditioning?"

"Don't know how she got this silliness with Walter Cronkite in her mind," she went on as if she hadn't heard me. "Couldn't *believe it* when I saw her in that fancy gown yesterday." She turned to me sharply. "What was it for, anyway? A costume party?"

"No," my face flushed, "just a dance."

Mama gritted her teeth and snarled, "If I'd had any idea that boy was involved in drugs—"

"Mama, please! Let's not talk anymore about Jon!"

She fell silent a moment, then straightened herself. "The old Sadie never would've been caught dead in a gown like that. She was a lot like my own mama, full of spit and fire. I think Sadie was part of the reason why I married your pa."

I looked at her curiously. "You've never told me much about Grandma."

"Well," she took a deep breath, "she was strong all her life, until one day, when she was only twenty-six, she caught the flu and it settled in her lungs. She dropped dead in a cotton field right beside me the day after my seventh birthday. There was a boll of cotton still clutched in her hand when they carried her away."

She paused as she massaged her kneecap. "After she died, Pa brought us down to Florida, away from the sad memories. But times were tough, and we had to go to work in an orange processing plant, like where your papa's now a supervisor. We worked there twelve hours a day, six days a week. The owners, who weren't nothing like your papa, didn't care that we were just kids."

She began to snatch at the stray blades of grass beside her. "There was a train that ran behind our shanty that always woke me up at one-forty-two every morning. You could set your watch by it, so they say. I couldn't afford one. I remember watching it race past my window one night when I wasn't much older than you, and thinking that my life was like that train, racing along into nothing but darkness." She tore at the grass, shredding it into pieces. "One night, I wandered down to the tracks and sat right down on 'em, waiting for that train. It felt so good just to *sit down*. . . ."

I stared at her profile, stunned. "Surely you didn't mean to—"

"But when I felt that train barreling down on me, I just couldn't go through with it. I jumped up at the last second and went back to bed. Never told a soul about it. Just got up at four-fifteen the next morning, same as usual, and went back to culling oranges on the conveyor belt.

"Years later, I'd still dream I was culling them stupid oranges. That was my job, twelve hours a day. Looking for split and rotten fruit and tossing it off. And sometimes in the mornings, I'd get up, fixin' to go to work, then find a surprise looking back at me in the mirror. *Who's that wrinkled lady with the double chin? Where'd her life go?* Because the truth is, something died inside of me that night on the tracks."

"Well," I said after a long, awkward moment of silence, "that was a long time ago. Things are better now."

"Yeah," she nodded. "But it took Rooster's mother's death for me to really feel—oh, I don't know—alive again."

"Rooster's mother's death!" I echoed, stunned. *What about when you married Papa? When you had us? Didn't you feel alive again, then? Or are we just the split and rotten fruit?*

She nodded absently, lost in her thoughts. "I was down at the end of the driveway getting our mail shortly after her death when I heard Rooster screaming at a car that had just passed: '*COME BACK! I'VE G-G-G-OT MY SHOES ON!*' I was afraid he'd get run over the way he kept screaming that, so close to the highway. So I grabbed him up in my arms and started to take care of him."

Her face transformed into a soft smile. "He'd be wearing a shirt that needed mending, so I'd sew it up. Or a scrape that needed tending and I'd pour on the peroxide. First time I used that peroxide I expected him to cry, but instead he howled with laughter. Couldn't figure it out until I noticed he was watching all the bubbles ooze up from where it was dirty."

She started to laugh, then stopped herself and slowly turned to me. "I can't believe that boy's in the hospital fighting for his life. Can't believe that you—that you—"

I felt sick. "Put him there?"

She didn't reply, just stared at me with that broad, sooty face.

"Oh God, Mama! How many times do I have to say I'm sorry?"

I woke up Saturday morning to the sound of chain saws. Papa and Wendell were cutting down the widowmaker tree. Another branch had fallen at dawn and Papa said he wasn't ready to become a widower. Mama was staring tight-lipped through the kitchen window when I got up. I started to say something, but decided against it. Things were bad enough as it was.

As the sound of chainsaws wore on throughout the morning, the tension in the house grew almost unbearable. With each falling piece of wood, Mama shuddered as if her own arms and legs were being ripped off. She kept me in the kitchen where we worked silently side by side, tending to the breakfast chores, then scrubbing down the kitchen senselessly and feverishly. I dared not leave, but grew more miserable with every passing moment. Not only did she want the floors mopped and waxed, but also wanted the cupboards and countertops washed down with Clorox. My eyes began to sting—and still she came up with things to do. I waited for her to tire so I could slow my pace, but she kept on toiling away.

Then, just after my waxed floor had dried to a nice gloss, Sammy spilled some chocolate milk on it and rushed out of the room without bothering to clean it up. I grabbed a wad of paper towels since I couldn't find any clean rags, and started wiping it up. The paper towels were no match for a puddle of liquid, though, and shredded in my hands. "Damn it!" I yelled, staring at the flimsy paper.

"I was thinking," Wendell said, helping himself to a meat loaf sandwich as we sat down for lunch, "it would be a waste to use all that wood just for firewood."

"Most of it's too rotten for anything else," Papa said.

"Yeah, but some of it's good. I know this sounds depressing and I don't mean it to be," he went on as he poured ketchup on his sandwich and spread it around with a knife. "I was thinking we could use it to make . . ."

"Go on," Papa prodded.

"Well, I thought it might make a nice coffin for Rooster," he blurted out.

"Lord sakes!" Mama gasped.

"I want him to live like everybody else does, but he's connected to that tree and I thought that if he doesn't make it, because he's not—you know—really responding, then—"

Mama slammed her fist on the table, knocking over her iced tea. "GET OUT!"

We all watched the tea wash over the table and drip on the floor without making a move to clean it up.

Wendell started backing away from her, his hands flung outward. "Mama, I didn't mean to upset—"

She came towards him waving a serving spoon. A piece of carrot flew off and landed on Sammy's plate. He stared at it, too scared to laugh.

"WHY, EVERYONE KNOWS HE'S GETTING BETTER! HE *SMILED* AT ME TODAY. I'M SURE OF IT! I'LL NOT HAVE YOU OR ANYONE ELSE SPEAK OF HIM AS IF HE WERE . . . WERE . . ." She started to shake and couldn't go on.

There was a long, awkward moment when the only sound was the tea dripping steadily onto the floor.

Then Papa cleared his throat and spoke up, "He meant it as a loving gesture, Mattie. Don't be ups—"

"Hush!" she barked at him. "Just hush! You the one who took down the tree, you chain saw massacrer!"

"Mattie! There wasn't a choice!"

"—And now"—pointing a finger at Wendell—"he wants to take down Rooster!"

"That's bull, Mama! I love him, too!" Wendell cried in a raspy voice. A tear spilled from his eye, ran down his nose, and dropped to the floor.

"And it all began with you, ma'am!" she cried, pointing her serving spoon at me.

I stared at her in horror.

"Hush, Mattie!" Papa demanded. "Can't you see how she's hurting? How everybody here is hurting!"

Mama clamped her mouth shut and dropped her hand. Yet I could tell by the way the serving spoon shook in her hand that she had plenty more she wanted to hurl at me.

But the words she'd said were already exploding in my head. I screamed back at the top of my lungs, "WELL, TOO BAD IT'S NOT *ME* ON THE BRINK OF DEATH, 'CAUSE YOU SURE WOULDN'T MIND USING THAT WOOD FOR *MY* COFFIN!"

A stunned silence swept the room, and for what seemed like an eternity, the only sound that could be heard was the slow, maddening drip . . . drip . . . drip . . . of the tea as it splattered on the hard linoleum floor. That, and the pounding of my heart as my eyes locked with Mama's.

Then all at once she was shaking her head, as if to shake the image of me from her sight. "STOP IT!"

"IT'S THE TRUTH!" I yelled back as my eyes flooded with tears. "BECAUSE I'M NOTHING MORE THAN—THAN THE SPLIT AND ROTTEN FRUIT!"

"STOP THIS CRAZY TALK!" she hollered back as she waved that ridiculous spoon. "STOP IT, RIGHT NOW!"

I heard the spoon clatter to the floor and for a fleeting instant I thought she was going to tell me, "Of course it's not the truth," and maybe even hug me.

But instead, she mumbled something under her breath that I couldn't hear, then shook her head again and fled the room.

I stood there foolishly, my toes curling to grip the surface of the linoleum floor as I sought something firm to hold onto. But its freshly waxed surface was too slippery to lend support.

"I'm sorry, Kady," Wendell said, his Adam's apple bobbing furiously. "I didn't mean to start something."

It was the first time I'd ever known Wendell to apologize for anything.

"It's not your fault," I managed to say as tears flooded my eyes.

"No, son, it's not," I heard Papa's firm voice.

And then Papa was pulling me into his wiry arms. "Here, here, my split-and-rotten fruit," he said as he pressed my head against his shoulder. He laughed a little. "Where'd you come up with that?"

"It doesn't matter, she doesn't love me," I cried hoarsely into his smoky shirt.

"She does," he replied, "in her own way."

Wendell put aside the wood he'd earmarked for the coffin and spoke of it no more. The freshly sawed-off wood of the widowmaker stump, which jutted about two feet off the ground, seemed a painful enough reminder of everything that had gone awry in our lives. Papa was going to pull out the hollow, charred stump just as soon as he could get ahold of a stump remover. Then, Jewel got the far-fetched idea that if we carved Rooster's name in the stump, his spirit would inhabit the tree and give it new life. And that the tree, in turn, would regenerate Rooster. Or something like that. Even though we didn't really believe it, Papa laboriously carved "CARLOS 'ROOSTER' ROSADO" in the dead wood anyway.

After that, hardly a day went by that someone didn't inspect the stump for some sign of new growth. Even Señor Rosado started coming around it. He told us not to scoff at the notion that the tree might have regenerative powers, that back in Cuba the ceiba tree was considered sacred.

Yet the only form of life that appeared around that old

widowmaker stump were termites, which began boring their way into the graying wood. Then early one morning, it was so foggy that I could barely make out the stump's dark, squat shape as I fed the chickens. It bore no resemblance to the towering tree it once was, but instead took on the eerie resemblance of a tombstone— one with Rooster's name already carved on it!

When I told all this to Jewel, she leaned over and gently cupped my chin in her hand and said, "That ole stump takes on more forms than you're giving it credit for. Sounds like your fears are getting in the way of a proper reading of the signs."

Early one February morning, as the sun began to slant through his window, Rooster woke up, turned to Tony and mumbled, "R-R-Rooster w-w-w-want *tostones*. . . ." Tony's cry of joy could be heard throughout the entire wing of the hospital. "*¡A DIOS GRACIAS!* HE CAN TALK! HE CAN TALK! HE'S GONNA BE OK!" Rooster grinned at him with bewilderment as he drifted back to sleep, wondering what he'd said to cause such a ruckus.

Two weeks later, Tony brought Rooster home in that piece of junk he'd finally turned into a pickup truck. It was quite a sight seeing them coming down that driveway past the orange trees. The trees' boughs were weighed with bright orange fruit that shone like welcoming beacons. The pickup had a motor louder than an airplane taking off as it rattled towards us, in sharp contrast to Rooster, who sat solemnly on the passenger's side. His pale head looked like a fragile egg carefully balanced on that stiff neck brace.

Only his ridiculous hair—as long as I'd ever seen it, and waving like bedsprings in the breeze—reminded me of the real Rooster. You would've thought the hospital staff would've given him a proper haircut before they sent him home, but they'd just shaved off an area near the base of his neck and let the rest go its natural, wild way.

Mama, Papa, and Señor Rosado were cramped together in the backseat, along with the big Snoopy dog, who was almost entirely shoved out the window. They looked like something from the cartoons.

As soon as the car stopped, Mama and Señor Rosado rushed out of the backseat and opened Rooster's door. I'd never seen Señor Rosado look as good as he did when he helped Rooster out of the pickup. His shirt was tucked in, the long strands of hair that usually fell in his eyes were combed back, and he even smelled good. Wendell, Sammy, Minnie, and I stood with eager anticipation just yards away.

Tony leaned over and steered Rooster into Mama's waiting arms, then quietly gathered up his things. We'd barely exchanged a single word since he'd tried to bar me from Rooster's hospital room. During the week after Rooster came to, Tony was so beside himself with joy that he talked almost nonstop to Rooster (who had remained subdued and bewildered by his surroundings), and to my family. He even hugged everyone—including Papa—but whenever he came near me, he stared through me as if I were air.

As soon as Rooster stepped out—a jumble of bony elbows, knobby knees, blindingly white new Keds that looked like giant teeth, and that oversized wobbly head—tears overwhelmed me. I rushed up to him and gave him a hug, and was stunned by how bony he felt. I pulled back as Dandy started honking from the chicken coop.

Rooster glanced up and blinked at his goose, who was hopping towards him. And yet, to the amazement of all of us, when Dandy reached him in a great big blur of feathers and joyful honks, Rooster shrunk back.

We looked around at one another, surprised. "Why, Rooster, Dandy's here to welcome you," Mama said encouragingly.

Rooster looked at her as if he were going to cry.

"Yeah, Roos," we all chimed in.

For the next several minutes, we tried to get him to respond to Dandy by keeping up a flood of encouraging talk while Dandy pecked and squawked at his feet. And just when we thought his face was transforming into a glimmer of a smile, his eyes widened in horror and his breathing came in ragged gulps.

"He sees the stump!" Mama whispered. She turned to him in her cheeriest voice. "Come on, Rooster, let's get you something to eat!" She started to whisk him toward his house, but he yanked himself free as a low, guttural cry came from deep within him. The sound grew in intensity until he was shrieking.

Everyone struggled to calm him down, terrified he might suffer a relapse. But his hands and legs flew everywhere at once. It took Tony, Papa, Señor Rosado, and Wendell to carry him into his house. And even from there we could still hear his screams.

After that, Rooster wouldn't go outside. Instead, you could hardly coax him out of bed. Before long, his limbs became as pale and thin as shoots sprouting from onions kept too long in storage, and his head looked even bigger and wobblier than ever. Sammy said he looked like Mr. Potato Head, but Mama made him hush up. And Dandy, who honked forlornly outside his window, only made him retreat more. "T-Tell him to sh-shut up!" he would yell, jamming his fingers into his ears.

I asked Tony what I could do to help Rooster, but he just slapped me away like a mosquito. I knew he was alone with Rooster a lot of the time, though, since Señor Rosado was off on another buying spree. This time he was stocking up on a new indoor-outdoor carpet called "Terrific Terrain." He envisioned carpeting all of Florida in the fake grass so nobody would have to mow their lawns again. For once, he bought something people wanted, if not for their yards, for their patios. They were carting it off as quickly as he purchased it from the wholesaler. He used some of the profits to buy the family's first color TV. After that, you couldn't even talk to Rooster. It was as if that TV had sucked him right into it.

Tony didn't slap Mama away like a mosquito when she came over to help Rooster. She brought him every sort of food she could imagine to get him to eat. Even chicken with *mojo* sauce! But he wasn't hungry. She tried to tell him stories, but he wouldn't listen. There was a physical therapist who came out to help Rooster, too, but even she had trouble coaxing him to do simple things like walking around and exercising his arms.

It was Minnie who came up with the perfect idea to bring back the old Rooster—make him a dollhouse of his very own. As she told me about her idea, her big blue eyes sparkled and her brown hair—as springy as Mama's—bounced, and I realized she was getting pretty. Together, we scrounged around the Rosados' yard and found an old wooden crate Señor Rosado said we could have. We covered the insides with shelf paper and started filling it up with homemade furniture and lots of PEE PULL.

It surprised me how creative Minnie was when it came to making furniture. She took a plain block of Styrofoam and covered the sides with some lace from an old dress, then the top with one of Mama's potholders to make a bed. When she was finished, it looked as if she'd put a quilted bedspread over a bed ruffle. We used old spools of thread for stools, blocks of wood for chests of drawers, and an upturned coffee mug for a table. We put a doily over it for a tablecloth and put some Cheerios on poker chips for a donut breakfast. Hooked potholders and washcloths worked great for rugs.

In the back of the dollhouse, we used old window screening to make a chicken shed and filled it with straw. We made tiny chickens out of balls of cotton and used aspirin tablets for eggs to put inside the nests, which we made out of Spanish moss. It was the first time in years that Minnie and I did something together without fighting. And Mama didn't get after us once about our neglected chores.

Yet, for all that work, when we carried it over to Rooster's house—where we found him half asleep in front of the blaring TV—he just shrugged.

"Rooster!" we exclaimed, stunned by his indifference. "This is your dollhouse. We made it for you."

He waited until a commercial—a boy transforming from a scrawny eight-year-old kid into a beefy teenager, all because he ate Wonder Bread that "builds strong bodies twelve ways"—before he bothered looking at it again.

I turned the volume of the TV way down so I wouldn't have to scream over the "Hmm Hmm Good!" Campbell's soup commercial that came blasting forth next. "Look, Rooster, we even put your school picture on the wall." If nothing else interested him about the dollhouse, I was sure that seeing his mug on the wall would!

"*Sí,*" he sighed, then turned his attention back to the TV as Quick Draw McGraw bounded onto the screen twirling his pistol.

Minnie was incredulous. "What's wrong with you, Roos? We spent days making this dollhouse just for you."

He shrugged, his eyes riveted to the TV. After a few minutes of watching Quick Draw McGraw save the day with his quick-drawing pistols, he forgot we were even there.

When I told Jewel how despondent Rooster was acting and how he wouldn't even go near the stump—which, in case she hadn't noticed, was as dead as a doorknob—she just shook her head. "Remember all them shoes he used to cart everywhere, thinking that if only he'd had his shoes on, his mama wouldn't have left him that day?"

I nodded.

"He never went without shoes because he never went without hope that she'd come back."

"But he stopped wearing them after a while."

"Only when time made her memory grow dim. But he'd still look for her from time to time."

I nodded.

"What he never faced was that she wouldn't always be there for him, that she had limits. And now he has to face the fact that he has limits, too. That he can't be the O Mighty Protector or whatever it is he thought he was."

"So you think that's why he's avoiding Dandy?"

"Avoiding everything. That fall shook him good, Miss Kady. Made him feel even smaller and weaker than he already felt."

"Then you shouldn't have had us carve his name on that stump, Jewel. Because the way it's turned out, it only makes him feel even more connected with death."

"Why, Kady Palmer, I told you that stumps take on more forms than what appears—"

But I wasn't listening to her. I didn't want to ever hear another word about stumps!

As February slipped into March, with the oranges scheduled to be picked the next week, winter came with a vengeance. Temperatures plunged overnight and were predicted to drop much lower before the week was over. The thin boards of our wood frame house did little to keep out the cold. From my bedroom window, I saw Papa at the shed with Elijah, his grove man, and Wendell. They were pulling out the oil heaters and stacking them in the truck.

Outside my window, a trumpet vine twisted and curved along the frame, its delicate hornlike flowers unfurling into the biting air as they heralded an early spring. I opened my window and plucked it before the cold killed it.

By afternoon, oil heaters were neatly lined up every few yards throughout the grove. It was a huge job setting them out and Papa hadn't wasted a minute. They were rusty heaters that had come with the house, covered with cobwebs from being kept in storage. Rats had even built nests in some of them.

As the sun began to set, Mama called me to the garden.

Minnie was already there helping her cover the flowers and vegetables. We used old blankets and towels for the sturdier plants and armfuls of Spanish moss for the tender shoots. There were broccoli, beets, carrots, onions, radishes, herbs, and marigolds. The pineapples had long been harvested.

We went ahead and picked the tomatoes left over from the fall crop even though many were still green. There was no sense leaving them exposed to nature's whims. Every winter since we'd moved here, we'd had to protect the plants at least once, but I couldn't remember it ever being this cold. Especially at the beginning of March!

Dandy trailed behind us, squawking pitifully. Papa and Wendell had set up an oil heater in the coop, but hadn't lit it yet. I scooped up the goose—who bit me!—and carted him over to Rooster's house.

I had to bang on the door a couple of times to be heard over the TV. Finally, Rooster stumbled to the door, rubbing his eyes.

"Here!" I practically threw the goose at him. "He's cold."

"Oh!" he gasped, "Oh! Oh! Oh!" His legs nearly buckled under Dandy's weight. Then he attempted to toss him back to me like a hot potato, but his arms were so weak that Dandy fell at his feet. Dandy started squawking loudly.

"Rooster! Dandy will freeze to death without you!" I cried. It wasn't exactly the truth, but I figured there was nothing to lose.

"H-H-He n-n-needs to go back to the c-c-coop!" Rooster cried, pulling away from Dandy as he pecked at his feet.

"It's cold in the coop!"

"Well-Well-Well—"

"My dad put an oil heater in there, though, and we need you to make sure it stays lit."

"Well-Well-Well, I can't-can't d-d-do *that*!"

"Sure you can. I'll show you how," I said, handing him a jacket.

He fixed his attention on the TV. "Oh, b-b-but G-G-Gilligan is stuck in in a *c-c-coco-NUT* tree. And—And—And—And—"

I helped him into his jacket, pulled a knit cap over his head, and said, "You're Dandy's O Mighty Protector, remember?"

His face flushed and his whole body began to shake. "No!" he cried.

I stared at him in shock, amazed to see such anger erupting from his shrunken body.

"I am *n-n-not* O M-Mighty Protector!" he railed at me. "And-And"—hot, angry tears filling his eyes—"you're *n-not M-M-Madrina!* You're n-not! Not! *Not!*"

"You're right," I said, swallowing hard. "I'm not. But I care about you a lot."

"I h-h-hate you! I h-h-hate you! I hate you! *I hate you!*" Suddenly he was kicking me and pummeling me with his fists.

"I'm sorry you feel that way!" I cried as I grabbed his fists and held them while he kept trying to kick me with his sticklike legs.

"And—And—And I-I-I hate *D-D-Dandy!*"

I looked at him levelly, then slowly shook my head. "You can hate me all you want to, but you don't hate Dandy."

"*¡Sí! ¡Sí! ¡Sí!* I *hate* D-Dandy!" he screamed, his eyes blinded by tears.

"*No you don't*," I repeated firmly, my eyes locking into his.

"Carlos! Get that blasted bird out of here!" Señor Rosado bellowed over the roar of the TV. "The last thing we need is bird crap all over the place!" His voice came from the kitchen, where Dandy had fled.

"Get Dandy and come with me," I told Rooster. "*He needs you.*"

"N-N-N-No, he d-d-d-doesn't!" He tried to pull himself free of my grasp. "Let *g-g-go-a-me!*"

"Get Dandy and come with me," I repeated. "*He needs you.*"

Rooster stared at me for a long moment, his chest heaving as tears began to stream down his face. Then he wrenched his hands free of mine and disappeared into the kitchen.

My head reeled with giddiness when I saw him return a moment later with Dandy, his arms straining under the weight of what had become a very large goose.

Papa and Wendell were so tired that night preparing the heaters that they barely touched the chipped beef and fried green tomatoes Mama had prepared from the garden. When the hard freeze forecast was announced on the radio, we fell silent. Outside on the front porch, I could see the soft glow of the oil heater inside the coop, keeping the chickens warm. Rooster and I had spent a long time there, Rooster sitting down when he got tired. I'd taught him how to light the heater and check the oil to make sure it didn't go out. Then we banked the straw to provide a warm area for the chickens.

He had been almost afraid of them at first, the same way he'd been afraid of Dandy, skirting around them when they pecked at his feet. It wasn't until one of the newly hatched chicks went skittering into the cold that Rooster showed any concern. He went after it—his slight body slow and deliberate—mimicking, "Eep! Eep! Eep!" Then, when it got late, I made him go home. His health was still too fragile for him to take any chances in the cold.

The wind howled, taunting me with its frigid breath as I went to bed that night. I couldn't sleep. From the living room, I could hear Papa's rocking chair rocking back and forth over the hardwood floor. He would be there all night watching the thermometer.

The Clarks had lost everything to the freezing temperatures of 1962. They hadn't relied on oil heaters, or fatwood fires, both common heating methods in those days. Instead, they had tried out their newly installed overhead sprinklers. The theory behind the sprinklers was to trap heat inside the trees by a continuous flow of water. Yet the results were disastrous. Mud daubers had built nests inside the pipes, which restricted the flow of water so much that heavy ice formed on the trees instead. Unable to bear the weight, most of the trees had split apart all the way down to the roots.

Freezes that severe were rare, I reminded myself. Otherwise there wouldn't be any groves in central Florida. And there were lots of groves besides ours, in spite of all the new developments cropping up.

The screen door slammed, and I heard the quick tread of Papa's feet padding across the front porch, then back into the house. He was checking the temperature, no doubt.

I could smell the aroma of his pipe wafting into my room, as rich and comforting as night-blooming jasmine. He rarely smoked in the house, and it was this smell that got me out of bed and brought me shivering down the hall.

A lone light from the kitchen bathed him in soft shadows. I lingered in the hall, watching him strike a match to relight yet another smoke. Although his body was slight, his hands were strong as he held the match up to the tobacco. Watching him bring the fire to life comforted me.

"What's the temperature?" I asked as I crept from the shadows.

"Twenty-nine." His voice sounded hollow in the stillness. He must have noticed my frightened expression, for his eyes crinkled into a reassuring smile. "Don't worry, if we'd had to light the heaters tonight, we'd have done so by now."

"Does that mean the danger's gone?"

"Afraid not. I just talked to a meteorologist at the Frost Warning Service who told me there's a mass of frigid air traveling down from the Arctic a thousand miles a day. Can you imagine that? It's predicted to drop to twenty in the next day or so."

"Twenty! It never hits twenty."

He looked at me levelly. "Not since sixty-two."

"That was the year of the freeze." An image of the splintery trees and rotting oranges flashed before me.

He nodded slowly.

"Well, at least we know better than to rely on those silly overhead sprinklers," I said. "That's why all the trees died!"

"Part of the reason. But what concerns me the most is that we've been having an unusually warm spell for this time of year and the sap's running high. There's already blossoms starting to form on the trees. That's the funny thing about Valencias. They can bud and bear fruit at the same time. You couldn't pick a worst time to have a freeze, Kady. It's like putting on your swimsuit, then finding yourself in a blizzard. The trees don't have any defenses to ward off the cold. And they're so young that it won't take long for the cold to penetrate their trunks. Maybe I should've planted them closer together, to protect them some from the cold. But I was thinking of the long-term, how they'd grow bigger this way. And I never dreamed another freeze would come so soon."

I nodded again. As difficult as his words were to absorb, at least he talked to me more than he would, say, a china doll in a pink sateen dress. He made me feel as if I was a part of what was going on. He'd always been that way, I realized, treating all of us as if we were equals.

His eyes crinkled into another smile as he set down his pipe and reached out to give me a hug. The warmth of his body quelled some of the fear that had risen inside of me like a fluttering bird.

*   *   *

The next evening the winds died down. The sun descended in a fiery ball, the calm surface of the lake mirroring its image like fine glass. I watched it sink, taking every bit of warmth it had accumulated during the day. The thermometer began to steadily drop. At eight o'clock, it was twenty-nine. At nine o'clock, it was twenty-seven. I knew that an orange tree can only withstand temperatures of less than twenty-seven degrees for a few hours. Anything less than that begins to split the wood. It would take a miracle for the grove to survive temperatures near twenty, which Papa predicted, probably wouldn't come tonight, but the next.

Papa called Elijah. "Light 'em!"

Within minutes, the grove was alive with the cry of Elijah and his two sons as they lit the heaters. He'd tried to bring more workers, but they were busy with other groves. All through the night, they would have to keep checking the heaters.

I dressed in my heaviest clothes and started out with Papa and Wendell to help however I could. High above us the stars flaunted their cold beauty. The voices of the guys on the north side of the grove could be heard as clear as a bell while the mass of frigid air settled in the trees. I braced myself for a long night as the sap began to surge through my own veins.

I'd just stepped into the truck when Mama hollered, "Kady! Get back in the house. I didn't give you permission to leave."

My heart sank. "Papa, can't I come help?"

"Barney, I need her to help with the food for all you guys. You're gonna be mighty hungry."

"Can't someone make a run to McDonald's?" I protested.

"Forget McDonald's!"

"Then get Minnie to help. Besides, there aren't that many guys."

"Minnie *is* helping. Now come inside before this house turns into a freezer!" The door started to close, then popped back open. "I'll let you go tomorrow if the snap keeps up," she added, her voice much gentler.

"All right," I said as a little smile formed on my lips. Lately, she'd been doing that a lot, stopping herself when she came on too strong.

Just last week, after weeks of scraping the paint off the entire garage (as well as the skin off my knuckles), she'd handed me an envelope. Inside it was twenty-seven dollars and fifty-three cents. Exactly. I'd looked at her, surprised. "What's this for?"

"Well," she'd shrugged, "I thought you did a good enough job that you deserved a little something."

"A little something? Why, there's twenty-seven whole dollars here." A slow grin formed on my face. "And fifty-three cents. Exactly." I counted it again just to make sure. "Yes. *Exactly.*"

"That right? I was just cleaning out my purse."

Mama never lost track of a single dime. Nor did she ever carry the huge sum of twenty-seven dollars and fifty-three cents in her purse. Because Lord only knew how many dented cans she could stock up on for that much cash!

"And what do you suppose I do with this money?" I asked her.

"Ohhhhh," she shrugged as if it were no big deal, "I thought you might put it in your savings account . . . or something."

"Or something?" The grin grew wider on my face.

"Or something," she said with a hint of a smile.

That night I was drawn to my dollhouse for the first time in a long time. It wasn't long ago that I used to dream about drinking from a little bottle like Alice in Wonderland did so I could pretend I was the mistress of that small world. But looking at it now, I felt as if I'd devoured the cake that said "EAT ME," for I seemed to be popping out of the house as if it couldn't contain me any longer. I wasn't sure what to do with the money, much as I'd longed to replace the china doll that Rooster had smashed. So I just kept it in the envelope for the time being.

After Papa and Wendell left, Mama set me to work frying circles of sausage on the griddle while Minnie made biscuits. Mama made a strong pot of Cuban *café* and filled a large pitcher with water, something I'd never seen her do before. I kept drifting over to the window and pressing my nose against the cold pane to see what was going on, yet all I could see was my own breath.

Then just before midnight, Papa burst into the kitchen along with Elijah.

Mama looked at him, alarmed. "What's wrong, Barney?"

"Went to start refilling the heaters and the tank's bone dry."

"It can't be! I just had it filled last month."

"There's a leak, ma'am," Elijah said.

"A leak! That could take hours to fix. We don't have hours."

"And meanwhile," Papa went on, then shook his head and fell silent.

"Meanwhile what?" Mama pressed.

"The oranges are freezing. . . ."

Mama drew back as if she'd been slapped. Then she took a deep breath. "Not all of them, are they? It ain't even midnight!"

"No, Mattie, not all of them yet. But—"

"Well then, we need that oil and we need it now!" she snapped.

"We think we know where the leak is," Elijah said. "Don't you worry none, we'll have it fixed in a jiffy."

"What's the temp?" Mama asked.

Elijah shifted his feet and looked down. "Cold, ma'am."

"How cold?"

"Twenty-four," Papa said.

"Twenty-four!" Mama echoed. "Well, no wonder the oranges are freezing."

Papa nodded.

"Dear Lord," she looked at him with sudden realization, "it ain't just the oranges we're fighting to save. . . ." She bit down hard on her lip as her voice trailed off.

I let a sausage patty burn before I remembered to flip it.

Papa put his hands reassuringly on Mama's shoulders. "We'll keep 'em going, tank or not. Call Clyde's Oil and have 'em send a truck out."

As soon as he was out the door, Mama was on the phone yelling at the owner's wife, her eyebrows arching like caterpillars on the run. "WHADDYA MEAN HE'S ON ANOTHER RUN? WE NEED OIL RIGHT NOW! . . . YES, I UNDERSTAND ALL THAT. . . . I KNOW IT'S THE MIDDLE OF THE NIGHT. . . . WHAT ABOUT YOU? CAN'T YOU DRIVE A TRUCK? . . . THEN I'LL DRIVE THE DARN THING MYSELF!"

Minnie and I exchanged looks.

"Well, great. Put him on!" Mama said brightly a moment later. She cupped her hand over the receiver and growled to us, "'Bout time that son of a you-know-what showed up." Then, sweetly to Clyde, "I'm so glad to have reached you, Clyde! We've got a major emergency here."

This time it was Mama who kept pressing her nose against the window as she waited for the oil truck to show up. Finally, she heard it rumbling down the driveway and breathed a sigh of relief.

It was long after sunrise before Papa and Wendell called it quits. "Got down to twenty-two," Papa said as he bolted down a sausage biscuit. "But we fixed the tank and got the heaters going full blast—the ones that worked, anyway, and plenty of 'em don't—so we can hope the trees'll be okay."

"Twenty-two is mighty cold. Trees have died at less cold than that," Mama said as she paced back and forth, an old shawl wrapped around her shoulders.

He massaged his eyes with a gloved hand and nodded. "I know it. Them heaters ain't miracle workers, either. Just raise the temperature a couple of degrees. Won't help much if it gets any colder."

"What about the oranges? Did they all freeze?"

Papa slowly nodded. "'Pears that way. We might still get some concentrate if the cold snap keeps up long enough to get 'em to the plant before they thaw. But even so, concentrate won't bring in nearly as much as fresh fruit."

"So we're fighting now to save the trees," Mama said flatly.

Papa slowly nodded again.

I gripped the stovetop to hold myself steady as I envisioned what would happen next: The pickers would show up like a flock of vultures, pick the oranges that were still frozen to turn into concentrate, and leave the rest to rot. Then the pungent smell of rotting fruit would fill the air, and hundreds of crows would show up to eat them. They would fly about like kamikaze pilots, slamming into the trees, the ground, and even each other, drunk. All about them would be rotting oranges, blue-green with mold and smelling like cheap wine. That's the way I remembered the grove when we'd first arrived in that old truck. It seemed as if a cruel circle was coming full swing.

The following evening, Mama kept her word and let me go with Papa.

It was so cold when I got outside that my toes felt numb even though I'd put on three pairs of socks. But I quickly forgot the temperature once we started through the grove.

Scattered on the ground, covered with hoary frost, were solid balls of frozen oranges that had already fallen off the trees. I picked up an orange and turned it about. It was a round, brilliant ball of seeming perfection covered with a fine sprinkling of ice crystals. And yet it felt rock-hard, like Grandpa's hand when I'd touched it in the casket all those years ago. I tossed it on the ground, repulsed.

Papa, watching me, picked it back up and cut it in half with his pocket knife. "Care for some orange slush?" he asked with a twinkle in his eye. I took it from him and bit into the icy juice. It was so delicious that tears welled up in my eyes. Then he handed me a twig covered with at least a dozen blossoms, each one incredibly beautiful, yet frozen stiff.

"There's no way all these blossoms would grow on this tiny twig even if there wasn't a cold snap," he said. "That's Mother Nature's way. What a grower tries to do is save as many as he or she can, then fret no more."

I nodded uneasily.

Before the sun had even set, I helped carry torches of fatwood pine through the grove to light the heaters. It was fun watching the heaters come alive with fire, knowing the power the fire had over the cold. But before long, it turned out to be hard work. Some of the heaters were so rusty they either leaked or didn't work at all, others burned the oil too quickly and wasted it, and others burned it too slowly and didn't put out enough heat. Then, once we'd finally gotten most of them lit, we had to begin refilling them! I didn't mind though, as it gave me a chance to thaw out my fingers. As we worked, you could hear the occasional sound of a frozen orange thumping to the ground as it fell off a tree. I heard a hissing sound as one hit a heater, followed by the sharp smell of burning orange peel.

I was already exhausted by the time darkness fell. But the night loomed ahead, colder than any I could remember. I didn't have the proper clothes for this type of weather, nor did the rest of us, and all the layers we wore made it hard to move freely. Every hand was needed, though, as once more Elijah had trouble finding help and had brought along only his boys. Papa even let Sammy help us. Only Minnie and Mama remained in the house, working feverishly to keep everyone fed and warmed as we trudged home in shifts. Rooster was back at the chicken coop where he'd been every night since he'd picked up Dandy.

At about eight o'clock, Papa studied one of the thermometers set in the grove and frowned.

"Seems colder than last night," I remarked as I followed him.

"Yep," he said, "and the night's still early."

As the night progressed, the temperature steadily dropped.

"We might as well put out the heaters and save the oil," Elijah said to Papa when it was only eleven o'clock. "It'd take nothing short of an inferno to save these trees."

Papa drew hard on his pipe. As smoke streamed through his nostrils, he remarked, "You know those piles of tires next door?" He pointed toward the Rosados'.

"I've seen 'em," Elijah nodded.

"There's a mighty lot of 'em. How about if we burn 'em *and* keep the heaters going?"

"I've seen it done," Elijah said as he scratched his chin. "Might be worth a shot in spite of the godawful smell. . . . But even so, with this type of cold . . ." He shook his head again.

Papa was already marching over to the Rosados' house. Wendell, Sammy, and I followed.

It was several minutes before Señor Rosado came to the door—red-faced, glassy-eyed, his hair on end. We drew back at the sight of him.

"*¿Qué diablos quiere usted?*" Señor Rosado snarled.

I knew "diablos" meant devil, and stared at him uneasily.

When Papa tried to explain why he needed the tires, the old Cuban yelled, "*¡TRAIDOR!*"

Papa motioned for us to back away.

"*¡TRAIDOR! ¡TRAIDOR!*"

Tony rushed up to his father. "*¿Estás loco?* It's only Mr. Palmer! He wants your old tires to burn in his grove!"

"*¡No, jeuga con dos barajas!*" he lashed back at Tony. "*¡Se va a armar la de Dios es Cristo!*"

"*¡Deje ya de hacer el tonto!*" Tony lashed back.

"It's *me,* Rosado. Mr. Palmer!" Papa spoke up. "I'm willing to pay you—"

"ROSADO?" his eyes blazed. "*¡ME LLAMA* SEÑOR *ROSADO!*"

I stared at Señor Rosado in shock as he continued to lash out at us in Spanish. His hands were gesturing wildly as he spoke, and at one point he called Papa "Fidel" and spat at him. He was so out of it that I think he thought we'd come to take over his sugar plantation!

"*¡BASTA YA!*" Tony cried to his father, and pulled him inside. I could hear him explaining something in Spanish in a voice fraught with anger and frustration.

After a few minutes, Tony came back outside, closed the door firmly, and leaned against it as if it contained an unbearable weight that would burst from the seams if he dared move. "Take all the tires you want," he said, waving his hand expansively toward the piles.

"Not if it's gonna create a problem," Papa said.

"No problem. He'll sleep it off and remember nothing."

"Thanks. I'll pay you a dime apiece."

"*No importa,*" Tony waved him off. "*You're* doing us a favor getting them out of here. *Papi's* spent years trying to figure out a use for them, and all they are is a home for snakes."

After Tony had gone back inside, I kept staring at the closed door, unable to move.

"You can tell Tony how *loco* in love you are with him tomorrow," Wendell said as he took me by the arm.

"What are you talking about? I just feel bad that he and Rooster have to live with a father like that. I mean, he seemed like he was doing better, selling all that fake grass and all. And now he's turned on a dime."

"This isn't about Señor Rosado. You're *loco* in love!"

"*You're* the one who's *loco!*"

"I know that look on your face," he said with a mischievous gleam. "It's the same look you had the day of the fire when you wandered around the yard with splinters in the back of your legs. You didn't even know they were there! I'm surprised you didn't have more after the way I saw you two kissing."

"What?"

Wendell rolled his eyes.

I thought back on that day. I hadn't even felt those splinters until hours later. But surely that didn't mean anything. *"I'm not even sure myself what came over me, except that the way you kissed me back made me think—well, never mind,"* Tony's voice came back to me. My cheeks grew hot in spite of the cold as it came rushing back to me: the passionate way I'd kissed him back.

"Come on now, we gotta save this grove!" Wendell cried.

Some of us began forming a line of tires along the north end of the grove where the frigid air was coming from. The idea was that the wind would pull the heat through the grove. Others built small fires throughout the grove where the trees were the most vulnerable, especially in the low pockets where the air was the coldest.

I stayed by the highway, which ran along the north end, unloading tires as they were brought to us on the back of the vehicles we'd pooled: Papa's and Elijah's pickups and Mama's station wagon, to which Papa had attached a trailer to the back. Unloading tires was far more backbreaking than I'd imagined. After the first few loads, my right shoulder was already throbbing. Wendell, watching me wince with pain, suggested I leave it to the men. But I brushed him off, saying, "Didn't you say we have to save this grove?"

"Step out of the way!" Elijah cried, then began lighting the line of tires. Suddenly, the night became alive with the choking stench of burning rubber.

For a moment, as I stared at the smoky blaze, I forgot all about the terrible smell. I'd never seen anything more beautiful than the orange grove lit by firelight, with the smoke floating through like orange clouds. In their hour of death, the green leaves had never seemed more vibrant, nor the oranges more brilliant. Joni Mitchell's melodious voice seemed to float through the very trees. *"We are stardust . . . We are golden . . . And we've got to get ourselves . . . Back to the garden."*

Why had it taken me so long to figure out where the garden really was?

I caught a glimpse of Tony's face lit by the fire—the jutting out of his chin, the furrow between his brow, and the fixed look that always seemed to focus on a point beyond wherever he happened to be. I hadn't realized he'd come out.

"Thanks for helping out," I called out to him.

"Who says I'm helping you?" he shouted back. "Did it ever occur to you that I'm doing it for me? That I wanted to get rid of those blasted tires so we could make room for some more Terrific Terrain, the most exciting ground cover ever?" He picked up a tire as if it were nothing more than an oversized donut and threw it on the fire, sending up a shower of sparks.

The tires kept coming as if they would never end. We kept throwing them on the fire line, making it as strong a blaze as possible. Each tire seemed to be heavier than the last, until I could hardly even drag them onto the fire without throwing my shoulder into spasms of pain. My throat burned from the smoke, my eyes were so watery I could hardly see, and I could taste rubber in my mouth.

Wendell shrieked as he pulled out a snake from the inside of a tire, startling me. It was half frozen from the cold, its body arched in the shape of a semicircle. "Have you ever seen anything like it?" he called out to everyone in disbelief.

I stared at him, stunned. Not so much because of the unusual shape of the snake, but because he was actually holding it without continuing to scream. He brought it close to the warmth of the fire and it began to wiggle. Finally, he set it down and watched it slither away. Then he picked up another tire and swung it onto the fire, his shoulders as broad and capable as Tony's. When had that happened? When had Wendell grown up?

As the hours crept by, the temperature continued to plunge. I had to stamp my feet to keep them from going numb in spite of the smoldering tires just yards away. Desperately, we kept piling on more tires to stave off the cold. I refused to go inside the house to take a break, refused to leave the grove. Not that my efforts seemed to make any difference. Then, in the wee hours just before dawn, Elijah came up from the south end of the grove and called out to Papa, "The bark, sir, it's starting to split on some of the trees."

Papa stared at him as if he hadn't heard him correctly.

"The bark, sir," Elijah repeated.

I felt queasy, for when the bark split it nearly always meant the death of the tree.

Tony threw another tire on the blaze and yelled at the top of his lungs, "IT AIN'T SPLITTING ON THE TREES NEAR THE FIRES!"

"NO, SIR! IT AIN'T SPLITTING NEAR THE FIRES!" Wendell chimed in as he threw on another tire.

"NO, SIR, IT AIN'T!" I added at the top of my lungs.

A rallying cry rose up among the workers as everyone renewed their efforts to burn every last tire.

For a while, everything seemed to be happening in fast motion as pickups rushed back and forth along the bumpy dirt roads, bringing tires. We piled them on the existing fires, as well as built new ones. While all this was going on, Sammy and Elijah's oldest boy kept the oil heaters going as best they could. Yet, in spite of all of our efforts, we couldn't completely stop the ominous rat-a-tat-tat sound of the bark splitting on the trees. I felt as if we were deep in a jungle, surrounded by the guns of guerrilla warfare.

By the time dawn broke, most of the tires had been reduced to smoldering piles of rubbery goo. We all stood about numbly, not knowing what else to do, except to pray for the sun to bring its warmth.

I wanted to scream at the icy stars, but instead I stared at the grove for a long while, trying to absorb the reality of what had been lost. Tears blurred my eyes as I finally trudged back home. *We'd done all we could and it wasn't enough. I felt as small and weak as Rooster must've felt in the hospital.*

"What's that on your hand?" Tony asked as he came up beside me. Much to my surprise, he took my hand in his and noticed blood seeping through my gloves. "You're bleeding."

"It's nothing," I said, pulling my hand away.

"That meant something, you know, the way you came around for Rooster the other day," he said after a moment.

I nodded as I felt a lump rise in my throat. "That meant something, you know, the way you came around for us tonight. Even if it was just to make more room for Terrific Terrain."

"That wasn't why."

I snatched a frozen leaf from a nearby orange tree and broke it in half. "Maybe Papa can become a partner in your family business now that we've lost . . ." My voice trailed off and I gestured wildly at the trees. Maybe the only dreams attainable on the property were man-made after all. If so, then it would only be a matter of time before Jon's father showed up with his big sign, HAMILTON ENTERPRISES—BUILDER OF DREAMS, and a set smile.

"Your father asked me to check the trees. I've only had a chance to look at those along the north side where we built the hottest fires, but it looks like we saved nearly all of those."

"How can you tell so soon?"

"*Ay*, lots of ways. Most of the bark's intact for one thing, unlike farther south."

"That doesn't necessarily mean they're okay. Lots of trees die without the bark splitting. Especially in these temperatures."

"I know, but it's a good sign, Kady."

"A sign!" I moaned. "You sound like Jewel and her stupid ideas about the widowmaker tree. It's alive alright, crawling with termites."

"*¿Qué te pasa?* Don't you believe we're the O Mighty Protectors of the Grove?"

His words took me by such surprise that I stared at him, unable to reply.

Mama and Minnie burst through the back door, laden with a thermos of *café* and another of hot chocolate, along with a package of Styrofoam cups. "I got some"—her voice rising in that sing-song tone she reserved for Rooster—"hot chocolate just for *Roos*-ter!" She looked toward the coop. "Where are you?" When he didn't emerge, she looked at us sharply. "Where is he?"

We looked at each other and shrugged.

"Why, I saw him in the middle of the night chasing that goose back into the coop," Mama said. "I took him straight home, told him it was much too cold for him to be outside. But he was back at that darn coop a short while ago, and when I tried to take him home again, he informed me he was wearing two jackets, four shirts, two knit caps, and was plenty warm."

She shook her head and sighed. "I would've offered to keep an eye on the chickens for him, but my hands were full with Grampsie. All the commotion woke her up and when she saw the flames from the grove through the window, she thought we were having another house fire! I just now got her settled back in bed."

"I'll check our place," Tony said, and disappeared for a few minutes. He came back to report no sign of Rooster.

You could almost see the ripple of fear spreading through the rest of us. As exhausted as we were, the thought of anything else happening to Rooster was too much to bear. Everyone started looking around for him, including Papa and Wendell, who pulled up into the yard just then.

I headed instinctively for the widowmaker tree without even thinking of where I was going. I stopped suddenly as the stump loomed before me. The early morning sunlight bathed it in golden light, the same golden light that lent the cruel illusion that the oranges were warm and juicy. Rooster hadn't gone near that old stump since he'd been back, and I couldn't really blame him, especially with his name carved on that dead wood. What was I thinking?

All at once, I found myself staring at the stump in amazement, for sprouting from its sawed-off top were sprigs of new growth fluttering in the breeze like fiery threads. The widowmaker tree wasn't dead after all! For a moment I could scarcely breathe, scarcely even move.

Then, as I crept closer, I realized that what I was seeing wasn't new shoots coming from the stump, but corkscrews of hair coming from Rooster's head! He was slumped inside the hollowed stump, fast asleep, with Dandy locked securely in his arms.

Tony cleared his throat, and I realized he was standing right beside me. The way he looked at me made me certain he'd seen the same thing I had. But he didn't say anything, just reached for my hand and held it. Then he turned to the others and cried triumphantly, "WE'VE FOUND HIM!"

Mama brought over her thermoses and Styrofoam cups and bustled into action. "I've got some nice Cuban *café*, strong as a fence post and hotter'n August," she declared in a blustery, no-nonsense voice. "And some hot chocolate for *Roos*-ter!"

As I sipped from the warm cup she thrust into my hands, I felt my strength begin to return.

Then Papa struck a match. My nostrils quivered at the familiar smell and I began to watch the smoke from his pipe rise whimsically toward the sky once more.